D0349974

DEC 10 2021

BROADVIEW LIBRARY

NO LONGER PROPERTY OF
SEATTLE PUBLIC LIBRARY

RICHELIO

DEC 1 0 2021

BROADVIEW LIBRARY

EDIE
IN BETWEEN

EDIE
IN BETWEEN

LAURA
SIBSON

VIKING

VIKING

An imprint of Penguin Random House LLC, New York

First published in the United States of America by Viking,
an imprint of Penguin Random House LLC, 2021

Copyright © 2021 by Laura Sibson

Penguin supports copyright. Copyright fuels creativity, encourages diverse voices, promotes free speech, and creates a vibrant culture. Thank you for buying an authorized edition of this book and for complying with copyright laws by not reproducing, scanning, or distributing any part of it in any form without permission. You are supporting writers and allowing Penguin to continue to publish books for every reader.

Viking & colophon are registered trademarks of Penguin Random House LLC.

Visit us online at penguinrandomhouse.com.

Library of Congress Cataloging-in-Publication Data is available.

Printed in the United States of America

ISBN 9780451481146

1 3 5 7 9 10 8 6 4 2

SKY

Design by Opal Roengchai
Text set in Adobe Jenson Pro

This book is a work of fiction. Any references to historical events, real people, or real places are used fictitiously. Other names, characters, places, and events are products of the author's imagination, and any resemblance to actual events or places or persons, living or dead, is entirely coincidental.

The publisher does not have any control over and does not assume any responsibility for author or third-party websites or their content.

For my mother, whose smile spreads magic

Chapter One

EDIE

When I wake to the chaotic sounds of the marina on this summer morning, I hear my grandmother in the houseboat's kitchen, chatting with our ancestors. Sun streams through my small square window. Temperance, at the bottom of my bed, licks her paw and her tail flicks idly. There is a scent of honeysuckle and my mother floats near the bedroom door.

I smush the pillow over my head, wishing for the oblivion of sleep. But it's no use. By the time I roll out of my narrow bed to slip my feet into flip-flops, Mom's gone. I peel off the tank top I slept in and pull on a sports bra and T-shirt. I slept in my running shorts. I'm efficient that way. I open my top drawer in search of a hair tie. Instead, my hand finds the dark purple velvet pouch. I open it, like I do most days. The silver necklace with the acorn pendant pools in the bottom, winking at me from the shadows. I pull out the tiny note handwritten by Mom: *For when you need me with you.* I close my eyes against the blaze of loss until it fades. Then I tuck the note back into the pouch with the necklace, tighten the drawstrings, and return it to my drawer.

After tugging my wavy mass of hair into an out-of-my-way ponytail, I head for the kitchen. Temperance leaps from the bed and slides ahead of me as if to say that it was her idea all along to go find my grandmother.

Sure enough, GG is surrounded by ghosts while she works with her herbs at the kitchen counter. She moves around my grandfather, Edward (cancer), to grab some calendula overhead, but then she backs into her sister, Mildred (heartbreak). GG's parents (old age for one, pneumonia for the other) come and go, as do some Mitchell witches who must be a century dead at this point.

As long as I'd been in Cedar Branch—two weeks today—not a day has passed that GG didn't talk to dead relatives, often while torturing some innocent plants. She chopped them or smashed them or hung them from clothespins that perched on the string crisscrossing the ceiling. The plants, not the relatives. As ghosts, the relatives were incorporeal. They were also silent, but that didn't stop GG from conversing with them.

"Should be nice weather tonight for the solstice," she says to her sister. "Pity the full moon isn't for a few days yet. That would have made for a very powerful evening."

GG mashes a pile of basil. Must be for the poultice that calms mosquito bites. Very popular this time of year. GG prepares and sells many salves and healing remedies. But what she's most known for is her honey. People describe my grandmother's honey as revelatory, illuminating, and lifesaving. It may be difficult to believe that all those claims are true, but I'm not saying that they're not.

"What did those herbs ever do to you?" I ask, my tone teasing.

"Good morning, Edie." GG glances up and smiles at me. Her long gray hair is braided down her back. Years of work outside has turned her white skin a weathered tan. She wears loose linen pants and over her cotton shirt is a smock, protecting her clothes from the messy war with herbs. Her feet are bare.

The houseboat rocks gently, an ever-present reminder that we are not on land—that I am far from the home I shared with my mother in Baltimore. When I first moved onto the boat, the constant rocking made me uneasy. I couldn't wait for my feet to feel solid, unmoving ground. Now, after only a handful of weeks, the rocking fades in and out of my awareness, but I still miss my house—and my old life.

The prisms hanging in the east windows cast rainbows of color across the room and through the ghosts, speckling me as I walk to the French press, avoiding the spirits in my path. Unlike GG, I choose *not* to interact with them.

The houseboat is bigger on the inside than it looks on the outside. I don't mean that it seems bigger. I mean that it's literally bigger. You'd imagine that GG would only have a tiny galley kitchen on this boat, but the counter is spacious (though there can never be enough room for me to avoid lingering ancestors). I had thought to ask GG how she'd managed that extra space, but she might mistake my curiosity for interest in our family magic, so I've kept my question to myself.

I duck to avoid getting smacked in the head by the bundles of herbs hanging like bats in a cave. There are also miniature plants and butterflies suspended in clear orbs. Bones dangle from the ceiling, too. Tiny ones stacked and strung together. They clack when you bump into them. I try not to bump into them.

"That coffee's is not likely to be hot anymore," GG says, her attention returned to the basil before her.

"I meant to get up earlier," I say.

"I'm not judging," GG says.

It's true. GG doesn't comment about my sleep or eating habits, so long as I do in fact eat and sleep at some point.

Same with Mom. Back at home, runners on my cross-country team had commented more than once how lucky I was that my mother allowed me to come and go whenever I pleased—sleep all day if I needed to and eat whenever I was hungry. They'd said I'd wasted all of that freedom because I didn't use it to stay out late at parties. But I had wished for parents like theirs, who had normal-people jobs and paid attention to when their kids left the house and returned. When I let this wish slip to Mom, it was cause for Tea and a Talk. For this, Mom brewed a mix of spearmint and lemon verbena.

Over steaming cups, Mom explained that she viewed mealtimes and sleep times as arbitrary. I'd argued back that adolescents crave structure and need it to develop a sense of safety. She asked if I'd ever felt unsafe. I admitted I hadn't. I *always* felt loved by my mother and safe in our home.

Ten months ago, when my days were turned upside down by Mom's death and I slept all day and haunted the house in the dark hours of night, no one stopped me. GG brought tea of lemon balm and hawthorn berries, sweetened with her own honey. It took me a month or so, but I managed to get myself back on a more conventional schedule. I had to if I wanted to get anything done and stay on track to graduate summa cum laude.

Now, in the kitchen of the houseboat on this humid June morning, GG looks up from her herbs to inspect me more closely. "Off for your morning run?"

"Soon." I slide into the bench seat of our dinette and lean my nose over the coffee. GG was right. It's not piping hot, but it'll do. Brigid's crosses made of straw and triquetras of iron perch on the heads of the windows. Witch balls hang in front of several of them. GG hasn't spared any magical protection symbols here. There's an iron triquetra over the window in my room, too. The only part of the room that GG said I could not change.

Mom appears across the table. I close my eyes tight, but when I open them, she's still there. Beautiful, as always, her wavy hair floating around her face. Her smile brilliant, like the last day I saw her alive.

"It's not getting any easier, Geege," I say into my coffee.

"Give it time. It's the way—" GG starts to say the thing she has said every time I bring this up.

I hold up my hand. "Please. Just don't."

There is a moment of quiet and then GG speaks again.

"What does this solstice hold for you?" she asks. "Or is it yet undetermined?"

"I'm working. Sundays are busy."

Even though I'd fought coming here, once I was here, it was obviously pointless to do nothing all day. I'd found Tess, my new running partner, on one of my first runs here. And then she got me the job at the ice cream shop. I planned my ACT and SAT study schedule around my work and training hours. And the rest of the time? Well, the rest of the time, I wished I could go home.

"I'm leaving soon for the perpetual woods and I'll be there into the evening to honor the day," GG says. "Would you like to join me?"

"No thanks." I guess I should give GG credit that she keeps trying, but I was not going to be carrying on these family traditions with her. I pour the lukewarm coffee down the drain, watching the brown liquid swirl counterclockwise before disappearing.

"You'll need to learn at some point," GG says.

"We've been over this."

And we had. At least once a day. GG was displeased to learn that Mom had not taught me the ways of the Mitchells. But Mom had understood. She knew that I hadn't been ready, and she never pushed me. Only now, she's gone. And I'm still not ready. Not after what happened.

"Edie, you cannot deny who—or what—you are forever. There are consequences."

I set the coffee mug in the sink with more force than I intend. "If you'd let me go home like I've asked, I could live in peace. Away from this." I gesture with my hand to the herbs, the bones, the witch balls. All of it.

"Well." She sets aside her knife and wipes her hands on her smock. "The plants need me." GG's terse words and clipped movements show me that she's not pleased with the way this conversation has gone.

Now that we are at the longest day of the year, the plants are beginning a quest to take over the entire roof of our houseboat. Tomatoes and herbs and flowers burst off the roof like abundant hair.

GG stops at the door that leads to the back deck of the boat.

"You are welcome to join me, should you change your mind."

I wish I were welcome to return to my home in Baltimore, not welcome to join her for her Celtic worship sessions in the perpetual woods.

"I won't change my mind," I say.

"So you say, but you know where I'll be?"

"Yes." Before I stopped learning about our magic, before I realized that it wasn't for me, there was plenty that I had learned. The names and meanings of trees, the eight major celebrations, basic recipes for basic problems, and the clearing in the woods where GG keeps her bees and where all the rituals take place. I almost miss that place—the magical clearing with its perpetually blooming trees, bees buzzing around hives, and the sense of peace that I always felt when I was there.

"I'm off to tend the plants, then," GG says.

As GG leaves the room, my eye catches on the handblown glass witch ball twirling in the middle window, casting purples and blues across the room as the light shines through it. Something shiny sparkles inside. My phone pings with a text and I pull my gaze away.

Tess wonders whether I'm bailing on her or what. I reply that I'll be there in five and get a GIF of a guy collapsing at the finish line of a race in response. I laugh, toss my phone on the counter, and trade my flip-flops for running sneakers.

Our boat is docked at the farthest slot in the Cedar Branch marina. We are the only liveaboards. GG must have some agreement with Jim, who runs the marina. I've never asked about it. In the mornings, Jim seems to be everywhere at once. Some boats need to be rented, others filled with gas, and still others pulled out of the water for spray washing and who knew what else. But he always takes a moment to say hello to me. No matter how busy.

"Mornin', Edie," Jim calls to me from the huge contraption that pulls boats out of the water. An Orioles baseball cap covers his sandy-brown hair, which is longish and curls a bit around his ears. "Going to be a hot one."

"Already is, but I don't mind," I call back. "Catch anything this morning?"

Jim fishes when he can sneak out before the marina gets busy. He's gone and back before I even wake up.

"Yup. Nabbed a bass for my dinner."

"Nice! See you," I say, waving.

His smile is quick and genuine as he waves back. Then I'm off, up the short hill from the marina entrance to the shaded lane and then out to the main street with its line of shops and restaurants. Cedar Branch is a tiny town with no stoplights and no national chain stores. It's somehow avoided becoming built up in the way of most towns around the Chesapeake Bay, maybe because it's sort of remote. Coming from Baltimore, it's unusual not to see a major drugstore, coffee shop, or bank on every corner. Then again, there aren't many corners here. I find Tess gazing into the diner's broad plate glass window. I stop next to her.

"Are you lusting after the pancakes—or the boy serving them?" I ask.

"Both?" She turns, smiling. "Almost gave up on you."

"Never give up on me."

"What's the torture plan for today?" she asks. Her short strawberry blonde hair is held back from her white, freckled face by a bright pink headband. A tiny nose ring glints in the sun. She's wearing a tank top with a picture of a unicorn pooping a glitter rainbow. Her running shorts match her headband. We must look startlingly different (her: adorably girly, me: boring jock), not to mention she's the super-extrovert and I'm the one who spends Saturday nights with test prep.

"Loving the retro shirt," I say.

"Right?" I'd met Tess on the bike trail the second or third day I'd been in Cedar Branch. We were waiting our turns at a water fountain when I asked about mileage on the trail. It turned out she could use some support for her new running effort, and I wanted someone to work out with. We've been running most days since.

"It's a hill workout today. Where should we go?" I ask.

"Ugh," Tess says. "Hills? In this heat?"

I grin. In these few short weeks, we've gotten to know each another pretty well. And Tess knows that I won't give up on a workout due to weather or whining.

"Fine," she says. "For what passes for a hill around here, we want to head to Shaw Road."

"Lead the way." I gesture for Tess to go ahead.

"You'll probably ditch me as soon as you learn these roads."

"I'll never ditch you."

Tess laughs as we start our warm-up down Main Street. The seafood place is stocking up for the day. Al, the owner, calls out to Tess, who smiles and waves back. We weave our way around the summer people in line for coffee. The bar is quiet, as is the so-called metaphysical supply shop. We branch off from Main Street and go a while until we branch off again to a smaller road, which turns out to be Shaw. As Tess hinted, it isn't much of a hill, but this area is so flat that I'll take any elevation.

"We'll do repeats to that giant oak up there. Let's take them fast to make up for lack of elevation, okay?"

Tess nods and we set off up the dirt-and-gravel road, kicking up dust as we go. I've run two seasons of cross-country, starting my freshman year. I did really well for a freshman, but sophomore season was rough because Mom had just died. Going into junior year this fall, I want to place better than ever. Since GG had to move me here because of her work, I'd lost my summer training group and my regular routes. So it doesn't matter to me that Tess is new to running. I crave company for my runs, and she wanted accountability.

After I've done eight repeats and I'm sure that my quads are going to curse me forever, I stop at the top to catch my breath. The oak is even more massive up close.

Tess crests the hill, breathing heavily.

"I've never seen an oak this big." I crane my neck to look at the top of the tree.

"Biggest one around," she says. She gulps from her water bottle and wipes her mouth with the back of her hand. "And I've always loved that cairn." Tess gestures to the rocks stacked in decreasing size from bottom to top. The cairn sits at the base of a very overgrown driveway that has a chain across the entrance.

"Doesn't look like the people who own it come here anymore," I say.

"Wait." Tess holds up her hand. "You don't know where we are?"

I look around. "On Shaw Road? Upriver from the marina?"

Tess looks at me with disbelief. She points to the driveway. "That's the Mitchell property."

"What Mitchell property?" I frown in the direction of the driveway.

"Edie. Oh my gods. That's *your* family's property."

I start to walk toward the entrance.

Tess joins me. "I can't believe you didn't know."

"And how come you know?" Peering down the path, I wonder what waits at the end.

"Because my family has lived here forever. We know stuff," Tess says. "People say the cabin is haunted."

"People say a lot of things about us." I step over the chain.

Tess's eyes go big with alarm. "What are you doing?"

"You tell me that my family owns property that I've never heard of and you think I'm not going to check it out?"

"Um, I did use the word *haunted*, didn't I?"

I've shared a little with Tess about me and my family, but she definitely does not know that I see ghosts. Not exactly something you tell people—unless you're *trying* to alienate them. I don't love seeing ghosts, but the fact of their presence makes haunted houses, well, just houses. With ghosts in them. But I hear the worry in Tess's voice.

"We don't have to go if you don't want to," I say, looking over my shoulder down the dirt track with its plants grasping from all sides. I can barely stand to know that our family owns a cabin just down that overgrown driveway and I can't see it.

"You really want to check it out?"

I place my hands together like I'm begging. "I really, really do."

"Fine." Tess sighs and walks toward me.

"Thank you, thank you, thank you!" I bounce up and down on my toes. My curiosity grows by the minute. Why did I never know that our family has property here? Why would Mom and GG keep this from me?

"But if I'm eaten by a ghost, I'll kill you," Tess says.

"After you're dead?" I say, as Tess steps over the chain.

"Yes, after I become a flesh-eating ghost."

I laugh. "That's a price I'm willing to pay." I grab two big sticks off the ground, and I hand one to Tess.

"Is this to fend off the ghosts?" She looks at the stick with doubt.

"It's to beat back the overgrowth," I say. "And spiderwebs."

"Great," Tess says. "More things that might eat me."

"Cedar Branch has human-eating spiders? That should have been on the news, or at least in the brochure."

I swipe the branch back and forth, giving us space to walk and pushing back the raspberry bushes, sumac, and sassafras.

"I wasn't aware Cedar Branch had a brochure," Tess says.

"If it does, it should definitely alert visitors of human-eating spiders." I smack at a mosquito buzzing by my ear.

Tess stops to smell the honeysuckle bordering our path. "And haunted cabins," she adds. She plucks a bloom and brings it to me, pulling out the stem to reveal a clear drop of nectar.

"Yes, and haunted cabins," I agree.

"Here." Tess holds up the bloom for me to lick the nectar. I pause and then lean in to catch the nectar before it falls. "Tastes like summer, doesn't it?"

I guess it tastes like Tess's summer, and my mom's too, probably. She spent all her summers here up until she was my age. But it doesn't taste like summer to me. Honeysuckle only reminds me of death now.

We walk tentatively forward, through trees that form an arch over the driveway, filtering the sunlight into a thousand shades of green. Cicadas drone around us and unseen birds call to one another in their singsong way. Eventually, the narrow drive ends at a plot of land that must have once been cleared.

"Whoa." I breathe the word out as I take in the sight before us.

"Whoa is right," Tess says in a quiet voice.

Goldenrod, Queen Anne's lace, black-eyed Susan, and more plants I can't identify have overtaken the plot of land, all growing up to our waists. But the plants are not what makes us gasp. There's a cabin, or what looks like a cabin, though it's barely identifiable as a man-made structure. It's completely engulfed by creeping vines that are growing up the exterior walls, covering windows and snaking through gutters and drainpipes. The roof sprouts grass and moss. The steps bloom with mushrooms.

I swim through the wildflowers and weeds until I land at the base of the three steps to the door. My shoes squish through fungi as I place my foot on the first and then the second step. I tug at the vines to expose the screen door. After unlatching it,

I pull it open, ripping more vines away as I do. The old hinges whine loudly. The knob of the main door won't give, though, and I can't get inside. I cup my hands around my eyes and peer through the windowpanes on the door, but it's too dusty to see much more than shadows.

Walking around the cabin, I'm greeted by a direct view of Eagles Cove. Battered wooden steps lead down to a dock that's half-submerged. Cattails border the edge of the water. The level of neglect doesn't match what I know of my grandmother or my mother. It must have been beautiful at one time, but that time is long past.

"Check this out," Tess calls.

I walk back to Tess. There's a large space beside the driveway where the plants aren't growing in the same willful way as they are all around the cabin. It's just empty.

"Strange," I say.

At the edge where the tall plants give way to scrubby grass and dirt, something sparkles in the sunlight. I bend down and find a rock, half-buried. I pry it out and rub the dirt from its surface, revealing a smooth, oval-shaped stone about the size of a golf ball. It appears black until the sun hits it, revealing its rich molasses-colored depths. I slide it into the pocket of my running shorts. "Ready to head back?"

"I am, are you, though?" Tess asks.

"Yeah, I mean, I want to see more, but I need a key to get in there." I give one last look at the foliage-encased cabin and we walk back down the dirt driveway toward Shaw Road. When we step over the chain, an intense shiver runs through me.

"Are you okay?" Tess asks. "You look pale all of a sudden."

"I don't know. Just got a weird chill." I shake out my arms and legs. "Probably just dehydrated," I say.

As we start an easy trot back into town, my mind is occupied with the cabin and wondering why I've never heard about it from Mom or GG. But mostly I'm wondering where I might find the key.

Chapter Two
EDIE

Flooded with curiosity about the mysterious property, after I leave Tess, I do exactly what I told GG I was not likely to do. I go to the perpetual woods to find her.

It takes me a while. Not only do I need to find the exact right hawthorn tree by memory, but I also need to remember the exact right words that GG and Mom used to chant. I search my mind. The chant had four lines and there was something about the woods and a secret and being a daughter. I try a few times and feel like I'm close, but nothing happens.

I would give up, but this is too important. I want to know why I've never heard about that cabin. So I keep trying. I count the syllables on my fingers to get the rhythm right. Finally, I've got it.

"With secrets deep, woods wise and tall,
Keep our garden hidden from all.
Know me as a Daughter in this place;
Reveal to me now our sacred space."

A gentle rippling sensation flows around me. A glow brightens the area and then recedes, revealing the clearing—just as I'd remembered it. GG and Mom had taken me to this place every year until I was fourteen and had decided that magic was not for me.

At the opening is a wood bower entwined with wisteria, a shade of purple that Mom loved best. As I walk through it, I realize that I've never been here without her. When I was little, before my magic showed itself, we'd hold hands to walk through here. The heavy blanket of grief settles on me. She should be here with me. I breathe slowly until it lifts.

The periphery of the clearing is a circle of towering trees that GG uses for her recipes. Oak for courage; birch for protection; elm for intuition; cedar for healing and cleansing. I walk by an old cedar to the inner ring of smaller trees in flower, always in bloom no matter what time of year. Cherry trees with their thick, lush blossoms. Apple trees with their delicate pale pink buds that spring open into white petals. Viburnum fills the space with her heady scent wafting from tiny white flowers.

In the middle of it all stands the ancient hawthorn that perpetually lives in all of its seasons at once. Part of the tree is barren, for winter. Another section is blooming with small white flowers for spring. A third portion is thick with green leaves for early summer, and the final area of the tree sprouts bright red berries for late summer and fall. As the naked branches of the winter side begin to sprout buds, the red berries of the autumn branches drop to the ground; the flowers disappear, allowing leaves to grow; and so it goes. In never-ending seasonal motion.

Behind the hawthorn, in a clearing that gets strong sunlight, is GG's herb maze with calendula, chamomile (which I thought were daisies when I was little), echinacea (which I thought of as Mom's daisies on account of them being purple), peppermint (which GG let me pick and chew whenever I wanted), elder (whose berries gave me a very sick stomach once), yarrow, and others whose leaves I don't remember or never learned.

All around, petals from the flowering trees float in the air, falling softly toward the ground, where they form a thick carpet beneath my feet. The bees buzz purposefully around their hives that sit beyond the herb maze. This is where GG harvests honey and the beeswax for her salves and candles. There is a huge stone slab beside the herb garden, where GG works when she's here. But at the moment, GG isn't working. She sits cross-legged before a low altar. Her eyes are closed, and her lips move in a whispered chant.

GG must sense my presence because her eyes fly open. "Edie!" She rises from her cross-legged position. "I see that your mind was changed. What caused it?"

I don't see any reason to beat around the bush. "I saw the cabin today."

GG says nothing for a moment; then, "I see."

I'm relieved that GG doesn't play dumb. Then again, I'm not sure she'd know how.

"Why didn't you tell me that we have property here?" I ask. "Why didn't Mom?"

Her hands drop to her sides. "That place is no concern of yours."

"You and Mom and Grandfather spent summers there. It must have meant something to our family."

GG opens her mouth. Closes it. She shakes her head.

"Do you still have the key?"

GG sets her lips in a thin line. Then she says, "You must stay away from that cabin."

A flare of anger flashes in me. "You won't let me go home. And now you won't let me go to the cabin either? If Mom spent time there, I want to, too." My hands begin to tingle.

"Restrain yourself. We cannot have your uncontrolled element in these woods."

I clench my fists, but my frustration grows. And so does the tingling in my fingers. The flower petals falling all around us, which seemed so beautiful a moment ago, smother me now.

"Do not disrespect me, Edie." She lifts one hand and the

leaves on the trees shiver in response. The falling flower petals swirl into a funnel cloud. GG has never used her magic against me, and I don't think she will now, but her point is clear. If there is a test of wills, I will lose. I don't even know how to use my own magic.

"Go home. We'll talk about this later."

My unanswered questions leave a bitter taste in my mouth. But GG has made it clear that this conversation is over.

"That houseboat is *not* my home," I say, and I leave her standing among her trees and herbs as a flurry of flower petals falls all around her.

When I get back to the boat, I strip out of my sweaty running clothes, and the rock I'd found falls out of my pocket, bouncing on the floor. It feels cold when I pick it up, despite the heat of the day. I set it in a dish on my dresser along with my running watch.

Throughout my shift at the ice cream shop, my frustration at GG grows and grows. By the time I return to the marina, the night is lit by the nearly full moon. The other docked boats dip and nod on the water. Jim's office is dark. I pace before GG's boat. I can't imagine sitting in there, and I don't want to face GG when she returns. I told her that this boat wasn't home, and I meant it. I step inside and lift the car keys from the hook by the door. Home—real home—is a bit of a drive, but I don't care.

GG's car doesn't want to start at first. I close my eyes. "Please," I say. "I need this."

I smell honeysuckle. Opening my eyes, I see Mom in the passenger seat. I close my eyes again, hoping she'll disappear. Her presence reminds me that she'd want peace between GG and me. I try to start the car once more and the engine turns over. I sigh my relief, and when I open my eyes, Mom's gone.

After checking my mirrors, I pull onto the lane and point the car toward the highway that will take me back to Baltimore and the home I lived in with my mother my whole life. I bring the old Subaru up to speed. No taillights appear on the dark country road unspooling before me and no headlights behind, either.

Something catches my eye in the rearview. A dark patch like a shadow. But when I look again, there's nothing there. Just me alone on the road. A sudden chill raises goose bumps on my skin. For once I wish my mother's ghost would come back. I fiddle with the temperature knobs and then roll the windows down to let in the humid June air. Moments later, the car starts coughing and wheezing. I didn't even know cars still coughed and wheezed. I'm at the sign for the town line when the car lets out one last strangled gasp and stops.

"No! No, no, no, no, no."

I try switching it off and on again, but the car will not revive.

"Please, please, let me go," I say.

But this time, the car refuses to give in. White smoke and

an odd smell billow from under the hood, sort of like when you burn green branches. I feel around for the lever that opens the hood, and finally I find it. Waving the smoke away as I look under the hood, the problem is clear immediately, even though I know nothing about cars.

"What the fu—"

I lean in because what I'm seeing makes no sense. Vines weave their way around the engine block and through every part of the mechanics of the car. I sigh and lean against the bumper. I'm not entirely sure how to get myself out of this mess.

Night has fallen fast, but the moon is bright. Mom is back, floating by my side. I sense a flickering in my peripheral vision, but when I turn, I see nothing. My nerves jangle and I tell myself to calm down. The song Mom used to sing to me whenever I was scared pops into my head. I start singing quietly.

> "Darkness, darkness, not welcome here,
> Return from where you came.
> Sunlight, starlight, please be near;
> I call you in my name."

A warm glow deep inside my chest brings instant comfort. But it's followed quickly by the burn of loss. I wish that I'd worn running shoes instead of these flip-flops, but I didn't exactly give any thought to this plan. I text Tess, and after a bit she replies that she wishes she could help, but she's at a party and she didn't drive.

"Got myself into this mess. Gotta get myself out," I say out loud.

When I pop the trunk, I'm not sure what I'm looking for, but it's definitely not an iron box containing a couple knives, a large container of salt, and a small jar of oil. I'm intrigued before I remember that I'm angry at GG, and at her useless tools. Then I realize the knives might not be useless after all. I select the largest one and return to the front of the car, where I hack away the vines. I only stop when it starts resembling an engine and not a jungle.

When I get behind the wheel, the car starts right up, but I'm not trusting it now. Admitting defeat, I turn the car around. I'm not going to try to drive all the way home in a car that might break down any minute. Mom sits next to me as we return to the marina.

When I arrive back at the boat, GG is waiting for me. The night is still dark, though dawn is only a few hours away now. GG doesn't yell or accuse or threaten. Instead, she says in an even tone, "I see you've learned about my anti-theft charm."

I can't decide if I want to give GG props for the most original anti-theft device ever or if I want to defend myself. I decide to defend myself. "I wasn't stealing the car."

"You took my car without asking."

She has a point. I run my hand over my head. "I wanted to go home."

"I know," GG says; then, in a softer tone, "I have something for you."

My eyes snap up to hers. "Is it keys to the cabin?" I know I'm being pushy, but I say it anyway.

GG gives a curt shake of her head and I know not to push further. From her lap, she lifts an object wrapped in cloth and tied with twine, and she holds it out to me. Despite my frustration with her, I step forward to accept this offering. I unwrap the cloth to reveal a small book with a red leather cover. The Celtic trinity knot is embossed on the cover.

"A journal?" I ask.

"Yes."

I frown. "You want me to write my feelings?"

Journaling was suggested to me by several well-meaning people over the last ten months. GG, thankfully was not one of them. I never saw the point of writing feelings on paper. For me, running is the best way through the bad moments.

"Wait." I turn the journal over in my hands. "This looks familiar."

"Open it," GG says.

When I open it, I see the pages are already filled, and I recognize the handwriting in deep purple ink right away. Any bravado

I had disappears, like the fake confetti that Mom conjured for my birthday one year.

I look at GG. "Mom's?"

GG nods.

"Why are you giving it to me now?"

"It is apparent that you need it now," GG says.

What I need is for GG to let me go home, away from anything to do with magic. What I need is a real mother who is here with me, not a ghost floating in and out of my days.

As if she's heard my thoughts, GG says, "It's hard to know, at times, what will help." She rises from the chair. "Sleep well."

Temperance follows GG to her room.

"Night," I say as I turn toward my room, the journal clutched in my hand.

Chapter Three
EDIE

"Hey, Car Trouble," Tess calls when I enter Ye Olde Ice Cream Shoppe through the back entrance. It's more of a stand than a shop, with two windows that slide open for us to serve customers. The ice cream is homemade, and I've learned that people will wait in pretty long lines for the good stuff around here.

I liked it better when she called me Summer Girl, which was my second nickname after Runner Girl. She's been calling me this new one since I asked her to come save my ass on Sunday night. Now it's Wednesday afternoon. I guess I'm stuck with this one until I do something that inspires a new nickname.

Today Tess's short hair is pinned back with multicolored plastic butterfly barrettes, and she wears a shirt plastered with a dog sporting pink sunglasses and surrounded by puppies. Over the image are the words BOSS BITCH. Can't make this stuff up.

"Did you run this morning?" she asks.

I nod. "Speed workout, but you and I are on for tomorrow, right?"

"You got it."

"Any prep?" I ask as I double-tie my apron.

"Nah," she says. "We had a lull after lunch, so I did it."

Tess's aunt owns the ice cream shop, so Tess works more hours than I do. She's even already made sure that we have an extra container of Chesapeake Mud up front, a big seller every night. And the milkshake machines are clean and ready to go.

"There's a party tonight. Want to come with?" Tess asks.

"I don't know," I say. Parties—at least the ones at home featuring people getting drunk and acting stupid—were not my thing, and I can't imagine it would be any different here. To avoid the subject, I busy myself with prep work that Tess already took care of. I check that napkin dispensers are full. They are. I wipe down the counter even though it appears clean.

"You've been here for weeks and you haven't come out at all. You can't just work and run the whole time that you're here."

"You really want to go to a party with your awkward co-worker who doesn't know anyone?"

"You are so much more than my awkward co-worker," Tess says. "You are my fellow Frozen Confection Dispenser."

"You make me sound like an ice cream vending machine."

Tess laughs. "Come on," she cajoles me. "I want you to meet people."

"I'll think about it," I say. "But right now it looks like we have a customer."

Okay, maybe I did want to get the focus off my nonexistent

social life, but it's not like I manifested the customer. I don't have that kind of magic. Tess and I head to the front, and the next four hours are full of ice cream cones, sundaes, and sprinkles.

Little kids take their ice cream choices super seriously, and the heartbreaker is when the top-heavy scoop plops to the ground, leaving the kid holding a useless, empty cone. You'd be surprised how often it happens. I hear a child crying and I know it's happened again.

"I've got it," I call to Tess, who is busy making sundaes for another family. I scoop a fresh cone for the little guy and call him over.

"Here you go, buddy," I say. "A new one just for you. And this one won't fall over. I promise." A glow brightens within me. I guess I like helping people. The ice cream cone seems to glow a little as well, but that must be the lighting in here. It's not magic. It can't be.

The boy gives me a wavery smile, tears still falling down his chubby cheeks, and his mom gives us a big tip.

"You have the touch," Tess says when he stops crying as soon as he licks his new cone.

I shrug. "I think it's the ice cream."

As the night wears on, elementary school kids trickle in— they come up with the strangest concoctions. Gummi Bears and butterscotch, really? The tweens with no parents are mostly hoping to see or be seen by others their age. We don't get many high school kids, and when we do, they're usually locals begging for free ice cream from Tess.

The night is over quicker than I expected, and Tess says it's time to go. I'm washing the scoopers. "Go where?" I say to buy time. I really like Tess, and she doesn't need to know how hopeless I am in social situations.

"Edie, for someone smart, you sure act clueless sometimes. Dry off those scoopers. We're going out."

I sense that there's no use arguing, so I do as she says. It can't be that bad. It probably won't be that bad. After all, Tess is nothing like those kids at home.

Inside Tess's Jeep, I fasten my seat belt and turn to her, mustering some confidence. "Where are we headed?"

"The barn," Tess says as she reverses out of the parking lot.

"*The* barn?"

"Yeah, it's this place where we party."

"Are you hoping a certain waiter from the diner will be at this barn?"

Tess grins. "Jorge? He'll be there."

"You sound pretty confident."

"I am, because there aren't many other places he could be. You probably had tons of places to party in Baltimore?"

"You mean Smaltimore. And anyway, I never partied much."

"You miss it? Baltimore?"

"Yeah, I do," I say. "Especially my house."

"Must be a weird change, living on a houseboat. Maybe your grandma will move back to your old house with you at the end of the summer."

"I definitely want to be back there for the start of school," I say. The end of the summer seems forever away right now. Especially when I think about the recent tension with GG. That cabin keeps grabbing at my mind, though.

After a couple miles, Tess turns off the paved road. The Jeep's tires crunch gravel as we park in front of the barn. It's already packed with cars and pickup trucks. Honeyed light spills from the open barn doors and music wafts to us on the humid night air. She flips the visor down, checks her makeup, and adds another dab of lip gloss.

"Ready to party?" Tess says. Then, when she sees my expression, she adds, "I promise you will not be the most awkward person there."

As soon as we get inside, Tess pulls me to the dance floor, which is in actuality the middle of the barn floor. As expected, I'm not sure what to do with my arms, and my feet are like two concrete blocks, but Tess's goofy dance moves make me laugh and I loosen up enough to bop to the music a little bit. After a few songs, though, the summer heat has gotten to her. Tess half yells, half mimes to ask me if I want to find something to drink. I nod and follow her off the dance floor. I'm sort of relieved to leave until I realize that all of the people not dancing seem to be drinking. And that's not something I do very well at all. I'd rather be dancing, which says a lot. At the first cooler, we find beer and hard lemonade. Tess asks if I want one, but I shake my head. I brace myself for her to give me a hard time, but she doesn't.

We root through a few more coolers before we find water. "Man, they're hiding the non-alky drinks, aren't they?" Tess says.

I feel immediately relieved that Tess isn't going to be one of the stupid drunk people. Then again, she *is* a designated driver, I guess. The edges of her blonde hair are darkened with sweat. She rummages in the cooler and comes up with one water and one soda, both of which she rolls all over her face and neck.

"Is Jorge here?" I ask as I grab a water for myself. I've only glimpsed him once through the window of the diner and I don't think I'd recognize him again.

As I take my first blessed sip, across the barn I notice a Black girl talking to a tall guy with brown skin. The girl's hair is a cloud of curls around her face just barely kissing her shoulders. She's wearing loose overalls over a tube top. Layers of necklaces drape down her chest. She gestures with her hands and rings sparkle from most of her fingers. But it isn't so much how she looks that grabs me; it's how animated she is, how open. I don't think I've ever felt that free, except when I'm running. I feel an unexpected quiver in my belly—maybe there *is* someone other than Tess worth talking to here.

"He's over there," Tess says, "with Rhia. Let's go."

"Who's Rhia?" I ask, following Tess and feigning a coolness I definitely don't feel. We make our way to the other side, where we stop in front of the dark-haired guy and the very girl I just noticed. I may be a Mitchell, but I wasn't aware that my thoughts were projecting.

The guy, who must be Jorge, smiles big at Tess. "Hey."

"Hey," Tess says, and I think she might be blushing.

"Nice dancing out there," he says.

"I've got moves, right?"

"You've got something. Not sure they qualify as moves though," the girl says, smiling at Tess. She's also just drinking water and is somehow not sweating profusely like Tess and me. Standing beside her in my damp Ye Olde Ice Cream Shoppe shirt and running shorts, I look like a schlub. I set my shoulders back and smile, hoping to at least look like a confident schlub.

"Oh, hell no," Jorge says, looking in the direction of the barn entrance. "My little brother just showed up. Be right back."

"Kay," Tess says. She watches him walk off and turns to us, waving her face with one hand. "Would it kill them to have AC in this place?"

"Tess, it's a barn," the girl says. "Besides, you're just hot for

Jorge." She turns to me. "I mean, have you ever heard of AC in a barn?"

"This is the first barn I've been in, so I'm probably not the person to ask."

The girl leans back to look me up and down. "First barn you've ever been in? Who *are* you?"

I open my mouth to speak, but the girl's large brown eyes have tied my tongue.

"And now you've met Rhia." Tess motions with a magician's sweep.

"Rhia"—Tess then gestures to me— "this is Edie, who I told you about. A lot."

"I knew that. Just messing with you."

And now I'm on the receiving end of Rhia's dazzling smile.

My voice finally decides to show up to the party. "Yeah, apparently I'm Tess's fellow Frozen Confection Dispenser."

"So you're a vending machine? For ice cream?" Rhia says.

I break into a smile. "That's what I said!" I give Tess an I-told-you-so look. "We need a better job title."

"How about Frozen Wonder Delivery Agent?" Tess says.

Rhia makes a face. "Are you a delivery person or a secret agent? And what even is Frozen Wonder? Is it bread? Is it snow? Just, no." She taps her lip with one long ringed finger. Then her eyebrows fly up. "How about Ice Cream Alchemist?"

I nod. "That could work."

The supposed hot song of summer comes on and Tess looks to the dance floor. Rhia fiddles with her necklaces. I fish around for something more to say, something that won't embarrass Tess and make her regret that she brought me.

"Edie lives on the purple houseboat," Tess says.

I'm not sure that's where I would have gone, but at least we aren't standing around in awkward silence.

"You're a Mitchell?" Rhia asks me.

I suppress a sigh. "You know my grandmother."

Rhia's laugh is big and open, the sort of laugh that invites others to laugh along with her. It reminds me of Mom's. "'Course I know Miss Geraldine. This is a small town."

I'm getting ready to ask Rhia how her summer's going because I'd like to move the conversation away from my family, but apparently the only conversation starters I've got fall into the category of Most Boring Questions Adults Ask Teens. I open my mouth, but she saves me by speaking first.

"I'm so sorry," Rhia says, her forehead crinkles with concern.

"Sorry for what?" I ask.

"About your mom. That was last summer, wasn't it?"

The whooshing in my ears blocks out all sound before the tsunami of sorrow crashes over me. My breath hitches in my throat. I'm brought back to that August morning last year.

And then she appears. My beautiful mother is floats behind

Tess and Rhia. It's not unusual that she's appeared. After all, it *is* the way of our family. But the timing isn't helping.

"I—I've got to go," I blurt.

Maybe I hear Tess calling my name over the pounding music. But I don't turn around. I push through the sweaty bodies and Mom bobs along beside me as I go. By the time I get outside, where it's not any cooler but at least not as crowded, Mom has disappeared again. I start to run down the gravel driveway and toward the main road. I have my running shoes on tonight— unlike the other night—and I don't care how many miles it is back to the marina. I need to run.

Chapter Four
EDIE

Panting when I reach the boat, I climb up to the roof and sit cross-legged, staring at a clear sky strewn with stars and a fat, nearly full moon while GG's plants nod to sleep all around me. Most of the other boats in the marina are quiet at this time of night. Just a few people are on the decks of their boats; the sound of conversation and strains of music drift to me. The warm air fills with the scent of honeysuckle, and Mom reappears nearby.

She made me the center of attention tonight. I don't tell her that though. GG thinks I'll feel better if I talk to Mom's ghost, like she talks to all of her ghosts. But I can't bring myself to do that. I don't see the point. So I watch her float nearby, a constant reminder of what I've lost.

My mind casts back to that hot August morning last year. I was studying at the kitchen table. Mom joked that I was the only teen in a mile radius who got up early in August to study. She kissed my forehead and told me that she'd just now finished a piece of jewelry for me. I begged to see it, but she said that she planned to ride her bike to the market to pick up a few things. When she returned, we'd have as throughout Tea and a Talk because there was something that she needed to tell me, and she'd show me the piece she'd made then. Tea and a Talk was what we did when we had something important to share with each other.

There was Tea and a Talk when I told Mom that I no longer wanted to be homeschooled. There was Tea and a Talk when Mom told me about the birds and the bees, as well as when she told me about sex. The former was related to how our family is connected to the earth and nature. The latter was what everyone else means by "the birds and the bees," a topic of zero interest to me, but the tea was nice. I always felt better after our talks. Mom had a way of doing that.

Except for just the one time it didn't help. I'd asked for Tea and a Talk to tell Mom that I was no longer buying her fairy tale about me not having a father. We lived in the real world and I wanted to know his identity. That time the tea was sharp and black, and no amount of milk would reduce the bitterness. It didn't come with any answers, either.

On the day of the bike ride, I remember her telling me about the jewelry and the Tea and a Talk and I remember her smile and I remember I told her to wear a helmet. I think I remember that part about the helmet, but maybe I only wish I had told her. I keep going back in my mind, trying to remember the conversation, as if remembering the conversation would change the outcome.

She'd been standing before me, smiling her big smile. A

canvas bag over one shoulder in case she found something that tickled her fancy while she was out and about (her words).

Then there were police officers, two of them, a man and a woman, at the front door. I'd started to get hungry for lunch and wondered if I should wait for Mom or go ahead and eat. You never knew where her adventures would take her or for how long. There was the knock at the door. I held the door open, halfway in the house, halfway on the porch. I remember thinking how hot the police officers must be in their uniforms in the humid August morning air. Thinking that someone must have been robbed on our street. They wanted to let us know. Ask us if we'd seen anything.

But instead they asked for Geraldine Mitchell. A breeze picked up and the scent of the honeysuckle bushes wafted toward me. All of the hair on my arms stood on end. I opened my mouth to say that my grandmother wasn't here, that she lived on the Chesapeake, but then I heard her voice behind me.

"I'm Geraldine Mitchell."

I turned to find my grandmother behind me in the foyer like some odd version of Mary Poppins. Her long gray hair was braided and twisted into a crown on the top of her head. She wore a long jacket and in one hand she held an umbrella like it was a walking stick.

"How—?" I looked around. "W-when—?" I stuttered, but

my grandmother walked past me to the officers sweating on our porch.

"I guess this is about Maura, then, isn't it?"

The officers seemed surprised, but then they didn't know GG. I did know GG, so I wondered how long she'd had this sense. And when she'd arrived. I'd been in the kitchen studying since Mom had left, so I would've seen her come in through the back door. But those thoughts dissolved when I heard the officer's words.

As the female officer spoke, GG was still as stone in contrast to the breeze that picked up around us. The wind ruffled the plants. The branches of the trees began to sway. The porch swing moved as though someone were rocking back and forth on it, and all of the wind chimes were set swinging; a cacophony of sound.

"Edie," she said. "We must go."

And then we were speeding to the emergency room of the closest hospital. Inside was a foreign space of white sterility. Eventually a doctor came to speak with us. She said a lot of things, but I only registered a few of them, like *too much damage* and *we did all that we could do*. They didn't let me see my mother, which only added to my sense that it hadn't truly happened. It could not have happened. She'd been right there. In front of me.

By the time we left the hospital, the rain was coming hard and fast. The ride back to the house was slow, with the windshield wipers thumping back and forth, our car a tiny boat in the vast ocean of my mother's death. On my lap was the canvas bag. The one that Mom had carried on her shoulder when she left for the bike ride. I didn't remember anyone handing it to me, but I clutched it to my body during the drive home.

Back at the house, I sat on my bed and considered the bag. It was blackened with road dirt. Inside, were two bruised apples, a decimated bag of cookies, a small purple velvet pouch with a silk drawstring, and a red leather journal with a Celtic knot on the cover. The book and the purple pouch had somehow remained unscathed.

Inside the velvet pouch was a beautiful necklace made by Mom. The chain flowed like a shining river, and the pendant was a perfectly rendered silver acorn with a tiny leaf at the top. And on a small card, my mother's handwriting. A note to me. This was the piece of jewelry Mom had made for me. I couldn't handle it. Too soon. I poured the necklace back into the pouch and placed it in the top drawer of my dresser.

Then I crawled under my covers to wait for the day when my world would stop threatening to capsize.

The seasons turned even though my mother was gone. I went back to school. I ignored the holidays. Somehow spring arrived, and I ignored my birthday, and then summer had the nerve to come around again. GG announced that we'd be moving to her houseboat, where she lived when she wasn't visiting us at the house in Baltimore.

I didn't want to leave my home, the space where Mom and I had lived together. But here I am, alone on the roof of a houseboat with a ghost for a mother. And now I've run away from a party and my only friend just because someone—that interesting girl—tried to be kind by expressing condolences.

I stand up beneath the starry sky and begin to climb down the ladder from the roof of the boat. Ten months since Mom died. Nearly three weeks since I moved onto this boat. I let myself into our living quarters and head to my room, where I fall back on the bed. Now, instead of stars, I'm staring at the honey glow of the wood-plank ceiling. My phone lights up with a text. Tess asking if I'm okay.

I'm not sure I'm okay, so I reply that I'm sorry I bolted. I include a sad face emoji.

Tess sends back a broken heart emoji and asks if I want to talk. I don't want to talk, but I don't want to be an asshole either. So I just don't answer. After a while she texts again, saying she'll see me in the morning. I start to type that I'm not up for our morning run. Then I remember telling Tess that I would never bail on her. I respond with a thumbs-up and a time to meet in front of the diner.

I reach over to place my phone on the bedside table. Mom's

red journal sits beside the lamp. I don't remember placing it there. I guess GG could have put it there, hoping I'd read it. Though GG doesn't come into my room much. She believes in privacy. Picking up the book, I run my hand over the smooth leather cover. I wonder if Mom ever bolted from parties. I flip it open to the first entry from June 2003, the year before I was born.

Chapter Five
MAURA

June 21, 2003

When Mama returned from the hospital that night, she came to my room and sat on the side of my bed. She placed her hand on mine and opened her mouth to speak, but instead of words, feathers spilled out, oily black like night. They drifted toward the floor before disintegrating into ash. That's how I knew my father had died.

Ever since he'd gone into the hospital a few days ago, I'd been wearing one of his old T-shirts. Every night, I wore it. So, when Mama came home late at night, I was wearing the shirt. My mother curled herself around my body as though I was still a small child and not an eighteen-year-old girl-woman.

We stayed like that while the house crashed around us, while the world remade itself in the shape of someone gone. When dawn slid her fingers around the blinds and into my room, illuminating our new world in cruel relief, my mother rose from my bed and left my room.

Mama did not speak, so I called my father's sister, a woman I barely knew at all. She arrived and handled all the arrangements—as they called them, as if they were a cluster

of Mama's flowers. Mama remained silent during the arrangements. Dad, it turned out, had planned everything fairly well on
his own. There was a letter with the details in his top drawer. It
had been there for a while, probably. Mama knew it had been
there, probably.

In the event of my death, it began. He had decided he would
be cremated, and that his ashes would be stored in a red cedar
box. I'm certain that he chose the wood because he loved working with cedar and not for its healing and cleansing properties.
It's not that he didn't believe in our craft. He lived with us, after
all. But he was a simple man when it came down to it.

Throughout all of it, Mama never opened her mouth. I made
her the calming chamomile tea with a sprinkle of the soothing
spell she'd taught me, but she didn't touch it. She nodded to the
people who came to hug us and clasp our hands in theirs. They
said things that couldn't help us. Not those words, anyway.

After it was all over and Dad's sister had left, Mama and I sat
in the silent house, looking at the cedar box that contained my
father. Six days since Dad had died and my mother still hadn't
spoken. And my father had not appeared to us. Mama stood and
went to the steps. I followed her up the stairs and to my mother
and father's room. Now it would only be my mother's room. I
watched as Mama pulled her travel bag from the shelf in her
closet. I watched as she selected a few things, and I understood.
I went to my room and did the same.

We met downstairs in the kitchen. We turned off the lights and left through the back door, not bothering to lock it. What we valued was in a red cedar box. We placed our bags in the trunk of the car. I settled into the passenger seat and Mama into the driver's seat. Then we pulled out of the driveway and headed for the highway. We traveled with the sound of the car swallowing the black ribbon of road, my hands resting on the flat top of the box.

We arrived at the cabin in early evening. I breathed in the familiar smell of pine and earth. I watched fireflies dance in the waning purple shades of the day. We didn't have keys because we rarely needed them. I whispered the words since Mama still wasn't speaking, and the door opened for me. I sighed my comfort at being back at our beloved cabin, the rich smell of cedar filling me with thoughts of my father. I placed my father's ashes in my room, on my dresser. One by one, Mama and I opened all the windows, inviting the evening air of the summer solstice to float through our cabin. Outside, the insects buzzed with evening chatter and the frogs croaked their replies. I walked down the steps to the dock, and I sat there, knees tucked under my chin, watching the water ripple before me, dark and alive. Mosquitos danced near me and away, never biting, one of the benefits of being my mother's daughter. The rickety old houseboat bobbed in the water.

Last season, Dad had shown up at the dock driving it. He'd

won it in a poker game, he said. Was he already sick then? Did his body know that it was beginning its march toward death? Did *he* know?

I wanted to see him, and I wondered if Mama's silence was the reason he hadn't appeared. I wondered if there was something we could do to bring him to us. An evening rain began to fall, so I climbed the steps back to the cabin. I'd expected that Mama would speak now that we were here. But on the porch, she rocked in her chair and stared out at the river, which met her silence with its own.

Chapter Six

EDIE

When I finish reading, I close the journal and hold it between my hands. Temperance lies on my pillow. Mom hovers nearby.

"I had no idea," I breathe out the words, and I half expect to see feathers.

I hadn't given much thought to the reality that Mom had been through what I'm going through now. That GG had now lost two beloved members of her small family. Mom still hadn't seen her father's ghost when she wrote this entry.

It had been days after the accident the first time I saw Mom. Maybe even a full week. I'd spent most of those days in bed, then I'd get up and run in the dark of night. Hours, days, dates—they held no meaning. But when I woke that day and I saw Mom, I was flooded with relief. She wasn't dead. She was here, at my bedside, like any typical morning.

Only . . . she didn't respond when I spoke to her, and if I paid any attention at all, I'd notice that her hair defied gravity, brown curls floating around her head. And she wasn't exactly standing on the floor. She was floating. Maybe only an inch or so. But still. Also, there was the issue of no shadow.

After the third time Mom appeared to me, I went looking for GG. I found her in the kitchen repotting a gardenia.

"Morning, Edie." GG examined me over her glasses. "It's good to see you up in daylight."

"I've been seeing Mom."

GG didn't stop sprinkling food at the base of the plant. "Oh, good! I hadn't seen her, and I was beginning to wonder, but I saw her just this morning as well."

"It's true, then," I said.

"Many things are true. Which one are you speaking of?"

I sighed. "That we see our dead?"

"It is the way of our family. Had you doubted that our dead stay with us?" GG stopped working with the gardenia to look at me.

"Maybe not doubted, exactly," I say. "Maybe I'd hoped that it wasn't true."

I never denied that our family was different, magical, witchy. How could I? Each child born to a Mitchell possessed power over an element. And they had other talents, too. GG's way with plants far surpassed the typical green thumb. And Mom's ability with jewelry, well, people came from very far away to buy from her collection.

"As logical as you are, and you hoped for that?" GG asked. "Did you imagine that your mother and I talk to the air?"

"But it's not normal."

GG made a noise of annoyance. "Normal." She shook her

head and washed her hands. "Why you became so interested in *normal* is well beyond my understanding."

I looked away. There were things that even GG didn't know. But all that mattered now was that I was not taking part in any of it—not the way that GG could grow plants and infuse honey with something that exceeded what the bees provided, not the way that Mom created jewelry that held emotions. Not the way that each of them could command an element or brew remedies and tinctures that solved everyday problems. Now I could add to that list that I definitely wasn't interested in seeing ghosts.

"Mom understood."

"Your mother needed to teach you. And I'm certain that she would have. She had not planned for this." GG gestures to indicate us being together and Mom being gone. "But your mother's death and the fact that she never got around to teaching you does not change what or who you are. Make no mistake: you *are* a Mitchell woman. And you will need to learn what all of that means for you."

Now, lying on my bed having read the first journal entry after bolting from the party because someone I don't even know mentioned my mother's death, the rocking of the boat maddens me.

I pull in a deep breath to steady myself the way Mom taught me when I was young. *What can you touch?* she'd ask. *What can you smell? What can you hear?* I try over and over, but it's so hard to yank myself from the past. I think of the cabin and feel my mother's grief overlaid with memories of how it was for me when Mom died.

There's a slight sheen on the last page of her entry. It's as if some wax was dripped or smeared on the paper. I run my finger over it. It's smooth. The moment my finger touches it, though, I sense the zing of magic. The room is illuminated with a golden glow. I am awake and alert. Then, as though I just read them and it was imprinted on my retinas, I see directions for opening a stuck door.

A CHARM FOR STUBBORN LOCKS

1. Blow three times into the empty keyhole.

2. Press your left thumb against the keyhole.

3. Say these words: *With my breath and words I've spoken, sticky lock, I bid you open.*

4. Twist the doorknob and the door will open! I know the spell doesn't sound very impressive. But it always works. I promise.

After a moment, the image dissolves. The room doesn't seem so bright and the hyper-alertness fades. Now at the top of the page are the words *A Charm for Stubborn Locks*. I admire how Mom magicked the spell into the book more than the spell itself. I mean, how often do you come across a lock without a key?

No sooner have I had the thought than I picture the locked door to the cabin. Here is a way I can get in without my grandmother knowing. A glimmer of hope on a suck-ass night. I almost smile as I turn out the light to go to sleep.

I wake flooded with thoughts of Mom and GG in that cabin alone with their heartache. I put on my running gear to meet Tess for our morning run.

"Morning, Edie," Tess says when I arrive.

"Are you greeting me with my actual name?" I ask. "No Barn Bolter or Soiree Sprinter?"

"Nah, not when you were obviously upset. Also, 'Soiree Sprinter'? Give me more credit, please."

That gets a smile out of me, which says a lot right now. We warm up at an easy pace down Main Street heading toward the bike trail that was once a rail line running alongside the river. "I'm thinking we do a tempo run today. Does that sound good?"

"To be clear—none of these runs sound good. I'm only doing this so I can catch my little brothers when I'm babysitting."

"Fair," I say. "Keep up with me and you'll outrun 'em all." I jokingly nudge her as I jog past.

"Oh, I'll keep up," Tess says, bumping me right back. "If by 'keep up' you mean fall down gasping for breath. Also, I have no idea what 'tempo run' means."

"It's when you push the pace for a sustained period," I say. "Not quite race pace. We'll do two miles."

"If you say so."

We fall quiet for a few minutes as we drop into our pace. "You want to talk about what happened last night?" she asks.

A motorboat roars down the river, pulling squealing kids on an inner tube.

"Any chance we can pretend it didn't happen?" I ask.

We continue on, the bright morning sun slanting toward us.

"How 'bout those O's?" Tess says, in an obvious bid to break the silence.

"Didn't take you for a baseball fan." I give her a small smile.

"I love all things summer."

We run another half mile before I speak again. "It's been ten months, but sometimes when it hits me, I feel like I'm drowning."

"You mean about your mom being gone?"

"Yeah," I say. We turn onto the trail and I start to pick up the pace. "It's like I'm stuck in this in-between place. Trying to move forward but also wishing to have her back."

The trail takes us toward the bridge that crosses over Cedar Branch River. The wood chips are soft beneath our feet and the trees shade us from the summer heat. It reminds me of the Stony Run trail at home where I loved to train.

"It's a lot though, losing your mom. Maybe be patient with yourself?"

Instead of answering, I push the pace a bit more. Patience is not part of my DNA. Tess impresses me by keeping up.

"You're doing great," I say. "You sure you've never run before?"

"Ha!" she pants next to me. "I'm actually dying. And maybe a little back in middle school."

A few people pass us coming from the other direction. A woman with a stroller, two guys running, a few people on mountain bikes. Tess greets every person with a smile and a wave.

"Do you know everyone in this town?" I ask.

"Almost," she says. "But I'm an equal-opportunity greeter. Hey—did you ask your grandmother about the cabin?"

"Yeah, it was a no-go."

"What do you mean?"

"She basically forbids me to go back there."

"Oh, wow," Tess says. After a beat she asks, "So when are you going back?"

We both laugh. "Anything happen with Jorge last night?"

"We hung out after the party."

"You like him?"

"You know what? I think I do!" Tess says between breaths.

We go a bit farther before I get the courage to ask about Rhia. I picture her carefree curls and the warm smile she gave me before she asked about my mother. "Are you and Rhia good friends?"

Tess's breathing becomes labored. She answers in short bursts.

"Totally. Since elementary school."

"She must think I'm bananas."

"Nah. Rhia doesn't judge," Tess says. "Anyway, you'll see her again."

We reach our turnaround point and head back.

"Because Cedar Branch is a small town?"

"Because being friends with me means being friends with Rhia."

I'm surprised to realize that my gut response is not to run away and hide. In fact, my gut—and other parts of me—might like to see Rhia again.

Back at the boat, I take off my watch, ready to strip down for my shower. The rock I found at the cabin still sits in the dish where I keep my watch. I pick it up, turning it over in my hand. I hold it in my palm and close my fingers around it in the way Mom taught me to hold crystals, to allow their good energy to move into you.

But this rock doesn't feel like good energy. It floods me with cold and nausea. I open my fingers to drop the rock back into the dish and I notice tiny black lines on my palm. The same sort of lines that run through granite or marble. I feel a little dizzy and I grab ahold of my dresser to steady myself. I may choose not to be a part of the family magic, but that doesn't mean I've forgotten all that I'd been taught. This rock is giving off very bad energy, and I want to get it off the boat as soon as possible. I use a sock to pick up the stone. I put that in a plastic bag and then run directly to Shaw Road.

At the giant oak and the precarious cairn, I turn down the same overgrown driveway. When I reach the empty space by the cabin, I look for the spot where I found the rock. On my knees, I dig a hole with my bare hands and dump the rock in there. I cover the hole up and sit back on my heels, wondering if there are some words I should say. But the only two spells I remember are the one for the perpetual woods and the new one for unlocking doors. Neither of those make sense for this.

Hoping I've contained that bad energy by burying the thing where it came from, I stand up and dust off my hands. I turn to take in the cabin. I try to imagine it the way Mom described it in her journal, absent of the unruly growth and sad neglect. I walk closer, drawn to this place where my mother spent her summers. I can get in. I know the spell. I turn back to look at the spot where I buried the rock. For what, I'm not sure. All I see is freshly turned earth patted down by my hands. Seems fine, so I figure I might as well check out the cabin. I crack my metaphorical magic knuckles and get in the headspace to do this spell.

I breathe in and let it out. I do that three more times until I admit that I'm procrastinating. I clench my hands and then uncurl my fingers. I can do this. It's just a simple spell. Like the

chant I said to get into the perpetual woods. Not like the magic
I tried to do before.

I close my eyes to call up the words. I kneel and blow into the
rusted keyhole three times. Then I press my left thumb against
it. What were the words? "With my breath and the words I'm
speaking, sticky lock open."

I open my eyes and try the knob, but it still won't turn.

I close my eyes again, picturing how the spell looked on the
page, how it had appeared in my mind. There was a rhyme. And
a rhythm, too. I flutter my eyes open and blow on the lock three
times again.

"With my breath and the words I've spoken, sticky lock, I bid
you open."

The brightening that comes with magic flashes and then
dims. There's a click of a bolt shifting. I turn the knob and the
door gives. A thrill rushes through me, but I tamp it down.
Bigger energy leads to bigger magic, and I do not want that.

I push the door open and a waft of air, cool and musty, slides
by me. The front room is dark, all the shades drawn. I step into
the center of the living area, my footsteps quieted by disintegrating rugs. I go to the large picture window and raise the yellowed
shade. In shocking contrast to the shadowed room, the view is
lush and full of color, overlooking the quiet cove and framed by
tall trees, leafy and bright green. From here, I can see the dock

that's slowly sinking into the river. Who gives up waterfront property? Makes zero sense.

Seeing something out of the corner of my eye, I turn. But nothing is there.

Despite the heat outside, I feel a chill. I run my hands over my upper arms. Maybe it's cold because the shades have been drawn.

Down a short hallway are three doors, all of them closed. The first door I open leads to a bathroom. Vines grow out of the toilet, overflowing the edge. They sprout from the sink and the shower drain, creeping across the floor, all of them tangling together. I tell myself it's a good thing I don't need to pee, and also they are only vines and vines can't hurt you, but I feel better after securely shutting the door, confining the vines.

I try the next door, opening it a sliver to reveal a slice of bedroom. Not overrun by vines. I push the door open farther. A shadow catches my eye at the edge of the room. But when I walk in, there's nothing. I feel chilled again, so I throw the shades open in this room, too. The sunlight that tries to break through is tinted green by the leaves covering the windows.

The room is not large. A queen-size bed sits against one wall and a chair perches in the corner where I thought I saw the shadow. I feel uneasy. But it's just an old, empty house. Nothing more. On the opposite side of the room is a tall dresser with three frames, facedown. I set them upright. In one frame is a photo of Mom on the dock, squinting into the sun. She's in her bathing suit and she's maybe ten years old. The backs of the other two frames are missing. The photos have been removed. I wonder why this photo of Mom was left behind. I slide it from the frame and stick it in my back pocket.

Next to the dresser is a closet, I learn. An old sweatshirt and a raincoat are the only items dangling from hangers inside. Except on the floor. A shadow curls on the floor in the farthest corner of the closet. No, that can't be right. Shadows don't curl. I pull the door open more fully and realize my mind is once again playing tricks on me. There's nothing there.

I quickly leave the room, making sure to shut that door behind me as well. I shake my hands out like I do before a big race. This is just a house. That's all. The last door opens into another bedroom, smaller than the first. I stand still with my hand on the doorknob as it hits me that this was my mother's room. I am hollowed by the realization. Two twin beds sit parallel to one another. Opening the shade on the window opposite the beds, I imagine my mother's hand touching this shade. My view through vines is of that barren land in back of the house and the driveway. In the haze of the hot morning sun, the light wavers above the dead grass near where I buried the rock. I blink and it's gone.

The dresser is dusty, like everything else. Closing my eyes, I place my palm on the space where Mom kept the red cedar box of my grandfather's ashes. If I'm hoping for some feeling conveyed across time through this wood dresser, I am disappointed. I feel nothing.

I sit on one of the beds. My mother slept here. I run my hand over the quilt and lie back on the bed. Is this the one she slept in? Did she have friends sleep over? Did they talk deep into the night and share private jokes? I reach my hand across the space between the beds as though I could reach my mother. As though she were in the bed next to this one.

The bedside table has one drawer, which I slide open. There's a tube of dried-out lip balm (cherry), two pens (one with purple ink, the other black), and some black satin cording. I pick up the purple pen and wonder if this is the same pen that Mom wrote with in her journal. I press it to my lips. I don't know why. When I set the pen back into the drawer, I see a yellowed envelope. I reach in the drawer. Suddenly, I am enshrouded in a deep chill. Way more intense than earlier. I snap straight up, looking around for the source of the cold air. Nothing. My breath plumes as though it's winter.

I'm not an idiot. I know that a sudden chill means that there is some sort of presence here. I turn back to the drawer. That envelope is my mother's. Something she wrote. I reach out. The drawer slams shut. I yank my hand back just in time. Good sense tells me I need to get out of here. That's when I see them. The room is filled with shadows—and they're moving. They yearn toward me, tendrils grasping for my limbs.

"Move," I tell my body, but I am frozen in fear.

Darkness closes in. The temperature in the room drops; my body shudders.

I fall to my hands and knees. I try to stand, but the shadows push me down, pressing the air from my lungs. My breath comes in short gasps. I crawl toward the door.

"That's it," I tell myself, the same way I talk myself through tough workouts. "Keep going."

The shadows suck at my foot. I shake my leg, but the shadows cling.

I try to move forward, but I'm pulled back.

"Come on, Edie." But I can't. I'm not making any progress toward the door and escape from here.

I don't understand what's happening in this place. First the strange rock. Then the drawer and the shadows. Mom would make sense of it. But she's not here. The unfairness strikes quick and hot. My hands burn. I slam them on the floor. "Move yourself!"

There is a burst of light and a buzzing in my head, like adrenaline before a race.

And then I am standing. The shadows slink back. On the wood floor are two blackened handprints. I don't think about what that means. I bolt to the front door. By the time I fling it open and slam it shut behind me, I'm quivery and unstable, like I've run a brutal 5K at race speed.

Chapter Seven

EDIE

"Edie!" GG says, when I collapse on the deck of our boat. Temperance leaps from her lap and pads over to me. She kneads my belly with her paws and curls up there, as if she knows that I need warmth.

I can't speak. I can't get warm enough. I lie on the deck, allowing the sun and Temperance's body to heat my skin.

"What happened to you?"

I squint my eyes open and make out the shape of GG over me, a pot of steaming tea already in one hand and a mug in the other. Mom, Mildred, Grandfather, and other ghosts crowd around as well.

"I want Mom," I say.

"She's right here," GG says.

I look away from the ghosts. "My real mom. My living mom."

GG sets the pot of tea and mug on the table next to her rocking chair. Then she kneels beside me and rubs my shoulder. "It's awful, I know."

I close my eyes. "I miss her so much, Geege."

"I know. I do, too. But, Edie, do not allow your grief too much power."

"I don't know what that even means, GG. I just want to go home." I imagine curling up in Mom's comfy chair in our sunroom, covered by her soft woolly blanket. I wonder if it still holds her smell.

GG helps me into the chair on the back deck of the boat. Then she presses a mug of hot tea into my hands.

"We are not like other people, Edie. Whether you like it or not, we have a lot of power. *You* have a lot of power. When emotions are muddled with magic, people can get hurt. Add an inexperienced witch into the mix and things could get very bad indeed."

With the terrifying ordeal at the cabin fresh in my mind, I have a hint about what very bad feels like. But I can't tell GG what happened—she was clear that I was not to go back to the cabin under any circumstances. And I'm starting to see why. But I *needed* to return that rock. A small voice whispers to me that I didn't need to explore the cabin.

"Is this about learning the craft? Because I told you that life is not for me. I'm not going to use magic, so you do not need to worry."

GG looks out over the back of our boat to the river flowing by us. Finally, she speaks. "You know how to drive, right?"

"You know I do," I grumble, leaning over the mug to breathe in the steam from the peppermint tea.

"Why did you learn to drive?" Her sharp gray eyes are focused on me now.

I sip the hot tea and frown, unsure where this line of questioning will lead. "Because that's what you do when you turn sixteen."

GG grips the arms of her chair and leans toward me. "Is that a good enough reason to learn how to operate a piece of heavy machinery? Try again."

I set the mug down with more force than I intend and hot tea sloshes over onto my hand. "To get places." I blot the spilled tea with my shirt.

"Why?"

I let out an exasperated burst of air. "For freedom. And safety, I guess? So that I can get somewhere if I need to."

"Exactly right." GG points at me like I'm a student who has given a perfect answer, which—if I'm honest—feels good. "Freedom, yes. But especially safety. That's why it's so important to accept who you are and learn the magic. It's how we Mitchells protect ourselves and our loved ones."

I perk up at what I think GG might be offering. "So if I learn the magic and you feel like I'm protected, you'll let me go home?"

GG shakes her head in confusion. "What's there for you, Edie? Why do you want to go back so badly?"

How can I explain to my grandmother that what I want is to be away from here, from reminders of our magical heritage? That I want to be back in my life as it was. "I just do."

GG sighs out her frustration with me. "If I believe that you can protect yourself, we can have a conversation."

In my room, I take out the photo of Mom and tuck it in the drawer of my bedside table. We have so few family photos and I wonder why. After a long shower, I settle in for a study session. I need to focus on unambiguous problems that offer clear solutions. Not on trying to master magic and definitely not on haunted cabins occupied by homicidal shadows. I shudder again with the memory of the shadows pressing the air from my lungs. I open my study guide to the algebra section, a refresher for the ACT. I took algebra freshman year as an honors course, so it's been a couple years. Working through math problems calms my mind. If magic worked like algebra, with clear, expected results, then maybe magic and I could be friends.

I'm only three problems in when I hear an insistent whisper, though it's so low, I almost miss it. GG is back on the roof, so it can't be her. I must have left a podcast playing on my phone. But when I check, the podcast app isn't even open. Maybe the noise is coming from the kitchen. But I don't hear the sound when I go there, only picking it up again when I'm back in my room.

I walk the tight confines of my room to figure out where the sound is coming from. It's loudest near my dresser. I open the top two drawers. Nothing. I look at the bottom drawer. The whispering grows louder, and I can tell now it's a woman's voice. I kneel in front of the dresser and place my hands on the knobs of the bottom drawer. I yank it open and immediately the whispering ceases. I frown and shut the drawer, standing to return to my algebra. I'm settled in with my study guide when I hear it again. I go back to the bottom drawer of my dresser. I open it quickly, rummage around until my hand lands on the journal.

"It's you, isn't it?"

"Who are you talking to?" GG has appeared in my doorway.

I hold up the notebook. "Mom's journal is trying to talk to me."

"Then I suppose you ought to listen."

"I have studying to do."

"Very well," GG says. "But in my experience, if magic wants to be heard, it will make itself loud."

GG walks away and I put the journal back in the drawer. Loud or not, I'm not in the mood for magical journals right now.

On Saturday morning, I find Tess outside the diner, our meeting spot. In the afternoons, the diner is packed with people coming

off the river or the bike trails, ready to inhale giant cheeseburgers
and crab cakes. But in the morning, it's mostly old people. And us.

"Today's workout is a pyramid where we'll incrementally
build up speed and then go back down. Make sense?"

"Good morning to you, too, Speedy Edie." Today Tess wears
a T-shirt that says I'M LIKE 104% TIRED.

"You know that's mathematically impossible," I say, pointing
to the shirt.

"That's why I wore it. To bug you." She smiles sweetly.

I pull my hair back into a ponytail. "Is Jorge working today?"
I gesture with my chin toward the diner.

Tess shakes her head. "But we're doing something next week."

"Go, Tess!"

Tess laughs. "We'll see. If he tries to pull my hair like he did
in third grade, he'd better watch it."

"Yeah, you'll have to tell everyone that he has cooties."

"That *is* always my go-to insult," Tess says. "How did you know?"

We run our intervals and I'm glad Tess doesn't seem to notice
that I'm dragging today. The terrifying experience at the cabin
two days ago drained my energy. We get through the workout
and run an easy pace back to Main Street.

"Hey, I have a question," I say. "You said your family has lived
here forever?"

"Oh, yeah. You should hear my grandpa go on about it. He
can tell you the history of most of these places."

Tess gestures down Main Street at the coffee shop with its window boxes overflowing with gardenias and impatiens, Al's Seafood with its rockfish on ice, and all the rest of the shops along this street.

"What about cabins?"

We come to a stop in front of the diner.

"You're wondering about your family's place?"

I nod. "I went back there after our run the other day, and it was . . . not normal."

"Whoa. Seriously?"

I nod. "What have you heard?"

"Well, there have been accounts or urban legends or whatever you want to call them of peculiar things happening around there. I remember one story where a guy trespassed up there with his dog. He said that they got a few yards from the cabin and the dog wouldn't move any closer. Just kept barking and barking. And there are other stories of people—like our age or even in college—who dared each other to sleep over in the cabin. One story goes that when they tried to get in the house, one guy was thrown like fifty feet backward. Nobody I know has ever even walked up the driveway. What happened when you went there?"

I blow out a big exhale. "I can't even explain it. There were these shadows and it was cold. Something's definitely not right, and I can't talk to GG because she told me not to go back there."

"You know . . ." Tess starts to say. "Rhia knows a lot about this sort of thing."

"The girl who I ran away from the other night?" I shake my head. "Hard pass. Not in a hurry to embarrass myself again. I've got to go. Text later?"

"She could be really helpful!" Tess calls after me as I jog toward the marina.

Tess's words about the cabin follow me back to the boat. While the guy getting thrown fifty feet sounds like typical exaggeration, the generally abnormal occurrences definitely track with what happened to me when I was there. While washing my hands, I notice that those faint black lines that appeared on my palm when I held that rock have not gone away. In fact, I think they might have grown, which definitely makes me nervous.

I take my time changing out of my running clothes because I need to ask GG about these lines on my palm, which means I'll also need to admit to returning to the cabin. Based on how she reacted back in the perpetual woods, I need to brace myself for a less-than-warm response.

"GG," I say after my shower. "Do you know what this is?" I show her my palm.

GG sets aside the herbs she's working on to take a look. But her usual calm demeanor disappears. "When did this start?"

"I just noticed it the other day. I thought it would go away, but I think the lines are growing."

GG presses on the spot and I feel a sudden and intense chill. Darkness begins to cloud around my vision. I snatch my arm back.

"Edie, it's very important that you tell me the truth. Where have you been?"

I look at the floor when I say, "I went back to the cabin."

"You did what?" GG's tone bristles with disbelief that I disobeyed her. I sense a surge of magic from my grandmother, but just as quickly, she composes herself. I can only dream of having such control.

"You knew I wanted to go there. I read about it in Mom's journal, which *you* gave me. I thought if I saw where she spent summers that maybe it would help me with missing her so much. And you wouldn't talk to me about it. So I went on my own."

"Is that where you'd been yesterday when you arrived here so upset?"

I nod. I don't mention the strange rock. A little at a time seems like the best approach. "I used Mom's unlocking spell," I say.

"Oh my gods and goddesses, Edie, you've no idea what you've done." She presses a hand to her mouth and paces. The canisters on the kitchen counter tremble in response to a flare of her magic.

"I didn't do anything wrong! I went to a cabin that belongs to our family."

"You weren't to go there. You've messed with magic that you don't understand."

"I didn't know!"

GG whirls on me, eyes blazing. "But you should have. You are a seventeen-year-old witch who should have learned her craft by now."

Her words sting as though she slapped me. "I wasn't ready. Mom understood."

GG shakes her head. "Being *ready* is a luxury we cannot afford, Edie. Your mother indulged you and now you're in danger because of it."

"What are you talking about?"

"You've gotten yourself infected."

I stare at my palm and the tiny lines that seem to be etched there. "Infected? By what?"

GG's sigh is as deep as the ocean. "Corrupted magic."

"But you can fix it, right?"

GG falls heavily into a chair. She looks at me. For as long as I can remember my grandmother has been strong, competent, no-nonsense. Except for now. Because now she looks helpless. And that scares me more than any shadow could.

Finally, she speaks. "I will do what I am able," she says. "But if we can't stop it, you'll be lost to us forever."

Chapter Eight
MAURA

June 25, 2003

It's been raining for days and I've barely risen from my bed. Dad's box of ashes sits on my dresser. The constant drizzle has caused the plants and trees to burst forth in an otherworldly green. Dad's ghost still has not appeared. In fact, I haven't seen any of the ghosts. I don't think Mom has either, though I can't be sure. She usually talks to them, but of course she's not speaking.

Even though it was late in the season, I'd bought some vegetable plants and herbs on my last trip to the market and Mama planted them yesterday. That seemed like a good sign.

But when I got up today, I found her in the kitchen boxing up Dad's things. He was barely gone, and Mama was gathering up his belongings.

I told her to stop. I asked what she was doing.

She looked up but didn't speak. Is this why she had wanted to leave our house in Baltimore? Because she couldn't be surrounded by Dad's things?

I went to her and placed my hands on hers. I begged her not to throw these things away.

Her hands stilled.

I asked her to talk to me.

She opened her mouth a tiny bit and I waited. The feathers spilled out. Mama clamped her hands over her mouth and turned away from me. When she turned back, her mouth was set in a grim line and she returned to her work. There was no talking her out of it.

I couldn't stay and watch her pack my father's belongings. I left, letting the screen door slam in the way that used to make Mama call out after me. But nothing. I spoke the words of the spell to keep dry and then I walked down to the dock like I did on the first afternoon we arrived. Dad's wreck of a boat nodded to me. I nodded back. He would have been working on this boat if he were here. It would have been this summer's project. Like the wooden porch chairs one year and the porch itself years before that. Dad always had a summer project when we came here. Mama said that because Dad is a Virgo, his form of relaxation is work. Was a Virgo. Was.

I cocked my head, studying the fiberglass hull and rain-slicked surface of the bow. I am not a Virgo, but that doesn't mean that I'm incapable of work. I went back up the steps. Mama was still looking at Dad's items, turning them over in her hands and placing them on the table in piles.

After I tugged on duck boots, I tucked Dad's box of ashes

under my arm and spoke the spell again. Then we walked outside into the rain. As I navigated the saturated earth to Dad's
workshop, I saw that Mama's plants had been drinking up the
rain, their leaves brilliant green against the dark, rich earth beneath them. The raindrops pattered on the leaves of the trees
above us and the earth gave off a rich loamy smell. Dad and I
remained dry.

I told Dad that we'd check and find out what supplies he had
already. The lock wouldn't give at first, but of course I knew which
whispered words would coax it. I couldn't remember a time that
I'd ever been in this workshop without my father. Right away,
the smell of sawdust assaulted me with memories of measuring
and cutting, of nailing and sanding.

I set the box on the edge of Dad's workbench. The workshop
seemed bigger without Dad's presence filling it. His tape measure sat nearby, waiting to be consulted about the size and scope
of the next project. I turned it over in my hand, feeling the blocky
weight of it. I hooked the metal edge of the measuring tape on
the windowsill and walked across the room.

"Fifteen feet, eight inches," I said to Dad's ashes.

The tape measure didn't care that I held it now, that my dad
was gone, that he would never again use it to measure twice
so that he would cut only once. Of course either Mama or I could
have magicked him the most accurate measuring possible. But

like I said, he was a simple man and preferred his old-fashioned ways. I dropped it into my bag, satisfied by the way it landed in the bottom like it knew its place in the world.

I told Dad that we needed to go to the hardware store.

With care, I locked his workshop, grabbed the car keys from the kitchen, and left. As I pulled into the hardware store parking lot, it hit me that I had no idea where to start and I couldn't ask my father, who was now a pile of ashes in a wooden box. I collected myself. I couldn't give up before I'd even started.

Inside, I held Dad under one arm as we walked by the wall of photos of people proudly showing off the projects they'd worked on. I wasn't sure when the Wall of Fame started, but I always remembered it. One time I had asked Dad why he had never submitted a photo to add to the Wall. He had said that he couldn't imagine that his projects were worth showcasing.

I smiled at the memory of his understated confidence as I cast around for some guidance in the store. The guy working the register looked around my age. He wore an Orioles baseball cap and a T-shirt for the cross-country team of the local high school. I told him that I wanted to rehab a boat. He asked me a lot of questions to get a sense of what I might need. I was even able to answer some of them. I loaded up on everything that he told me—steel wool, a handheld sander, cleaning supplies, primer, paint. He double-checked the color, asking if I was sure. I confirmed that I wanted purple. Just because I was rehabbing Dad's boat didn't mean I had to choose a Dad color. Then he told me that I'd need to wait for the rain to stop before I could sand and paint the exterior of the boat. I didn't want to wait though, so we talked about how I could rehab the inside, until the rain let up.

As I was paying with Mama's credit card, the guy asked what was in the box. His warm eyes made it impossible for me to lie, so I told him that's where I keep my father. He laughed and said that was a good way to keep him out of trouble. It hurt my heart to hear joy. Even so, he had a nice laugh. I let him think that my comment was a joke.

Chapter Nine
EDIE

After GG's terrifying declaration, she told me she'd need some time to pull together a poultice for my hand. When I asked if she wanted me to help, she said it would be better if she worked on her own. That was her way of sending me to my room, I guess.

I had pulled out Mom's journal for answers and—if I'm honest—maybe comfort. Now, after reading the entry, I try to imagine Mom working on this boat. But I'm too agitated to dwell on the fact that Mom sanded each panel of wood with her own hand. Or the mystery of why Grandfather's ghost hadn't appeared after his death.

I rub the page in the journal hopefully, and there's another smooth spot at the top of the entry. This time, when I touch it, the same thing happens as before. The room grows brighter. I feel more awake. And a new spell appears to me, superimposed over Mom's journal entry.

CHARM TO KEEP DRY

1. First of all, note that this will <u>not</u> work if you are already wet.

2. Before going out in the rain, touch the crown of your head,
each eyelid, and your belly button.

3. Say these words:

From crown of head to baby toe,

Hear these words and make it so.

Whether it be sprinkle or it be storm,

Let dryness on me be the norm.

4. Go out in the rain and stay dry.

This one seems pretty useless. The memory of it seeps back to me, though. Mom tried to teach it to me a couple years ago when we had a heavy rainstorm. I told Mom that I could get wet like normal people do, that I wasn't going to melt. But she convinced me to do it with her, just us in our backyard. She said the words and out we went in our bubbles of dryness and danced in the pouring rain and stomped in puddles—and not a drop of water landed on us. I shut the journal with care, the memory of my time with Mom blossoming in my mind.

GG calls me and I find her in the kitchen. Mildred floats nearby and Temperance bats at a purple-and-blue witch ball. "Come here. And give me your hand."

With the obedience that comes from seeing fear in an adult, I give her my hand. She spreads one of her honeys on my palm.

I yelp in pain. The honey sends a burning sensation through my hand and up my arm. GG nods to herself. "That's good."

"It doesn't feel good."

GG doesn't respond. She layers mashed basil leaves over the honey.

"Will this cure me?"

GG's eyebrows pull together. "I'm not certain," she says. "At the least, it should arrest the infection."

"You know people say that place is haunted."

"I'm aware of what people say."

"Is that why I got infected? Is there some sort of curse?"

"That's one way to look at it."

I watch while GG works, her movements sure. She's now layering cabbage leaves over the honey/basil mixture. After she wraps it all in gauze, I ask her the question that's been on my mind.

"What did you mean when you said that I could be lost forever?"

GG looks me in the eyes for the first time since we started this discussion. "We've got to stop this progression before it reaches your heart. But let's not worry about that just yet."

"You can't say something like that and then tell me not to worry! What if your remedies don't work?"

GG eyes me as if gauging if I can handle the answer. "If this doesn't work, our next course of action will largely be up to you."

GG embraces me then, sudden and fierce, and that's how I know that I'm in real trouble. No matter what she says about not worrying, I can see worry etched in the lines around her eyes and in her brow when she thinks I'm not looking. I want to go home, back to a normal life, but obviously I can't do that if I have a magical infection working its way toward my heart. And if learning the family magic could help me—could've helped me avoid this mess to begin with—then I need to learn.

After we clean up the mess from the remedy, I say, "Okay, where do we begin? What do I need to know?"

"What?" GG wipes out her mortar and pestle with a clean dishtowel.

"You've sufficiently scared me. I'm ready to learn."

"Good." GG gives me one of her nods and then hands the mortar and pestle to me. "Crush these herbs. When you're finished, come find me."

As I work, Mildred, GG's dead sister, watches over me, shaking her head. I imagine she'd be tsking if she could speak. I look past her to the rows of small glass jars of dried herbs labeled in GG's neat handwriting. Beside the sink, several mason jars full of GG's honey wait for her wax seal. It's a whole production line in here. Too bad I can't put the ghosts to work. My wrist hurts by the time I finish mashing all the herbs and I can't stop sneezing.

I find GG rocking in her chair on the back deck of the boat. A family paddles by—the parents in a canoe and the children in kayaks. They're struggling against the flow. I think what easy paddling they'll have on their way back.

"My great-aunt made sure I did everything correctly," I say.

GG smiles. "Mildred always was a busybody."

I sneeze again.

"Here." GG gives me a palmful of sunflower seeds, which she'd harvested from her own sunflowers the summer before, I'm certain. I pop a few salty seeds into my mouth, spitting out the shells in the river and chewing up the rest. I sneeze again.

"Do you need a tissue?"

"I thought you gave me those seeds to help with my sneezing."

GG shakes her head. "I was simply sharing a snack with you."

"I don't need a tissue," I say.

GG rises then and I follow her into the kitchen, where she begins to melt wax to seal her jars.

"So is there like a rubric or something?" I ask.

"A what?" GG says.

"A guide for what I need to learn and a measurement of my proficiency."

"There's no *rubric*." GG says the word as though it tastes bad in her mouth. She pours the hot wax over the lids of the jars, then presses her seal into the wax before it hardens. A honeybee within a Celtic knot appears on each lid down the line.

"How will you know I'm ready? That I can protect myself?"

GG doesn't stop her work. "You will survive. That's how you'll know."

"Harsh." I frown. She must be kidding, right?

GG turns to look at me. "This isn't child's play, Edie."

"You think I don't know that?" I can't forget what happened three years ago, when I decided to stop learning about magic.

GG sets down the pot and wipes her hands on her apron. "How did you learn to drive?"

"Not that again."

"What was the process?"

"I practiced. A lot."

"There you go."

"But there was a book I studied with all of the content I needed. And then there was a test." It's only Day One and I'm already exasperated with my grandmother—my fear notwithstanding.

"You have your mother's journal, right?"

"Yes," I concede. "But it's not exactly a study manual."

"Between that and my teachings, you'll learn what you need."

I should have known that GG would believe in student-led instruction. "Okay, what do you want me to work on now?"

"Light the candle there without a match."

I do *not* want to light that candle. The simple idea of it makes my fingers curl into my palms. I might even be sweating a little. "Is there something else I could start with?"

"Perhaps. But learning to manage your element—your fire— is necessary."

I clear my throat. "So, this candle?" I walk over to GG's Brigid candle. Mom had one, too. She lit it every night at sundown and I knew GG did the same. She's made this candle of beeswax, and whenever she lights it, it smells of lavender.

"That very one."

I wiggle my fingers, and then clench them into fists again. "No problem," I say, but I'm procrastinating.

"Do you have a lighter?" I'm still stalling.

"No."

"Flamethrower?"

"Edie." GG's tone tells me she's had enough of my nonsense. I stand before the candle. Nothing to be afraid of. Just a candle. I lift my hands, trying to remember the guidance Mom had given me during our lessons so long ago.

I'd been excited then, eager to learn our craft. I can picture her clearly with her long wavy hair pulled back with a tortoise-shell clip. She wore a loose dress with a batik pattern of blues and purples. She'd just shown me how she could conjure a ball of water. When she let it splash into the sink, she'd laughed with delight. I wanted to experience that same joy, but I was scared of my element.

"Don't be frightened," Mom said to me. "Anger and fear bring chaos to our magic. We seek balance and order. Slow your breathing. Calm your mind. Relax your body. Then, when you are ready, hold your palms up and ask the fire to come to you. And remember, Edie, I am here. My water can put out any fire."

Now, as I stood before GG's candle, I focused on all of the steps that Mom taught me. But when I hold my palms up, a spasm of fear goes through me. I tighten my hands into fists to tamp down the fire and let them drop. I sigh loud enough for GG to hear.

"Sighing won't light the candle," GG says. "Or at least sighing alone won't light the candle."

"I can't do it."

"You *can* do it. It's a part of you. You're blocking your magic from coming to you and I can't imagine why."

"No, you can't," I say, frustrated. GG can't imagine why because she's never done something terrible with *her* magic.

As I'm heading out for my evening shift at Ye Olde Ice Cream Shoppe, GG hands me a list and tells me that I need to stop by Cosmic Flow.

"That phony metaphysical store? Seriously?"

"Cosmic Flow has some hard-to-find items that we'll need."

I wave the list at GG. "Mom always said that those stores

sell fake products and they propagate a misleading view of our craft." Maybe GG won't make me go if I make a strong enough case against it.

"That is true of many such stores. But it's not true of this one."

Conceding defeat, I leave with the list. Near the marina office, Jim is helping a young couple with a boat rental.

"Hey, Edie, how's it going today?" he calls to me.

"Meh, been better, to be honest."

"You know what they say, don't you?" Jim says, grinning.

"Nope."

"A bad day on the river is better than a good day on land." He turns to the couple he's helping. "Especially on a beautiful Saturday like today. Am I right?" The man nods, but the woman eyes the boat with doubt.

"If you say so." I can't help but smile; Jim has that effect. "Got to run. See you!"

Jim dips his head in response.

I take my time getting to Cosmic Flow. I've never liked those sorts of stores with their overpowering incense and dim lights intended to lend a mysterious air to totally ordinary items. I tell myself it's because of Mom, but part of me knows it's because I've never felt that I belonged in that world, even a fake version of it. I stop at the general store on the way for a Coke and a bag of Gummi Bears, because everyone knows that sugar makes failure taste less bitter. That's not magic, that's just truth.

But there are only so many detours I can take in this small town.

A brass bell jingles when I open the door to Cosmic Flow. I'm immediately hit by scents of lavender and sage mingling with sandalwood. Tall shelves on the left showcase countless tinctures in tiny amber bottles. On round tables draped in hand-dyed cloth, carved wooden bowls hold bird wings, seashells, and bones. In the back, despite myself, I'm drawn to an altar woven with wildflowers and lit with flickering candles.

"Welcome to Cosmic Flow." A female voice floats across the darkened space. "The source for your mystical, magical tools and supplies."

I try not to roll my eyes as I step toward the counter. I am about to pull out my list when I stop. It's Rhia, the girl from the party at the barn. *The girl I ran away from*, I think, and I cringe inside. She's changed her hair and I can't take my eyes off it. Gold thread, pearls, and tiny shells are woven into skinny side braids that end in her natural curls. The tips of those curls are dyed blue. She's wearing a cropped white tank top with the moon phases printed in black. She has a silver ring on every finger. A small tattoo of a squirrel perches on one shoulder. Three tiny stars wink at me from her inner wrist. And I'm the one who is supposed to be magical.

"Um, can I help you?" she says, and I can't tell from her tone if she remembers me or not.

I'm embarrassed by the way I ran off the other night and I'm hoping I can get this errand over with and not do any additional damage. She uncaps a marker and writes on something I can't see from my angle. I step forward.

"Hey," I say. "My grandmother needs these items." I hold the list out to Rhia. "I was wondering if you could help?"

She slips the cap on the marker and tucks it into her back pocket. "Miss Geraldine sent you this time, huh?"

"Yeah, I was on my way to town for work anyway." I pick up a piece of rose quartz from a dish sitting on the counter. I close my fingers around it. Cool and calm. Nothing like that strange rock from the cabin.

"Right, the Ice Cream Alchemist."

So she remembered. I drop the crystal back into the dish and smile to myself while Rhia scans the list. She levels a gaze at me. "Looks like you all are getting into some serious magic."

"Well, you know my grandmother. Never met a chicken foot she didn't love." I bite my lip, willing myself not to say anything else stupid.

But Rhia laughs in that big open way that I noticed at the party. "Tess didn't tell me you were funny." Rhia comes from around the counter and hands me a tote bag. "For your discoveries."

"This is cool," I say, holding the bag at arm's length so I can fully see the way the store's name is depicted with Celtic knots surrounded by spirals and stars.

"I designed that."

I look at the bag again. "Wow. I like it even better now."

"You know, I worked hard on it and hardly anyone comments. So thank you. You sort of just made my day."

"Glad to be of service." I bow a little bit. Oh my gods, I must be the most awkward human on this planet.

Rhia's smile looks like it knows something I don't. As I follow her, I wonder if I just accidentally flirted. I feel like maybe I did, which would be a first for me. Rhia takes me throughout the shop, dropping various items into the bag. As she gives a running commentary on the selections, I'm amazed by how much she knows about the magical world. I'm mostly quiet because—let's face it—I barely have anything to add due to very little witch training. Also, I'm pretty dazzled by watching and listening to Rhia. By the time we are finished, the bag's contents include bird's feet, dried fungi, feathers of various shapes and colors, and two powders—one crushed horn, the other crushed antler.

As Rhia slides everything back into the canvas bag, she assures me that no animals are harmed; they harvest everything from what they find on foraging trips. She slips in the receipt and hands the bag to me.

"Thanks for your help," I say. "Otherwise it would have taken me forever and I would have missed my shift and Tess would have had to make all of those sundaes and milkshakes and twists by herself." I lean toward Rhia as if I'm sharing a secret. "And between you and me, she's not that great at twists, so you've basically done a service for the town."

Rhia's laugh makes me realize that I could get used to making this girl laugh. That's not a feeling I expect, and I push my hair out of my face as I let that sink in.

"Now I'm the one who's glad to be of service," Rhia says. Then, she gives *me* a little bow. And now whose day is made?

"Hey," she says as I'm leaving. "Say hi to Tess for me."

"You got it."

Tess glances at the tote bag when I enter the ice cream shop. "Cosmic Flow. Was Rhia working?" She's rinsing off a scooper, something we do approximately three hundred times a shift.

"Yeah, she said hi," I say, trying to keep my tone casual as I grab a clean apron.

The thing is, I've never found a girl so interesting before. Or a boy, or anyone, for that matter. As people at school began to pair up like they were ready to board Noah's ark, I started to assume that the world of attraction and romance wasn't for me. Mom and I had even had Tea and a Talk about it. She'd made a peach tea with some of GG's honey for that one. I was sure there was something wrong with me because I hadn't felt the same stirrings everyone else at school seemed to be feeling. Mom made me feel so supported, saying that human desire exists on a very broad continuum from none to a lot, and wherever I landed, it would be exactly right for me.

But now I'd met a girl who I found *interesting*. I have no idea what to do with the bubbling feelings. And no mom to talk to.

I peer into my bag and pull out a card that Rhia must have slipped in. I sense a blush creep up my cheeks, even though Rhia isn't here and even though she probably gives these cards to everyone who comes in. It's a tarot card. The Wheel of Fortune. On the back of the card, Rhia has written the name of the store, a phone number, and a doodle of herself.

After hanging up the bag, I show Tess the card. I hope that I'm not blushing anymore. "What does this mean?"

"You'd have to ask Rhia. I told you, she knows about all that shit—tarot, witch history, Wiccan rituals, paranormal shit. All of it."

I tuck the card into my pocket. As I'm wrestling my long hair into a fresh ponytail, Tess says, "Know what? You can ask her all about her witchy knowledge tonight."

The *idea* of seeing Rhia again spreads tingles through me that have nothing to do with my magic, but the *reality*, well, the reality makes me want to run. Far away and very fast. "What do you mean?"

"We'll hang tonight. After work," she says as she taps out a text. I open my mouth, but Tess holds up a hand. "Don't even. I already told Rhia that you're coming to hang with us. We'll go to the beach."

I pull the bill of my baseball cap low over my eyes. "Ugh. But I'm so awkward!"

"Stop talking about my friend that way." Tess loops her arm in mine. "You're awesome. Let's finish this shift and then we'll go. It'll be great."

I brace myself for another gathering with a lot of people I can embarrass myself in front of—especially Rhia. Tess blares music as we fly down country roads until she stops suddenly to turn onto a dirt road flanked by fields. This definitely does *not* look like a beach. On the left, in the middle of an empty field rising toward the waning moon is one huge tree. Tess veers off the dirt road onto the field.

"Whoa!" I say, clutching the oh-shit handle.

Tess laughs. "This is why we all drive trucks and Jeeps out here. Four-wheel drive, baby!"

We bump along the field until Tess puts it in park and hops out of the car.

"The *beech*," I say, finally understanding that our destination was never somewhere flat and sandy bordering the river.

"Yeah, what did you think?"

"Well, I was mentally preparing myself for skinny dipping."

"What?" There is a pause and then Tess giggles. "Oh! You thought—"

"Yeah."

Chapter Ten
EDIE

The tree is a huge weeping beech—the tree of knowledge—and right now all I know is that my stomach is trying to come up through my throat. Rhia is already there, her white shirt luminous in the glow of the waning moon. She holds back some hanging branches for us as if they were a beaded curtain. Tess flashes her camera light around the space. Beneath the twisting, weeping branches of the beech is a space larger than some apartments. On a circle of tree stumps, candles in glass jars flicker, radiating a warm glow near and deepening the dark beyond.

"Welcome to our sanctuary," Rhia says, opening her arms wide.

"This is an incredible tree," I say. Looking up, branches soar way overhead before they drop back toward earth dressed in leaves. This tree must be so old that it would have been here even before my mom's time. Maybe even GG's.

"This is where we come to get away from life," Tess says. "Or just to hang."

"I brought soda since two of us are driving. Is that okay, Edie?" Rhia says.

"Soda's great. Unless it's ginger ale, in which case, *blech*."

"It's ginger ale," Rhia says.

And there it is—my first foot in mouth of the evening. Nice job, Edie. Mortification must be written on my face because Rhia bursts into laughter.

"Kidding! It's orange. Because Tess loves orange soda."

"Truth. It makes me happy," Tess says, pulling out a huge bag of chips. "And I brought these. Because salty and sweet are the best together."

At first, I feel bad that I don't have anything. Then I remember. "I have Gummi Bears!" I root around in my backpack and pull out the bag.

"You didn't need to bring anything," Tess says.

"I happened to have them," I say. I don't need to mention that I got them while trying to avoid going to Cosmic Flow.

"And I, for one, am grateful. I love Gummis!" Rhia says, holding out an open palm. I'm absurdly pleased that Rhia likes what I brought. I try to shake a few out, but they fall in a clump. Smooth move there, Edie.

"That's like a mob of Gummis," Rhia says, peering at her palm.

"Or a scrum," I offer. I take a seat on the ground, cushioned by leaves that have fallen seasons before.

"Or an orgy," Tess adds.

"Ugh! I don't want to think about Gummi Bears getting nasty in my belly!" Rhia says, still peering at the candy in her palm.

"You'd rather they were playing rugby in your belly?" Tess asks.

"Those two things don't seem all that different to me. I mean, have you *seen* a rugby scrum?" I say.

Rhia and Tess cackle.

I crack open an orange soda and look around the space where we all sit. "Doesn't this field belong to someone?" I ask. "Don't they care that we're on their property?"

"It's my uncle's," Tess says. "He doesn't care as long as we don't leave any trash. And we don't."

"We would never," Rhia says, craning her neck to look up into the tangle of branches overhead.

I hear in the way that they talk about this space the same reverence for nature—and especially the wisdom of trees—that Mom and GG instilled in me and which I still feel, especially sitting beneath this old one as night presses in around us.

"I still can't believe that you're Geraldine Mitchell's granddaughter," Rhia says as we break open the chips.

"Why's that?" I ask, even though I'm not sure I want to hear the answer.

"No offense, but you seem so, I don't know—athletic?"

An unexpected laugh bursts out of me and Rhia laughs, too. I grab a handful of chips. "Are you saying witchy people can't work out?"

"I'm saying I can't exactly imagine Miss Geraldine running a 5K in her day."

"Yeah, well, my grandmother and I don't have a lot in common. Her whole scene is *not* really my thing," I say. Though it looks like it's getting ready to be my thing, whether I like it or not. I catch myself rubbing my left palm with my right thumb. A shiver of cold rushes through me. I stop.

"Not your thing?" Rhia's tone is incredulous. "Is that even possible? You have magic. It's as much a part of you as your two arms or the fact that your eyes are hazel."

"That's pretty much what my grandmother says. Especially lately," I say. But I'd rather focus on the fact that Rhia noticed my eye color than what GG has shared.

"If I were a Mitchell, I'd be all about the magic."

"In my experience, being a Mitchell is the shortest distance to having no friends." I toss a handful of Gummi Bears in my mouth so I don't have to make eye contact with the two of them.

"Maybe you've been looking in the wrong places for friends," Rhia says.

Rhia's words have teeth. They won't let go. It's true that here,

I'd made friends with Tess easily, and without having to hide anything. She knew who my grandmother was, and she didn't care. Rhia maybe cared a bit too much about my family, but—in a way—that was sort of a welcome change.

"Do you do anything your grandma does?" Tess asks. "Like the salves and honey and stuff?"

I shake my head. "You two are believers, then?" I ask. "In magic?"

"How can anyone know about it and *not* believe in it?" Rhia says. "I've been studying the craft for years."

"Yeah, since eighth grade at least," Tess says.

Around the same time Rhia was beginning to learn the craft, I'd decided that I wasn't meant for that world.

"I've read everything that I can get my hands on. I'm learning how to cast spells," she says, and I hear the excitement in her voice. "But I don't have innate magic, so I'm pretty limited." She says this last part with a sigh, and she seems to shrink a bit. It's the first time I've seen anything except pure confidence come from Rhia.

Mom and GG had told me how spells were basically recipes. As long as you had the right ingredients and a true intention, they could work for anyone. But mastering elements was something that could only be done by those born with innate magic. Like the Mitchells. Like me.

Rhia might be limited, but she clearly knew way more than I did. I remember the card in my back pocket. "What does this mean?" I hold out the tarot card. "Or do you give them randomly to whoever comes in?"

"Not random." She takes the card from my hand and I can practically see the glow of her confidence return. "Right, the Wheel of Fortune. This one was meant for you. It's about external forces and being powerless. It's sort of ambiguous, though. Could be good stuff is coming that's out of your control or could be things are going to suck. Are you feeling tossed around by Fate right about now?" I expect her to laugh at this last bit, but her expression is earnest.

"You could say that," I say.

Rhia holds the card out to me and I take it. I feel a tingle when our fingers touch. Maybe there are more forces out of my control than I originally thought. And not all of them are bad.

"What are these forces?" Rhia asks. "I mean, if you want to tell us."

Do I tell them that I've somehow gotten myself infected with corrupted magic? Not sure I'm ready for the oversharing portion of the evening, so instead I say, "My grandmother wants me to learn about . . . all of *this* faster than I'm ready to. And I don't think I can do it."

"That's rough," Tess says.

Rhia practically spits out a mouthful of soda. "Rough? Having your grandmother teach you magic? That sounds amazing."

"It's complicated," I say in a quiet voice.

"I get it," Tess says. "Here, have more Gummis." I grab a handful and pass them to Rhia.

"Okay, yeah," Rhia says. "Sorry. I *love* magic. But family. Not always the easiest." She reaches in the bag for more Gummi Bears, and I notice she keeps putting back the green ones.

"We could help, though," Tess offers.

The first feeling that zips through me—which I do not expect and therefore can barely give a name to—is something like . . . joy? Or maybe wonder. I've never had anyone my age to talk about magic with. But in the next beat, I'm worried that it could all go wrong. Like what happened before. "That's okay. Learning magic—it's a lot of work."

"Edie." Rhia levels me with a grin. "I love magic. This isn't work to me."

"Really?" I ask, my heart fluttering with hope.

"Really."

"You're not setting me up so that when I get real about this, you two can laugh at me behind my back?"

"Whoa, what?" Tess says. "Somebody must have been a real bag of dicks."

I watch the dance of the flame from the candle. "Somebody was."

"We promise that we are not setting you up," Rhia says quietly. "So tell us."

I breathe in some courage, hoping that I can trust them. "My grandmother thinks if I master my element, I'll be safe."

"Safe? From what?" Tess asks.

"I told you I went back to that cabin, right?" I pick up a dead leaf sitting in front of me. It's brown and as smooth as paper.

Tess nods. "You said it was not normal."

"What cabin?" Rhia asks.

"The one on Shaw," Tess says to Rhia.

"Oooh, bad energy up there," Rhia says.

"Yeah, and I was really wigged out"—I'm still not ready to spill the truth of the infection—"GG figured out that I went there, and she said that she won't feel I'm safe until I learn magic and how to master my fire."

Both girls are quiet for a moment and I wonder if I said too much, even though I was trying not to. I fold the leaf in half and then half again until its brittle edges break apart. I sprinkle the pieces back to the ground.

"What does she want you to do exactly?" Tess asks.

"Light a candle, no matches allowed." I hear Tess let out an *oooh*.

"You could try now with us," Rhia says.

"Really? Here?" I'm full of doubt, not to mention major amounts of self-consciousness.

"Sure, use this." Rhia picks up one of the candles sitting on the tree stump. My eyes linger on her lips as she purses them to blow out the flame. She places the candle on the ground in front of me. The smoke from the blown-out wick drifts between us.

Tess leans in closer.

I slow my breathing and hold my palms up. I close my eyes, ready to call the fire. But then I remember that day three years ago. I pull my hand back and clench my fingers into a fist.

Of course, nothing happens.

Rhia scoots closer to me. She smells like the sandalwood incense from the store. I realize I don't mind the scent on her.

"Maybe you need to channel your thoughts toward light or fire or heat or something," she says. "Try again. Embrace your inner witch."

Rhia's probably onto something. Mom and GG talked a lot about our elemental connection to nature. Mom's element was water and GG's earth. But by the end of eighth grade, it seemed safer to keep my elemental connections to logic and the real world. And I definitely stayed away from embracing my inner witch. And my outer witch, too, for that matter. "I'm not sure I want to."

I look at Tess for support, but she says, "You never let me slack off on a hard workout. I'm with Rhia."

"We're here with you. One more time," Rhia says, placing her hand on my shoulder.

There's that sizzle again at her touch. Effing Wheel of

Fortune, tossing me around. I hold my palms up again, but I'm too agitated.

"I can't, okay?" I say. "I can't do it!"

The tingle in my fingers is sudden and intense. I push myself up to stand and then walk through the curtain of draping branches, into the murky night.

"Whoa!" Tess exclaims.

"Crap! Where's some water?" Rhia's voice is tense. "Protect the tree!"

"Edie!" Tess yells.

I hear a splash. I run back through the branches to find Tess and Rhia staring at leaves smoldering on the ground. Tess holds an empty can of orange soda.

"You set the leaves on fire!" Tess says. She looks at me the way I've been avoiding ever since that time when I was fourteen. Like I'm something to be afraid of.

"I didn't do that." The denial flies out of my mouth as if words can make something true. I clench my hands and hold them behind my back. I couldn't have done that. Could I?

"Edie, come on," Tess says.

"Your fingers brushed against a leaf and it caught on fire," Rhia says excitedly. "So you *can* do it. But that was a little too close to the beech for comfort, especially when it's been so dry."

I wipe my hands on my shorts as if they are dirty, as if I can wipe away my magic. "I need to go back."

"But we just got here," Tess says.

"That's okay, you stay, I can run back."

"It's late and dark and it's far. Are you sure you can't hang for a little longer?"

"I'm not asking you to leave. I'm sorry. I really am."

Tess and Rhia exchange a glance, communicating in that way of friends who've known one another forever. A way that I, an outsider, am not able to read. I start to walk back toward the dirt track that leads to the road. I tuck my hands under my armpits and try not to cry. I don't get very far before I hear Tess calling me.

"Come on, Edie," she yells to me. "I'm not going to let you walk home." I turn back and see her gesturing from the Jeep.

"Thanks," I say quietly when I get in.

"Did you do this at home, too?" Tess asks as she drives me home.

"Do what?" I can't stop rubbing my thumb across the pads of my fingers. I didn't set those leaves on fire. I couldn't have done that. I swore I would never let it happen by accident again.

"Run away when you're uncomfortable," Tess says. She glances at me before turning her eyes back to the road unspooling before us.

Her words hurt, but they strike true. "Probably. After all, running is what I'm good at." I attempt a laugh, but Tess isn't fooled.

"You want to know what I think?" Tess says.

"You're probably going to tell me whether I want to or not."

"*I think that you have a lot going on and you think you can handle it all on your own. But guess what? You don't have to do that.*"

I don't trust my voice, so I just nod. When I return to the boat, I shut my bedroom door and slide to the floor. I hold my head in my hands. My hands. I look at them. I haven't conjured fire for years. I wasn't even sure I could anymore.

I'd been in eighth grade. Mom had been teaching me about the elemental nature of our magic. By that time, I'd been to the perpetual woods with Mom and GG and I'd helped with gathering ingredients for salves and potions and infusions. I'd been told that a particular talent would emerge for me at some point. But first I needed to learn how to manage my element.

Mom could bring rain, roil water, or calm it. GG's earth magic is very powerful, which is why the perpetual woods always blooms and why her bees produce the best honey. Everything is connected, Mom had told me more than once. My element would be fire because that was the order of things in our family.

I had wanted to impress the girls in my class. I could create fire from nothing, I'd told them. We'd gone to an empty lot near the school and I'd been trying to set a piece of paper alight. One of the girls called me a useless freak. The others giggled and chimed in. They all started chanting *freak, freak, freak.*

I felt the anger and then the tingling, only back then I didn't know what the tingling meant. Or how anger could feed it. I pointed at the girl to tell her to shut up, and a flame bloomed from my fingertip. She started screaming. I tried to quaff the flame, but suddenly all of my fingers sprouted flames. Then all the girls were screaming. Someone squirted her water bottle all over me.

The girls left me behind, drenched in water and shame. Now, three years later, that sense of shame clings to me like an odor. What if I'd accidentally set fire to the ancient beech tree or worse—to Tess's shirt or Rhia's hair? I tentatively rub my hands together. They seem completely normal. And I *didn't* set fire to the tree or Tess or Rhia. It was only a few dry leaves.

But now I'd proven to myself that I still don't have any control. How can I do what GG asks of me without control? I look at the black lines veining my palm. GG's attempts haven't cured me yet. And I can't wait around for the Wheel of Fortune to decide my fate.

I go to the top drawer of my dresser and pull out the purple velvet pouch, allowing the necklace to spill into my open palm. I've never been able to put it on. It hurt too much to know that my mother would never make another piece of jewelry ever again. It made her death too real. I consider the shining necklace in my hand. My mother is dead; I can't change that. But she made this for me, for when I needed her near. And I've never needed her as close as I do now. I lift the necklace and clasp it around my neck. I touch the silver acorn and feel a bead of golden warmth there, a sense of comfort against everything that's troubling me.

Her journal whispers to me now. I crawl to my bedside table and retrieve it, the red leather worn and smooth in my hands. With my finger, I trace the trinity knot. Mom isn't physically here to help me. Maybe her journal is the next best thing.

Chapter Eleven
MAURA

June 27, 2003

Today when I woke, the gray skies didn't give away the time, but the clock told me that it was well into morning. I guzzled some water and grabbed a granola bar and headed to the boat. Mama sat in one of the chairs on our porch, staring at the river. She looked up when I came out with a bag on one shoulder, Dad under the other arm. I let the screen door slam. She didn't say a word. But this time, I expected the silence.

I started where I'd left off the day before, sanding and more sanding. I wondered how I'd thought that I could do this by myself when I was completely clueless about rehabbing boats or even just about boats in general. But I kept sanding because I had no idea what else to do. And also because when I was inside the cave of the boat, sanding, I felt connected to my father. I sanded and sanded. As the day moved toward late afternoon, I heard the bell from the porch of the cabin. Mama had always rung the bell to let Dad and I know that food was ready when we were down here. The clanging resounded with normalcy.

I set aside the sander and was surprised to realize that the rain had let up. Outside the boat, I leaned down on the dock to rinse my hands in the water, watching tiny whirlpools form. I pulled my hands from the water and idly twirled my fingers and the water obeyed, swirling in response. I used to love my element, playing with the water for hours at a time. But now the idea of it just made me tired. As I climbed the steps to the cabin, I hoped that Mama was ready to talk today.

I asked Dad's ashes why Mama would not speak. He didn't speak either, but that was probably for the best.

Mama had grilled some fish and I prepared a salad. But we ate in silence again because hearing only my voice in the cabin made me lonelier than if I kept quiet. After cleaning up our dinner dishes, we sat on the screened-in porch overlooking the river. The rain had started again, and we listened to it drip onto the leaves of trees and ping the surface of the river and the top of the boat. Mama cleared her throat and I looked at her in surprise.

She pointed to me, but I didn't understand what she was trying to communicate. I asked her to speak to me, but Mama shook her head and kept her lips closed tight. She pointed at me, then pointed to her shirt. It took a minute to realize she was asking about Dad's T-shirt.

She held her nose, and I understood she was telling me it was time to wash it. In any other moment, I might have laughed. But I wanted my mother to talk to me. I needed to hear her voice.

I knelt before her and begged her to speak. But all she did was grab the sleeve of my T-shirt between her pointer finger and thumb and lifted it. And still, she refused to speak to me. Frustration spiked, hot and red. My fingers began to tingle.

She grasped the hem of the shirt again.

I pulled away from her, wiggling my fingers to try to calm them. Mama saw what I was doing and stood up, her own hands at the ready. I didn't want to be wrapped in vines and I didn't want my magic to be bound. When Mama did it to me once, the whole world felt muffled, like I was experiencing it through cotton. I felt the magic building inside me, but I couldn't let it out.

I found a bind-breaking ritual in one of her old books, but it wasn't easy magic, and I didn't have it in me to perform it now. I yanked the shirt over my head and tossed it at her.

She reached out for me, but I shook her away. I went to my room and shut the door. Dad's ashes looked at me from my dresser.

Dad, when I close my eyes, I can picture you walking in the door, smiling. You always arrived on Fridays after work. You would unload your pockets on the kitchen counter. Keys, mints, change, and whatever else you'd accumulated during your workday. It always drove Mama a little crazy, didn't it, the way that you'd dump your things there like that? Then you'd crack open a beer, take a long swallow, and ask who wanted to walk down to the dock? Or who wanted to walk to town for ice cream?

I don't remember doing either of those things last summer.

What was I doing that seemed so important that I couldn't walk to the dock with my father? What held my attention so much that I wouldn't go with him to get an ice cream cone?

You know what? After I wrote that, about Dad, I read it out loud and I sort of saw him for a few seconds. His ghost, I mean. It was faint and flickering, but it was there. I wonder if there's a way that I can use magic to make him appear permanently.

Chapter Twelve

EDIE

OLD BIND-BREAKING RITUAL

This is a powerful one. The ingredients are specific, and your intention must be pure.

INGREDIENTS:

Soil cleansed under moonlight or soil from perpetual woods

Hawthorn bark

Crystal quartz

Feather

Three strands of hair from yourself and three from the one
who bound you

INCANTATION:

Dirt of earth and feather of sky,

With bark and crystal here do lie,

Hairs of mine and the caster twined,

Hear my words and break this bind.

On Tuesday, when I return from my morning run after leaving
Tess at the diner with Jorge, GG stops me on my way to get

changed out of my running gear. My grandfather floats just behind her, as does Mildred. Ever since I told GG that I'm ready to learn, we've been spending our time in the kitchen, with GG showing me how to prepare salves and infusions and decoctions. But whenever she asks me to practice my fire, I am still reluctant.

"I'm working on a new remedy for you. I need you to run an errand for me."

She hands me a mason jar with a thick brown liquid sloshing around in it and then she gives me something long and thin wrapped in a muslin bag.

"I need some bark from a beech tree. This isn't the ideal time to harvest bark, so in the jar is the enrichment to help heal the tree. The other item is a sharp knife. Do you remember how to ask a tree for bark?"

"Yes." It had been a solemn lesson with Mom, but one I couldn't forget. I'd gone into it rolling my eyes. Why did we need to *ask* a tree for bark? Mom had explained that bark for a tree is like skin for us and that we only harvested it when we truly needed it. If we wanted something from a living thing, we needed to show respect and gratitude and we needed to give something in return. That lesson had stayed with me.

I grab my helmet and a water bottle and walk to the marina, where Jim keeps a couple bikes.

"Jim?" I call.

"In here." His voice comes from the office. I enter the space,

which is dim compared to the bright light of the midday sun outside. Jim sits at his desk working on a tablet, which seems out of
place in this weather-worn building. He's got his beat-up old O's
hat on and a navy-blue T-shirt with CEDAR BRANCH MARINA over
the left breast and, beneath that, the coordinates for the marina.

Behind him are a few framed photos. One with a group of
people in an unfamiliar landscape catches my eye. On one corner
of the photo hangs a medal like people receive after finishing a
marathon. On the other corner hangs a black corded necklace
with a round pendant that looks sort of like a coin.

"Are you a runner?" I ask, pointing to the medal.

Jim turns to look where I'm pointing. "Was. In another life-
time." He turns back to me and I think I catch a bit of sadness
before he smiles and asks, "What can I do for you?"

Maybe it's not sadness; maybe he's just busy. "Could I borrow
a bike?"

"Of course. You've got a helmet?"

I hold up the helmet. I'd never ride without one, not after
what happened to Mom—but Jim doesn't know that.

"Okay, be safe," he says.

I smash the helmet over my unruly hair and slide the water
bottle into its holder. Gently, I lay the knife wrapped in cloth in
the basket alongside the jar of brown liquid. Then I point the
bike toward the only beech I know.

The ride is longer than I expect, but I don't mind. Flat roads mean easy riding and heat doesn't bother me. After a while, I come up to the turnoff and pedal my way down the dirt road, bumping across the field to the weeping beech.

When I part the low-hanging branches to let myself in, I realize someone is there and I freeze. Rhia sits on the ground with her back against the trunk and her knees pulled up to her chin. It seems like she might be crying, but I'm not certain because her face is pressed against her knees. She's obviously having a private moment, so I step back as quietly as I can. But of course I step on a branch, which cracks loudly. Rhia's head snaps up. She quickly wipes at her eyes.

"Edie." Rhia stands and wipes off the butt of her shorts. "What are you doing here?"

"Nothing," I say. "I'm—" I can't seem to speak. I point behind me. "I'll go."

A warm breeze ruffles the leaves around us. A lone bird calls from a branch far above our heads.

"No, it's fine. You can stay."

"Are you sure?" I'm still frozen.

"Yeah, yeah." She gestures for me to come into the enclosed area beneath the draping branches. "Join me."

I enter the space and hold my breath for a moment, caught by the peace of this place.

"What are you up to?" she asks, before I can ask if she's all right.

She eyes the jar in my one hand and the cloth-wrapped knife in my other hand, which she doesn't know is a knife, and now I'm suddenly wondering if I should, in fact, leave, because who brings a knife on a bike ride? Then I remember that she studies the craft.

"My grandmother asked me to harvest some beech bark. Would that be okay with you?"

"I guess?" Rhia looks at the broad trunk of the huge old tree. "Will it hurt the tree?"

I wobble my head back and forth. "Well, yeah. It will. But I'll help it heal."

"Really? You can do that?"

I hold up the mason jar with GG's tree enrichment. "I can. Through my grandmother."

Rhia steps toward me, her hands in her back pockets, and I can't help but notice the way that her breasts push out her LOVE IS LOVE tank top. I force my eyes away, and they land on her long legs. *Effing Wheel of Fortune.* Her hair is pulled back in a pineapple with tiny braids tracing her hairline in the front. Rhia could wear a potato sack and make it work, I think.

"I thought you didn't want to deal with magic," she says.

"More like magic and I don't get along very well. You saw what happened the other night. I'm basically clueless."

Rhia takes a small step forward. "Do you mind if I watch?"

A quiver goes through me. I'm not sure what it means. Maybe I sort of like the idea that Rhia wants to watch me.

"Sure," I say. "Come over here."

I set the jar on the ground and I kneel before the tree as Rhia circles around and kneels next to me. I pull the knife from the cloth bag and set it in front of me. Then I rest my hands on my thighs and close my eyes.

"Is that an athame?" Rhia asks.

I open my eyes. She's pointing at the knife.

"No," I say, and I pause. Rhia knows so much about the craft that I'm surprised she doesn't know this, and I feel bad correcting her. "My mom taught me that athames are only to be used for directing energy. Not cutting actual things."

Rhia's sudden smile is as welcome as the sun emerging after a storm. "You're not as clueless as you let on."

"That was a test?"

Rhia cocks her head and grins. "Yup."

"And I passed?"

"With flying colors." After a moment, her face takes a serious, more vulnerable expression. "Can you actually teach me what you're doing?"

The joy of pleasing Rhia is tempered by her question. It's so foreign for me to share this part of myself with anyone. And last time I was here, it didn't end all that well. It takes me a moment to respond.

"I can show you what I've been taught." The words come out slowly.

"But . . ." Rhia hears something in my tone.

"I'm new at this and I've never taught anyone."

"I just want to be a part of it."

"Okay," I say, relieved. "First, we sit in a way that shows respect for the tree, like this."

Rhia mirrors my position: kneeling with her butt resting on her heels.

"Now close your eyes and press your hands on the trunk of the tree."

Rhia follows my guidance. I try not to get distracted by the fact that if I scooted over just a foot, we'd be touching. Being so close to her, my body is electric, like before a big race. I breathe out to calm myself.

"Okay, now you can repeat after me: Great Beech, whose memory is longer than ours."

I wait to go on until Rhia says her part.

"We request bark from your strong trunk, which feeds your many branches and roots."

Rhia repeats my words.

"We thank you for your sacrifice."

Rhia's voice catches with emotion.

"We leave you this nourishment for your soil so that you may live on after we depart this world."

My mother taught me this and now she's departed from this world—and here I am now teaching someone else. My mother lives on through the passing of her knowledge. The realization blooms big in my heart.

As if she senses my thoughts, Rhia grabs my hand and gives it a quick squeeze. I squeeze back and I don't want to let go, but I have to for the next step.

"Okay, I'll carve a bit of bark from the tree. Like this." I make a swift and shallow cut into the trunk, carving a piece about two inches long, which I place into the cloth bag that held the knife. "And now I'll use this enrichment to mend the area that I cut."

I rub GG's salve on the cut and then hold my hand there for a moment longer. "Thank you," I whisper to the tree. When I remove my hand, the bark has already begun to knit itself back together.

"Wow," Rhia whispers.

"GG's preparations are very powerful," I say.

I pour the rest of the salve onto the soil at the base of the tree. "This should help it to stay healthy."

Rhia scoots over and places her hand over the spot where mine had just been, whispering her own thanks. After we're finished, we sit next to one another on the exposed roots with our backs against the smooth trunk.

"I've never met anyone—not even Tess—who has the same respect for trees that I do. I could see it in you the first time you came here," Rhia says.

The branches of the weeping beech rustle in the breeze.

"Sometimes I think I like trees better than people." I catch what I've said and look quickly at Rhia. "Not all people."

She laughs. "It's okay. I get it." Rhia picks up dead pine needles and twirls them between two fingers. "People can be hard."

"Agreed," I say. I look at her. "Do you want to talk about it?"

She squishes her eyes closed tight and then opens them. "It's my grandmother. She's got dementia. We used to be so close. But now? She can't remember things." Rhia's voice catches. "She can't remember me."

Impulsively, I reach out and grab her hand. "I'm so sorry." She nods her appreciation, squeezing my hand and letting it go.

I've lost sight of the possibility that the people nearest to me could be going through hard stuff, too.

"When it first started," Rhia says, "when she first started forgetting things and asking the same questions over and over— that's when I turned to magic. Gods, I know it sounds ridiculous." She closes her eyes and shakes her head. "But I thought that maybe I could find a way to cure her, you know, through the craft."

"Doesn't sound ridiculous to me," I say in a quiet voice. I understand wishing for a magical solution to an unsolvable human problem.

"Obviously, I didn't find a cure," she continues. "But the rituals and the focus on energy and nature gave me comfort." She shrugs. "So I stayed with it. And I come here when it gets hard. Instant mood adjustment sitting under this tree." She draws up her knees and rests her chin on them. "Do you have anything like that?"

I look at her. "An instant mood adjuster? Running. No matter what's bugging me, a good run can get it out of my system."

"Did you need to run after the last time here?"

"What do you mean?" The memory of my shame prickles.

"You were angry."

I give her a rueful half smile. "It wasn't anger, exactly." I rub the back of my neck with my hand while I figure out what to say. "I guess when it comes to fight or flight, I'm all flight. Speaking of which"—I look at Rhia and sigh—"I've got to go. Sorry. Feels like bad timing, but my grandmother is waiting on me to bring this back to her."

Rhia shakes her head. "No, it's totally fine."

I gather my items and we both stand. "Could I . . . could I hug you?" I ask. I sort of wince, bracing myself for a no.

But Rhia nods. I step forward to give her a quick one-armed hug, but the feel of her against me is so right that both of my arms wrap around her to pull her closer. She tightens her arms around me in response. I turn my head and bury my nose in her neck, breathing in her scent of sandalwood and summer air and trees.

"Thanks," she whispers in my ear. "I needed that."

We pull apart and immediately I miss the feel of her soft body close to mine.

"Happy to be of service," I say, reprising my role as most awkward human to ever walk the earth. "And now I'll go."

Rhia giggles and waves to me. The feel of holding her close and the gift of her parting smile carries me back to the boat.

At the boat, I hand GG the knife, the bark, and the jar that held the enrichment. GG peers at me.

"What?" I wipe my hand across my mouth. "Do I have schmutz on my face?"

"No." She peers at me some more. "Your energy is different."

"Different how?" My mind goes to Rhia and our shared hug.

"Not as heavy as it was."

I turn my head as I feel the heat of a blush come on. "Is that a good thing?"

"I believe it is," she says as she begins shredding the bark.

"What are we working on today?"

"A healing decoction," GG says. "For your hand. Please put that copper pot on the stove and fill it about two-thirds of the way with water."

I do as she says. "Done."

"Now toss in a couple cinnamon sticks, dandelion leaves, and a few peppercorns, and stir."

As I stir, Rhia's smile comes back to me. It's such a new experience to spend time with someone and not pretend that I'm different than I am. I can't be sure, but when we were together I sensed that she was feeling the same.

"Be mindful that you do not pollute the decoction with your emotions, Edie."

I stir some more, but now my thoughts are clouded not with Rhia but the mystery of the infection and GG's focus on my instruction. "How does me learning all of this help with my infection?" I ask her. "And mastering fire. I don't get it."

GG is quiet for a moment. "If I'm ever . . . compromised in some way, I need to know that you can take care of yourself. Defend yourself."

My mind goes to what Rhia shared about her grandmother. I can't even think about something happening to GG. She's all I have left.

Chapter Thirteen
MAURA

June 28, 2003

I went back to the hardware store today to restock the supplies I'm already running low on. Standing in the sandpaper aisle, I tried to remember the correct size for my sander. Behind me, someone asked if I needed help. Over my shoulder, I said that I needed a boatload of sandpaper. The person laughed, asking if the pun was intended.

I hadn't realized I'd made a joke, so I turned around to see the same guy who had helped me before. His smile crinkled his eyes in a way that made the grip on my heart loosen just the tiniest bit. He asked how the boat project was going and I said it was a lot of work. He reached out to grab the right size sandpaper that I needed and I noticed his nice build. He turned to hand me the packets and I hoped he hadn't caught me ogling.

He told me that he thought it was cool that I was rehabbing a boat. As we looked for sturdy work gloves that would fit my hands, I told him how I was doing it for my dad. He would be working on the boat this summer if he were still here, but he wasn't. I felt like I owed it to him, to his memory. Maybe I was starved for conversation because I hadn't planned to say all of that.

Then the guy said his name—Jamie. And I noticed how his sandy-brown hair curled around his ears and the way his hazel eyes held so much compassion. I had liked that we were sort of anonymous, but I told him my name. Maura, he said, sounds Irish. My name on his lips, from his mouth, sounded to me like a wish. I wanted to hear him say it again. He asked what else I needed as we walked toward the front of the store.

I wondered about how to get the old boat out of the water so I could clean up the hull. Jamie barked out a laugh. I stopped walking, irritated by his reaction. He turned to look at me and realized I'd stopped following. He hadn't thought I was serious, and when I said I was, he moved the bill of his cap, rubbed his forehead and adjusted the cap back down. He let out a big *whew* and said it's a whole thing, getting a boat out of water. Then he said that working on the hull would be no joke. He explained that there's a lot more boat under water than you realize.

I told him sharply that I was raised on boats. Dad always had a boat. He didn't always keep them, but as long as we'd been coming to Cedar Branch, I'd been on boats.

I expected Jamie to surrender and apologize. He didn't. He had the nerve to look at me with skepticism! Then he rattled off all these questions that he knew I wouldn't be able to answer.

Like about the engine and the septic system. And how to start it
if it stalled.

He told me that I was a boat tourist. So I told him that he
was a dick.

My fingers started tingling and I wasn't sure I had full control over my element, so I walked out. The last thing I needed
was to accidentally create a rainstorm inside this store. I was outside before I realized that I was still holding the sandpaper and
the gloves. And I hadn't paid. I sighed, waiting for my anger to
calm down, and then I went back into the store.

We didn't speak as Jamie rang up my purchases. After I paid,
Jamie slid the bag of items to me. And still we said nothing.

But of course when I arrived at the car, I couldn't find my
keys. I whispered a quick charm to reveal where I'd left them.
The keys were back in the hardware store. I stood by the car trying to talk myself into going back in for them and then Jamie
walked up with my keys in his hand.

When I took the keys from him, our fingers brushed against
one another. He apologized for being condescending and I apologized for calling him a dick. As I dropped the bag into the back
seat of the car, I casually suggested that he could come help
me with my big boat project if he knew so much about it. I told
him that we were in Eagles Cove, if he decided to come by. As I
pulled the car out of the parking lot, I noticed the afternoon sun
peeking through clouds for the first time in days.

Chapter Fourteen

EDIE

RETRIEVAL CHARMS

There are two main ways to search for a person or a thing.

FINDING A PERSON:

This is essentially scrying, using something from the person's body (hair, nails, something that has touched their skin) to direct a crystal.

1. Attach the item to a clear quartz crystal.

2. Suspend the crystal from a chain or cord.

3. Spread out a map.

4. Place four additional clear quartz crystals at the corners of the map.

5. Hold the crystal suspended from the chain just above the map's surface.

6. Slowly swing the crystal counterclockwise, while saying the following:

With this crystal and the items I bind,

Reveal to me the one I wish to find.

After a few turns, the crystal will pull toward a particular
location as though it were a magnet. When this happens,
you've located your person.

FINDING AN ITEM:
If you are searching for a lost item and you know what it is,
but you don't know where it is, that's much simpler. For the
strongest result, light a candle and burn some rosemary.
Say these words:
As I hold this image in my mind,

Help me see what I hope to find.

It's the last day of June, which means a full week has passed since
I went to the cabin. The decoction that GG and I made from
the beech bark seems to be helping. At least those black lines
aren't progressing, and I don't feel nauseous or dizzy. I still feel
cold sometimes though, and—even more peculiar—I sometimes
think I see shadows just in my periphery. But when I look, they
disappear. I continue to seek comfort in Mom's journal.

"I remember this second one!" I say to Temperance. "Mom
was always losing her car keys." I laugh a little when I remember her repeating the words while rushing around, rummaging
under couch cushions and in the kitchen drawers. When she left
a room, it was like a hurricane had come through. A friendly
hurricane with a good sense of humor.

"And how about Mom meeting a boy and telling him to come help her with the boat? Bold move, Mom."

It doesn't surprise me; she always had an easy connection with people. I consider trying the latest spell that's been revealed to me. Mom hovers at the foot of my bed, which feels encouraging. Maybe I can start with finding something small, something that I know the location of. Like a pair of earbuds I left in Baltimore.

My time with Rhia the day before at the beech comes to mind. If I want this spell to work, then I need to give it the same respect that I gave the beech. I grab some rosemary from GG's herb stash, light a candle, and say the charm with intention.

As I finish the charm, there's the sensation of warmth on my skin and that brief shimmer of light that comes with the magic, and behind my closed eyes, a bright image flares: a ceramic dish sitting on my dresser in my bedroom in Baltimore. And in the dish are the earbuds.

"Huh," I say to Temperance. "It works!"

Temperance looks at me like she's known the whole time that the charm works.

"Guess I'll hang on to that one."

After our run on Thursday morning, Tess and I stop at the diner for coffees for Tess and me, tea for Rhia, and donuts for all. Arguably, the coffee shop has better coffee. But Jorge, who

Tess is now officially seeing, doesn't work at the coffee shop. So the diner it is.

"Nectar from the goddesses," Rhia says when she sees our goodies. "And you two are the goddesses, obviously." It's the first time I've seen her since our moment at the beech. After she gives us each a peck on the cheek, my hand goes to the spot she kissed. Rhia's lips on my cheek.

"Are you blushing?" Tess asks.

"What? No," I say, dropping my hand.

Over donuts, Rhia lays out a favor she needs. "I could use some help with something. Bachelorette weekend. I got a last-minute order and I need to make twenty aromatherapy spell bottles. Will you two help?" She presses her hands together. "Please?"

"Count me in," Tess says, dusting powdered sugar from her hands.

"Sure," I say.

Under Rhia's direction, Tess and I gather bath salts, crushed herbs, and dried flowers while Rhia organizes the glass bottles.

"What spell are we casting on these?" I ask, as we start our assembly line.

"Oh!" Rhia laughs. "These aren't *real* spell bottles. They're just pretty bottles full of items that smells good."

"That makes this easy, then." I fill the bottom of a bottle with bath salts and hand it off to Tess.

"What's up with your hand?" she asks. "I noticed that bandage before but forgot to ask."

"I cut it," I start to say, but I am the world's worst liar. "On something. And GG thought it looked infected, so she's got one of her remedies on it."

"With your grandma on the case, I'm sure you'll be better soon," Rhia says.

"Yeah," I say, "I hope so." And truer words have never been spoken.

Tess says, "Hey, so I'm hoping we can all get together for Fourth of July."

"You know I'm in. Wouldn't miss it," Rhia says, as she funnels crushed sage into a bottle.

Tess presses a cork stopper into the mouth of a filled bottle and sets it aside. "You don't have plans, do you, Edie?"

"I take offense at your suggestion that I have no other social life," I say. I'm measuring out portions of bath salts.

"So you do have plans?" Tess wrinkles her brow.

"I'm joking." I'm glad to have Tess's invite, but can't help feeling a twinge. This will be my first Fourth of July without Mom.

Last July Fourth, we decided to decorate our front yard for the annual parade that passed by our house. Mom took it to a whole other level with a ten-foot-tall Statue of Liberty made of papier-mâché she'd found. We dressed her in the Maryland flag.

Then we bought all of the American flag motif pinwheels that we could find and planted them all around her. One hundred and eighty-seven pinwheels. It seemed there was no end to the quirky plans she came up with. How could I have known that I'd only have her for six more weeks? What would I have done differently if I'd known? For one, I would have been ready to learn the magic.

"Edie, you *have* to party with us. July Fourth in Cedar Branch is amazing," Tess says. "First, there's the town crab fest, and then at night there's a band and fireworks. The band sucks. It's totally for old people. But we are going out on Jorge's boat to watch the fireworks from the water."

"Okay, you've convinced me," I say. The fact that Rhia will be there is a highly motivating factor. "And thanks."

"For what?"

"For including me. Even though I can be a pain in the butt."

Tess puts a hand over her heart. "As a member of one of the founding families of Cedar Branch, it's my birthright to welcome all newcomers into our amazing traditions," she says with mock solemnity. "Even the ones who are a pain in the butt."

"I haven't had crabs this good in so long." I tap my wooden hammer lightly on the knife I've positioned just so on the claw. I crack the claw open, and a beautiful intact piece of meat waits for me.

"That's because Al's does the best steamed crabs, and also, you're a landlubber," Tess says. She's opened her crab and is cracking the body in half.

"Excuse me, Baltimore is a port city," I say.

"Doesn't matter how close to water Baltimore is. It's about how you're so clueless about boats and life on the water."

She's not wrong. Mom's journal shows how much she knew about boats, but it's not knowledge that she passed on. The missing of her washes over me. My body goes still for a moment while I wait for the wave to recede.

"E, you okay?" Tess asks.

"Yeah, fine."

"I never did like the look of their beady little eyes," Rhia says, pulling me from my thoughts. Rhia stares down her crab.

"You like to eat that lump crabmeat though," Tess says.

I smile. It feels good to be with friends tonight.

"That's right, I do. The one exception that I make to my dedication to not eating living creatures."

"Could you pass the pitcher of lemonade?" I ask Tess.

"I've never seen you drink a beer or anything," Tess observes as she hands me the pitcher, now covered in steamed crab spices.

"Yeah, me and alcohol do not mix."

"Same," Rhia says.

A happy little spark flares inside me, knowing that Rhia and I have this in common. Though I doubt that Rhia's reason for not drinking is the same as mine. Alcohol affects witches in unexpected ways. One time, Mom started to levitate after drinking a glass of champagne on New Year's Eve. And when I drank just one beer at a party freshman year, I burped iridescent bubbles. Then—to play it off—I tried to conjure a bottle of bubbles, but I hadn't done magic in a while and I ended up with a stuffed Powerpuff Girls doll. It was a whole thing.

Tess has tried to introduce me to the people gathered at this crab fest, but they all sort of blend together. Jorge sits at the next picnic table over with a couple of his buddies. They seem all right, but I'm happy to be sitting at this table with Rhia and Tess. We all continue to pick crabs until there's a pile of carcasses before us and the flies are starting to become bold.

After we get cleaned up and twilight falls, we board Jorge's boat. Tess hands Rhia and me life jackets.

"Seriously, Tess?" Rhia says.

"Safety rules are safety rules."

"I guess I can't argue with that," Rhia says.

I secretly don't mind wearing the life jacket—I've never been as at home in the water as Tess and Rhia seem to be. And definitely not like Mom, who was practically a mermaid. But then it was her element, after all.

As we motor up the wide river, Tess points out huge osprey nests sitting on channel markers. We pass by boats anchored together in pods with music blaring. Perched along the shore are all kinds of houses from modest cedar cabins like ours to enormous multifamily vacation homes with their windows looking out over the water. Jorge maneuvers his boat to what he assures us is the best viewing spot and then he kills the engine and drops an anchor. Tess sits with him at the helm while Rhia and I take seats side by side in the back of the boat, or stern, as our captain keeps calling it.

"Jorge, is that Eagles Cove?" Tess points off the port side of the boat.

"Sure is."

"Hey, Edie, your family's cabin is over there," Tess says.

Night is falling fast, and the cabin is little more than a black shape amid tall trees. "I see it." I hadn't missed the fact that GG had skirted my question about why people say the cabin is haunted.

Rhia leans in close to me, a welcome distraction from my thoughts. "I love fireworks," she says, "don't you?"

I nod. "Mom and I never missed them." I'm quiet, remembering times when Mom and I would jump in the car in search of the most impressive displays.

Rhia grabs my hand. "This must be hard for you. Tonight. Not being with her."

"It is. But it's also good to be out. With you," I say, enjoying the feel of my hand in Rhia's. "And Tess," I add quickly.

Rhia leaves her hand holding mine for a little while, and even though I've obviously had physical contact with girls—on the cross-country team the girls were always hugging or high-fiving or braiding each other's hair—this feels different in a delicious tumbling Wheel of Fortune way.

"How are things with your grandmother?" I ask, not sure if it's the wrong time or not.

She shakes her head. "Really hard. She didn't know what day it was today, even though she's always loved Fourth of July. When we were little, her barbeque was legendary." Rhia smiles to herself. "You should have seen her. This little old lady working the grill like a boss."

"She sounds awesome."

Rhia nods. "Thanks for asking." She squeezes my hand and lets go.

My hand feels emptier now than it ever felt before Rhia's hand was in it. Like Rhia's hand was meant to be in mine. I absently rub my palm with my thumb.

When darkness falls completely, the first fireworks soar into the sky. Rhia and I lean our heads back to watch them burst overhead and then shower down, reflecting in the water where our boat bobs. I slide my leg closer to Rhia's until our bare thighs touch. I keep my face turned toward the sky. More fireworks explode over our heads. We *ooh* and *aah*. Rhia's leg, warm and smooth against mine, kindles sensations in my body that I've never felt before.

"What are you smiling at?" she says into my ear.

"This," I say. And maybe she thinks I mean this night and these fireworks, but what I really mean is sitting here with her, like we are in our own private world.

She scoots even closer to rest her head on my shoulder, and—even though she's really just resting her head on the shoulder of my life jacket—I can barely breathe. I want to grab her hand again, but this is all new to me. So instead, I sit as still as possible, relishing the nearness of Rhia. The fireworks build toward the finale, booming faster and faster.

When Rhia grips my arm, I think it's the next step in our dance. But she points. "Does something look odd over there?" she says.

I follow the line of her finger toward Eagles Cove and sit forward in my seat. At first, I don't see anything. Then, when a huge display of white fireworks goes off overhead, I see them. A swirl of shadows seeps from the cabin. I glance at Tess and Jorge, but they are staring at the sky. Looking back in the direction of the cabin, the shadows drift toward the river and appear to dissolve into the water. The magic of the moment with Rhia is eclipsed by worry.

As the finale of fireworks blast their staccato overhead, my eyes remain trained on the cabin, but nothing more occurs. After the display is finished, during our ride back to shore, Tess invites us back to her house, but I decline. After what I just saw, I need to talk to GG.

"Geege," I say, tapping her awake when I return to the boat.

"What? What is it?" She comes awake in her sitting chair, raising her arms as if to fend off someone—or something.

"Tonight on the boat, we were anchored across from Eagles Cove."

"Yes?" GG looks up at me standing over her.

I squat next to her. "I saw these shadows coming from the cabin. They didn't look natural."

GG sits forward, blinking away sleep. "This is not good." She turns her sharp eyes on me. "It sounds as if the protections have been breached." She frowns, her mind working through a puzzle. "When you were there, did you touch anything? Remove anything?"

I think about everything I touched in the cabin and of the photo I removed. My stomach sinks. "Yes."

"I see." GG pushes herself up and goes to the kitchen area to make tea.

I follow her, hoping for more information than she'd shared so far. "What does that mean, though?"

GG pulls down a tin of tea leaves and she selects one of her honeys. "Something's been disrupted and whatever is meant to be kept in could be getting out."

"*What* is meant to be kept in?"

The water begins to boil. GG turns off the burner and lifts the kettle using an old oven mitt. She begins to pour water over the tea leaves in a slow, steady stream. Her brow wrinkles.

"A terrible mistake."

I'd like a more direct answer, but I've already learned that GG will not answer when she doesn't want to. I try a different question. "Shouldn't we banish whatever it is rather than renew the protections?"

GG sets the kettle down firmly. "You have learned some of our craft. Do not presume that you know more than I do."

In reaction to a rise in her magic, all of the canisters on the counter jump; the prisms and witch balls shudder. The bones stacked on a string clack. Just as quickly, she contains herself and everything goes still once more.

"I'm sorry, Edie," she says. Then, more to herself than me, she mutters, "I had hoped that this would never happen."

I'm rattled, but I do what I do best. I focus on the outcome. "What do we need to do?"

GG pours a cup of tea and adds two teaspoons of honey. "We need to make a protection spell, and because there's no full moon, it will need to sit for twenty-four hours." She pushes the cup toward me. "But first we need our wits about us. Drink up."

"You weren't exactly the Ice Cream Alchemist tonight. What's going on?" Tess asks.

She, Rhia, and I are sitting cross-legged in a circle, enveloped beneath the arms of the old beech tree. Rhia has lit the tea candles and some incense. We've met up here because I'd been so distracted at work that Tess had to save me from making career-ending mistakes, which, in an ice cream shop, boils down to wrong orders and incorrect change.

"Last night, Rhia and I saw strange shadows coming from the cabin. When I told GG, she said that we need to create a protection spell, so I was up most of the night doing that with her."

"Whoa, sounds intense," Rhia says.

I take in a breath and blow it out. "That's not all." I unwrap the gauze covering my hand and hold out my palm so that they can see the tiny lines there. "GG says it's an infection from corrupted magic. From the cabin. And her cures aren't helping." I drop my hand back into my lap.

"*That's* why you needed those powerful items from Cosmic Flow," Rhia says.

I nod.

"But it isn't working?" Rhia asks.

I tug on the bill of my cap. "What if—?" I start to speak, but I can't get the words out. I try again. "What if I can't be cured?"

One of the candles gutters out, so only parts of the girls' faces are illuminated by the two remaining candles. One side of Tess's face and one side of Rhia's. I wonder what they see when they look at me in this dim light with my face shadowed by a cap.

"Don't think like that!" Tess says. "You've got to stay positive."

"What will happen?" Rhia asks. "With this infection if it's not cured?"

I shrug. "All GG says is that if it reaches my heart, I'll be lost forever. She wants me to reinstall the protections, but I don't see how that will help me. Doesn't it make sense to banish whatever bad magic is residing there?"

Rhia taps her teeth with her fingernail. "Did she say what sort of bad magic is up there?"

"Nope."

"Props to Miss Geraldine and all, but I'm with you," Rhia says. "Banish the baddie and the associated magic goes, too."

"Where would you even begin though?" Tess asks. "I mean, if your grandmother doesn't want to tackle this, it must be very hairy."

Rhia stands up and begins to pace. "Bad magic is usually connected to objects. There must be something at the cabin that you need in order to get rid of this thing. Did anything really bananas happen?"

"The whole thing was bananas! Shadows tried to kill me. Vines grew from the toilet. A drawer tried to eat my hand."

"Wait!" Rhia exclaims. "What was the order of things?"

I dread putting my mind back there because it was so terrifying, but I close my eyes. "The whole place was dark and cold." I shiver at the memory. "But things got really weird in my mom's room. I opened this drawer. There was some random stuff in there. And an envelope. When I tried to grab it, the drawer slammed shut and then the shadows basically attacked me."

Tess reaches out to rub my arm. "I'm so sorry you went through that. I had no idea."

"That's it, though." Rhia jumps up and down. "That's it! Whatever is up there is protecting that paper. I'd bet my Wiccan license on it. You need that paper, Edie."

"There's a Wiccan license?"

"No, kidding. But I'm serious about that paper though."

I wonder if it's too much to hope that even though Mom isn't here to teach me, I can get help from my new friends.

"Would you two . . . consider going with me?"

A second candle gutters out. The last one illuminates only the small area in front of us, leaving us surrounded in shadow. I open my mouth to take back my plea when Rhia speaks.

"I would definitely go in daylight," she says.

Relief cascades over me like when Mom would summon warm water to wash my hair when I was little.

"Aw, man, if you two are in, then I'm coming, too," Tess says.

"Wait." I can't believe that this could be happening. "Really?"

"It'll be good for me," Rhia says.

"How?" I ask. I can't imagine how going to a cursed cabin can be good for anyone.

She twists the ring on her left pointer finger as she speaks. "I've been *studying* magic, but not actually engaging with it. When you showed me that ritual with the tree? I felt more connected to all of this." She gestures around us. "It's time for me to come out from behind the counter, you know? Especially if it would help you," Rhia continues, giving me a small smile. "And I've got plenty of tools to deal with the paranormal. Nothing to worry about."

"When should we go?" Tess asks.

"How about tomorrow?" Rhia says. "I don't need to work until later."

"Tomorrow works for me. Edie?"

I nod, "Yeah, me too." I'm relieved that I won't be alone. But I'm not convinced when Rhia says that there's nothing to worry about. Not at all.

Chapter Fifteen

MAURA

July 3, 2003

Jamie showed up the other day! I was beginning to give up on him. It had been days since I told him to come by—days filled with missing Dad and Mom's silence. But then he showed! And bonus points, he really knows boats. Even old boats like ours. That first day, he spent time on the engine compartment, assessing everything, and then made me a list of what we needed to buy to get the boat running. Then he showed me the septic system.

I told him that I wasn't planning on living on the boat, but he said that it was a good idea to know how everything works anyway. I told him he was so helpful I wondered what his hourly rate was. He blushed, even though he tried to hide it.

This afternoon, his boat approached our dock again. *Back again so soon?* I asked. He gave me a cute smile and said that he thought I was renting him. His smile caused a gentle flutter in my low belly and I felt my face offer a small smile back. The first in a long while. Jamie tossed the ropes to me and I tied them around the cleats on our dock. He went right back to work on the mechanics while I kept sanding the wood.

As dusk began to fall, Jamie gathered his tools and asked me what I was doing for the Fourth. I had to wait a moment before I could speak. We usually watched fireworks from our dock. The words were simple. *We usually* . . . But usually my dad hadn't just died. I looked down and toed the deck of the boat. I told him I didn't know what I was going to do.

Then he said that he could pick me up if I wanted to go watch fireworks with him tomorrow. I looked up at the cabin where Mama was up to who knew what and I thought about another night spent in silence. A night that would be so different from how we'd spent every July Fourth that I could remember.

Dad and I would go crabbing early in the day and then we'd steam the crabs with his special concoction of beer, vinegar, and Old Bay. Sometimes it was only the three of us and Mama would say that it was way too much work for three people, but she also loved that we did it. And sometimes Mama and Dad's friends would come and then it was a real party. When it started to get dark, we all trooped down to the dock and set ourselves up to watch the fireworks. Even though Fourth of July is practically the middle of the summer, it always felt like the beginning of the summer here on the river.

I ran up to the cabin. I could tell I had surprised Mama by the look of shock on her face when I burst through the door. She was bent over a piece of paper, writing, but she flipped it over as soon as I came in.

I frowned and wondered what she was doing, but I didn't

want to keep Jamie waiting so I asked if she planned for us to do the same July Fourth tradition as always.

She began to open her mouth and I couldn't believe it. Was she actually going to speak? A single feather slipped out of her mouth. She shut her mouth tight and shook her head vigorously.

I told her that I was going out with Jamie then. A part of me broke inside when I said it. But I didn't take it back.

When I told him that I'd like to watch the fireworks with him, he looked up at the cabin and I followed his gaze. Mama stood on the porch watching us, her mouth set in a thin line. A soft rain began to fall, and I whispered a few words to keep us dry. Jamie asked what I was doing. I told him I was saying a little prayer to make the rain stop, which wasn't the truth, but it was good enough for the moment. Mama had taught me that you needed to truly trust someone before you shared your magic with them. I hoped Jamie could be someone I truly trusted.

Chapter Sixteen

EDIE

After I charm the lock and remove the chain crossing the driveway, Tess's Jeep makes its way through the overgrowth to the clearing. Rhia lets out a long whistle when she sees the cabin.

"How long did you say it's been since your grandmother lived here?" she asks.

"Longer than I've been around."

Tess pulls supplies from the back of the Jeep. She straps a bike helmet on her head and pulls oven mitts over her hands. When I look, she raises her eyebrows. "What? I have zero interest in a magical infection."

I hold my hands up. "Not judging."

"Rhee, can you believe how completely the cabin has been taken over?" Tess asks.

"It's unusual for sure," Rhia says.

I look over the directions that GG gave me while Rhia and Tess discuss the cabin. Rhia walks all around the property.

"Wild" is all she says. She accepts a bag of supplies from Tess.

"So you'll stay out here and wait for us or get help if something goes sideways, like we said?"

Tess claps her oven mitt hands together. "I'm very much fine staying out here." She smiles, but I'm too nervous to smile back.

"Ready?" Rhia asks me.

I sigh out my nervousness. "Ready as I'll ever be."

Tess and Rhia look at one another. "It's now or never," Rhia says in a serious tone.

Tess nods sagely. "No time like the present."

"Need to strike while the iron's hot," Rhia says.

"Early bird gets the—" Tess dissolves into helpless giggles and Rhia starts laughing, too. Even though my stomach is in knots, I join in.

Then, in my best deadpan, I add, "I mean, never put off till tomorrow what you can do today."

They both burst into laughter again. Rhia gives Tess a big hug.

"It'll be fine," Tess says. "Between the two of you, what could go wrong?" She smiles, but it's obvious that she's nervous, too.

The grass and wildflowers swish around Rhia and me as we approach the front door. I swat away insects that buzz too close. Turning, I notice a slight ripple in the air over the empty space behind the cabin like I'd seen last time.

I tap Rhia on the shoulder. "Do you see that?" I ask, pointing.

"What?" She leans close to catch my line of vision.

"Sort of wavery over there. Like when you see heat coming off asphalt." When I look at the same spot again, the strange rippling effect has disappeared. "Not there now."

"Hmm, let me know if it happens again." Rhia turns back to the cabin and gestures with her hand toward the plants overtaking the building. "Nature is always trying to achieve balance."

I take a moment to digest her comment. GG's abundance of plants on the roof of our boat pops into my mind.

"Do no harm," Rhia says.

Instead of tearing the vines away from the entrance as I'd done earlier, she holds them open for me to slip through. I hold my breath, preparing for the worst. I step through the doorway. No shadows. No vines. I breathe.

When I turn to Rhia, the door slams shut. Me on the inside; Rhia on the outside. Immediately, I begin to hyperventilate. Rhia bangs on the door.

"I can't get in!" she calls through the door.

I grab the doorknob and twist. A wave of relief washes over me when it clicks open. I hold the door open this time, so it can't slam shut. Rhia lifts her foot to step through, but she falls backward. She dusts herself off and steps back up to the door. She tries again and is again pushed back by an invisible force.

"This cabin doesn't want me inside," she says. "Guess those urban legends weren't wrong."

"There has to be a way to get you inside." I remember that before my magic showed itself, Mom had to hold my hand in order to get me into the perpetual woods. Maybe this is the same. "Let's try this." I hold out my right hand and she grabs it. I try not to focus on Rhia's long fingers enveloped in mine and whether or not my hand is sweaty. "Don't let go," I say.

Rhia's fingers squeeze mine. "I definitely won't."

I pull Rhia and just like that, she's able to come through the doorway with me holding on to her.

"I don't know what will happen if I let go of you," I say.

"Let's not find out," Rhia responds.

We walk hand in hand into the living area. It's chilly, like last time.

"Where did the drawer try to bite off your hand?" she asks.

"My mother's bedroom."

Rhia leads me to the middle of the living area. "Okay, let's set up here. Center of the space. Feels right."

It's awkward to hold hands while trying to get everything we need out of Rhia's bag. I hold the bag open with my free hand while Rhia reaches in. First, she pulls out the canister of salt.

"You think there could be unsettled spirits in here," I say, as she sprinkles a ring of salt around us. Settled spirits, like the ghosts on our houseboat, wouldn't be affected by salt. But unsettled spirits are repelled by it.

"I don't know what's in here. But apparently a shadow tried to murder you, so we might as well take precautions."

"Precautions are good."

"Let's test the ring. I'm going to let go of your hand," Rhia says.

I look down the hallway for evidence of the shadows I saw last time. "I don't know, Rhia. That makes me nervous."

"We can't do much while holding hands."

As much as I'd like to continue to hold Rhia's hand—both because Rhia's hand in mine is all good things and also because it seems to be keeping her here—I know that she's right. I release her hand. We wait. Nothing happens.

"Okay, cool. Salt works," Rhia says, as though she's making a mental note.

At least we have that going for us.

We set out the rest of the items from the bag. A candle, a small vial of salt water, a jar of soil, and pieces of black amber, black tourmaline, obsidian, and crystal quartz. GG had given me the list of items and directions on what to do. And we *are* doing what she expects. We're just *also* going to try to get the paper out of here. Maybe it'll be nothing. But maybe Rhia is right and it could help.

"Are you sure you have enough crystals?" I ask Rhia with a teasing tone.

"We want these protections to be powerful. You have the tri-quetra?" Rhia asks.

I pull the iron trinity knot from my bag. GG had told me that this triquetra, which normally hung over my window, repels negative energy and could create a sort of shield along with the spell. She just doesn't know that I'm using it for another reason, too. As I tie a satin cord through it, Rhia pulls out the spellbook that GG gave us.

"This will only work for a short while," Rhia says.

"How short a while?" I ask.

Rhia shrugs. "The book is old. No specifics. You'll need to be speedy."

"That's one thing I'm good at." My attempt at a smile is wobbly.

"Can you light the candle?" Rhia asks.

"Sure," I say. "Where're the matches?"

Rhia looks at me, her expression serious. "If *you* light it, the flame itself will hold power."

I shake my head. "I can't, Rhee."

"You can," she says. She pours the soil in the bowl and then drips the water over the soil. She places the triquetra in the bowl and sets the candle on top of it. Arranged around the bowl are the crystals. She gestures for me to light the candle.

I clench my hands and then slowly allow them to open. I huff out a breath, close my eyes, and ask the fire to come. There is the tingle. I open my eyes. Sparks jump from my fingers. *It's happening. Be calm. It's okay. You can do this.* The sparks grow into flames and my anxiety spikes. Instead of touching the wick, I sort of flick my fingers toward the candle, like I want the flame to get off me. But I miss the wick and my fire hits the spellbook instead.

"No!" Rhia tamps out the catching flame.

I clench my hands tight, extinguishing the sparks in my fingers.

"It's okay," Rhia says. "I can still read it. Here." She hands me a box of matches and I notice her hands are shaking a little bit.

I light the candle with the matches, the stain of failure seeping through me.

We place our hands over the bowl and together we say the words:

> "With the power of water, fire, and earth we ask,
>
> Charm this talisman so that we may complete our task.
>
> Erect a barrier around this place,
>
> Contain what's within and keep us safe."

The last word has barely left my mouth when the windows begin to shake. The kitchen cabinets bang open and closed. The doors down the hall rattle.

"Well, that didn't work," I say, pretending that I'm not terrified. "We need to leave. Grab my hand."

Rhia squeezes my hand tight. She's scared, too, despite her earlier bravado. The doors down the hall burst open.

"Rhee, look."

Shadows slide out of the rooms and down the short hallway toward us.

"Maybe we shouldn't leave the circle," Rhia whispers as the shadows draw nearer.

Vines emerge from the bathroom and up from the kitchen sink.

"We've got to get out." I'm remembering last time. I barely made it out and I don't want anything to happen to Rhia.

"We're safe in the circle, we're okay. And you need that paper."

"I'd rather skip the paper and stay alive."

"It seems like getting that paper could help keep you alive."

The strange shadows on July Fourth come to mind. Something is leaking out of this place. Something ugly and corrupted. It had already infected me. Could it hurt others too? "Right. Okay."

"Here." Rhia reaches into the bowl with her free hand. She sets aside the candle and grabs the triquetra. "Put it on and see what happens."

I loop the cord over my head and there's an immediate shift. The shadows down the hall slow their creep. The doors stop banging and the cabinets stop rattling.

"Go!" Rhia says. "You don't have much time."

I step toward the hallway.

"Edie!"

Rhia points down. The toe of my shoe has brushed through the circle of salt. I bend down to try to repair it. Rhia's face moves from surprise to fear in the second before she's sucked backward and away from me.

"Rhia!"

I reach out to catch her foot, but I miss. I leap for her. She's moving too fast for me to grab her. She's pushed out the front door. The door slams shut. My stomach plummets. *Leave*, every fiber in my body screams at me.

But I need to get that paper. If there's any chance that it could help me get rid of this infection, any chance it can prevent anyone else from being harmed, I don't have a choice.

I force myself to turn to the short hallway leading to the bedrooms. The shadows seem to be holding. For now. I feel the acorn necklace beneath my shirt, against my skin, reminding me of Mom. And the heavy triquetra, reminding me of GG. I whispersing my mother's lullaby. My voice betrays the fear quaking through my body, but the familiar warmth and calm still flow through me.

I reach the door to Mom's room.

I look over my shoulder. The shadows seem closer than before. And I have no idea how long this enchantment will last. I step into the room. When I look back again, the shadows are only a yard away and they block my path out. I start singing again. I step up to the small bedside table. Vines are slithering over the floor toward me. I rip open the drawer.

It's still there. The yellowed envelope. I wait a moment to see if the drawer wants to cut off my fingers. But it stays open. I grab the envelope and shove it in my back pocket.

I turn to prepare myself to run through the shadows to the front door. Pure dread rises up when I remember how it felt when the shadows tried to grab me last time. Then I notice something puzzling. The vines are snaking their way toward the shadows, not toward me. But there's no time to examine why because they've opened up a path for me and I can't let it close. I sprint to the living room, scoop up the candle, Rhia's bag, and the bowl, sloshing its contents as I go. I race to the door, yank open the doorknob, and fly out of the house.

Tess stands in front of the car, looking completely freaked out.

"Where's Rhia?" I ask, breathless.

"Are you okay?" Tess says.

My body starts to shake. Whatever tiny amount of composure I had has crumbled. I lean over, bracing my hands on my knees. I close my eyes, but that's scarier. I open my eyes and try my mother's calming technique: *What can you see? What can you feel? What can you smell? What can you hear?* Someone touches my back, and I jerk upwards to find Tess looking at me with concern.

"Is Rhia here? Is she okay?" I ask.

"She's okay. She's in the car. Let's get out of here."

"What about completing the rest of the spell?"

"Rhee did it while you were inside."

I stand up and nod. "Okay." Shadows creep at the edges of my vision. I blink and they are gone. I pat my pocket to make sure the paper is there. "Let's hope this has some answers."

Chapter Seventeen
MAURA

July 5, 2003

I'm sure that Jamie had no idea what he was getting himself in for when he took me out last night. Even I didn't expect all of the emotions that came up. By a little before seven, Jamie was going to show up any minute and I hadn't even showered. I peered in the mirror and took care of some blemishes with a few whispered words and then put on some clean clothes. When I came out of my room, Jamie was there in his clean T-shirt and jeans, ready for me. Seeing him smiling at me made me feel almost as good as floating on the river after working on the boat all day. But as soon as we left the cabin, I felt off. It felt wrong, leaving Mama, even in her unrelenting silence. I felt as if I were leaving Dad, too. I know he's dead. I know that.

We parked in a big field among a lot of other trucks and cars. Most people had spread blankets next to one another on the grass, but I asked Jamie if we could stay in the truck. He said yes, but it still felt all wrong. Wrong to be lying on a truck bed rather than the dock. Wrong to be away from Mama. And most wrong not to have Dad nearby. As the first fireworks cracked open the sky, I felt a tear trickle down my face. I tried to wipe it away so that Jamie wouldn't notice. But as each new explosion illuminated the sky, the tears fell one after another, too many to catch. By the time the finale beat its staccato all around us, I was shaking with tears.

Jamie was so sweet, he asked me to tell him about Dad. But I couldn't. I had the tiniest sense of how loss leaves silence in its wake. Then he asked how long ago it had happened. I had to count in my mind the days of June and today's date. I told Jamie it had been about two weeks. It was too dark to see his face, but in his silence, I felt the shock.

He'd hadn't realized that it was so recent, and he said he'd take me home. But I asked if we could drive around for a bit or something. I missed Dad, but I didn't want to go to that silent cabin just yet.

We didn't speak as we got settled back in the cab of the truck. Jamie didn't try to fill the silence with meaningless chatter. This was different from my mom's silence. It felt comforting.

He drove the country roads and I leaned my head against the window, letting it all blur by. After a while, he turned off the main road and we bumped along a gravel driveway until he stopped the truck. He told me that this was where he went when he needed quiet.

We walked down a dark path, lit by the moon, to a building

sitting at the edge of the water. We entered through a door in the back and Jamie flicked on a light, casting a warm glow around us and illuminating the boathouse.

The space was like a huge garage, but for boats and on the water. Two motorboats bobbed gently in their boat slips. An old wooden canoe gleamed against one wall. A couple kayaks were stacked on arms built into another wall. Paddles hung by their blades and life jackets hung by their necks. The boathouse smelled like wood and water and fuel. It reminded me of Dad, but in a good way.

We ascended some wooden steps and then we were in a loft area, with a small balcony that gave us a bird's eye view of the river.

Jamie plopped on the ground and we both laid back so that our heads were on the balcony. Above us, the sky was carpeted with diamonds. It filled me with awe. I hadn't seen the stars in so long.

Jamie said that he liked to imagine those stars over people and land all over the world. That he couldn't wait to get out and experience it all. He told me how he wanted to travel internationally and help people. I told him how I was admitted into UPenn, where my dad went, and that I knew I'd be crazy not to go. Jamie said it sounded like maybe I wasn't sure that I wanted to.

We lay like that for a long while. I inched my hand closer

to him until my fingers found his. He interlocked his in mine
and we lay like that, holding hands and staring at the gems em-
bedded in the night sky. Jamie's warm palm against mine woke
something deep inside me, like ordinary magic.

Back at the cabin, I thought about how much Dad would
have loved that old boathouse. On my bed, I rolled over on my
belly and retrieved the bag of Dad's belongings that I'd hidden
in the space between my bed and the wall. I pulled out Dad's old
watch. The watch face glinted in the low light of my bedroom
lamp. I slid it onto my slender wrist and fastened the metal clasp.
Dad wore this watch every day.

This cheap, old watch had gotten me into trouble a couple
years ago. I'd gone to a concert with friends. After it was over,
we'd all been too amped to go home, and I lost track of time.
When I realized how late it was, I performed a quick charm to
change the clocks at home. But when I arrived home, Mama and
Dad were awake, sitting in the kitchen chairs in their pajamas.
Mama's face was etched with worry that quickly gave way to dis-
appointment. Dad was angry. He tapped his watch and asked if
I knew what time it was. He knew exactly what time it was because my little charm had only affected the digital clocks in the
house, not Dad's analog Timex. I never forgot Dad tapping his
watch and telling me that I was inconsiderate or Mama telling
me that I'd abused the gifts I'd been given. Now, I unclasped

Dad's Timex from my arm and placed it back in my bag. I wondered about the power of Dad's things—how they could bring back memories so clearly. And I wondered again if there might be a way to bring on Dad's ghost.

Chapter Eighteen

EDIE

NO UNWANTED MARKS CHARM

This one is very simple, but you need to be careful about your intention or else you might get rid of something else by accident.
Unwanted marks I clear away,
Leave the rest untouched as I say.

Tess and I are sitting in the back room at Cosmic Flow, which has become our de facto meeting place. Rhia helps a customer out front. I'm staring at the note that I'd pulled from the cabin. The paper itself is thick and yellowed. Handwritten on it are five puzzling lines.

"I've been looking at this for the last two days and it makes no sense to me," I say.

I push the paper over to Tess and she reads it out loud:

"'Watch the passing of time. Unlock the place where memories are built. See a moment of joy, captured. His name, times two, hangs on a chain. Love, worn in a never-ending circle.'"

"Does it mean anything to you?" I ask.

Tess shakes her head. Rhia comes in after ringing up a customer. She seems like a light turned down today. I wonder if she's feeling regret from going into that cabin with me or if maybe things are hard at home.

"We can't figure out what this means. Do you have any ideas?" Tess says.

Rhia picks it up. "It's phrased oddly, huh?" She flips the paper over. "And there's not much to it. Just these five tiny handwritten lines on the whole page."

I sigh out my frustration. "Why did we think this paper would tell us anything about what's in the cabin or how to get rid of it? This is nothing but an old note that my mom must have written and then forgotten about."

Rhia sets the paper down and walks over to a table stacked with boxes.

"Come on, Brainiac, think," Tess says.

I *want* to think, but my brain has been foggy ever since leaving the cabin. The lines on my palm are progressing up to my wrist. I'm frustrated, and a little scared, too.

"If Rhia thought the bad magic was protecting the paper then it's probably more than an old note. I believe in Rhia," Tess says.

I wanted Rhia to be right, too. But I don't see how these five lines are going to help me at all.

"Come on," Tess cajoles me. "You would never give up this

easily on a run. Or a math problem either, probably."

"Ugh, you're right." I stand up and pace. I interlock my hands and rest them on my head, willing my brain to work through this puzzle. I had hoped that this paper would offer me a clear answer, not more ambiguity. But life doesn't work like that. And neither does magic.

"Maybe they're clues or riddles. And maybe each one will lead us to something or someplace that will give us some actual answers. 'Watch the passing of time.' How do we watch the passing of time?"

"Maybe when we watch a sunset?" Tess says. "Or watch people grow older?"

"I don't know. By looking at a clock?" Rhia says from across the room where she seems to be organizing antlers by size.

"Yeah, like when we're bored at school," Tess says.

"Wait!" I say.

"What? Clocks?" Rhia sets down an antler.

"Mom talked about a watch in her journal. What if the clue is actually the word *watch*?" I say.

Tess pulls the note closer. "If the clues are that on the nose, then what could these others be? 'Unlock the place where memories are built' must be keys or a lock, right?"

"Maybe. But keys to what?" I say. "And why would we need them? How does a watch and some keys help us banish whatever is in that cabin?"

"Is the watch meaningful in some way?" Rhia asks.

"It was my grandfather's. Why?"

"I'm not sure. But you know about scrying, right? Using something that belonged to someone to find them?"

I nod.

"Items that hold a person's energy can be powerful in magic."

I frown. "I don't get what you're saying."

"If we figure out the rest of the clues, maybe it will give us the big picture that we need. So, where are memories built?" Rhia asks.

My gut response is *everywhere*. But when I close my eyes and think about where memories are built, I think of my mother and of the house we lived in together. "A house," I say. "A home."

"E, focus on your mother, grandmother, and grandfather. This is somehow connected to them. Where were memories built for *them?*" Tess says.

I consider what I've learned from my mother's journal. I straighten up. "My grandfather had a workshop where he *built* furniture. My mom wrote about helping him."

"Perfect. So now we know we are looking for a watch and some keys to a workshop," Tess says.

"Where is your grandfather's workshop?" Rhia asks.

I think back to Mom's journal entries. "It was behind the cabin."

We all look at each other. There's no workshop behind the cabin. Just an empty plot of land.

"I guess it was demolished at some point," I say.

"But maybe we only need to find the key," Rhia says. "Maybe we don't need to get into the actual workshop."

"Maybe," I say, doubtful.

I look at the paper again. "And how do we know where to even look for this stuff—assuming we guess correctly what it is we are looking for?"

The sense of impossibility settles down on me again.

"Edie, you said your mother magicked spells into her journal, right?" Rhia asks.

I nod.

"Do you think there could be something magicked onto this paper? Something we can't see right now?"

I press the heels of my hands against my eyes. Feels like anything is possible at this point, which also feels totally overwhelming. "I need a minute." I go outside where the heat and humidity are a welcome change from the dim incense-filled shop. I breathe in the summer air and get a whiff of honeysuckle. I wait for Mom to appear, but this time the scent comes from actual honeysuckle that sits near the back entrance of the store. Rhia comes out like a woman on a mission. She stops in front of me, arms crossed over her chest.

"You're pissed that I talked you into using your magic at the cabin and it got a little crazy," Rhia says in her characteristically direct manner.

I blink a couple times, trying to make sure I'm understanding what she's saying. "Wait. You think *I'm* mad at *you*?"

"Yeah," she says, dropping her arms to her sides. "Aren't you?"

I shake my head. "I thought *you* were pissed at *me*."

Rhia shakes her head and her curls shake, too. "Why did you think that?"

"Maybe because I dragged you into a potentially homicidal cabin? And I suck at the whole fire thing. Also, you didn't say a word the whole ride home. But mostly the homicidal cabin part—what if you'd been hurt?"

"I was totally freaked out. Way out of my depth," Rhia confesses. She steps toward me. "But it was my choice to go in there with you."

Rhia's words give me a happy tingle, even though it might not mean anything more than the fact that she was helping me—like friends do.

"And it was *my* choice to agree to the magic. Besides, your plan worked. We cast the spell *and* got the envelope. Bonus: neither of us was eaten by shadows. Truth is—I couldn't have done it without you." I look at the ground and then back at Rhia. "Wouldn't have wanted to."

"Oh." A small smile plays at the corner of her lips. "Okay then. That's . . . good to know."

"And you're not mad at me?" I ask.

She shakes her head. Then she looks up, brown eyes catching mine. "You were great in there. I was scared shitless."

"Except for the epic fire fail. But you stuck it out with me."

"You'll get it," Rhia says.

I wonder if she's right. She cocks her head back toward the store. "Come on."

We walk back into the shop where we find Tess posing for a selfie.

"Stop sexting Jorge. Time for a group hug," Rhia announces.

"What?" I say.

"Bring it in." She holds her arms out and wiggles her fingers, indicating that Tess and I should join her.

Tess drops her phone and flashes an innocent grin. "No idea what you're talking about, but I never say no to a Rhia hug."

I allow myself to be enfolded and wrap my arms around them, appreciating the way that this grounds me and—if I'm honest—savoring this closeness to Rhia.

"Are we all good now?" Tess's voice is muffled by the hug. "Because you are both taller than me and I'm sort of suffocating."

Rhia laughs in that big, open way, and now she's the same Rhia I remember, with all the lights turned on.

"Hey, you know what we should do?" Rhia says when we pull apart, an impish smile lighting her face.

Both Tess and I look warily at Rhia. "What?" Tess says.

"Tattoos. To commemorate our first haunted cabin experience together," Rhia says.

"You say it like there will be more haunted cabin experiences," Tess says.

"There might be!" Rhia says. "What do you say? Little ghosties right here?" She gestures to the soft skin of her inner arm. "You know I always have my needle and ink. Ready to stick and poke."

Tess shakes her head.

"Still not ready?" Rhia asks, disappointed.

"You know I want one. I just haven't figured out the perfect image yet."

"There are no perfect images, Tess. Pick something that you want on your body." She turns to me. "Edie?"

"Not this virgin."

"Virgin?" Rhia raises an eyebrow and quirks a smile.

My stomach does backflips in response and the heat of a blush creeps up my neck and across my cheeks.

"*Tattoo* virgin," I say, as though I'm not also a virgin in other ways.

"My favorite kind of virgin," Rhia says, grinning. "Technically, I guess some would say I'm a virgin, too, if—"

"Enough about virgins!" Tess says. "Focus. How are we going to figure out if something is magicked onto this paper?"

"Wait!" Remembering how the spells appear in the journal, I inspect the paper for a waxy mark. But I can't find any. I frown and pull Mom's journal from my bag. "Maybe if I look at the spells that have appeared, I can figure something out."

Rhia leans over my shoulder as I flip through the journal to the latest spell. "What's that one?" she asks.

"For removing zits, I think." I laugh a little.

"Maybe we can reverse it," she says, reading it. "Let me think." She closes her eyes. Her brows pull together in concentration. A moment later, her eyelids fly open and she looks excited.

"Marks erased I wish to see,

Reveal yourself anew to me."

I hold my palm over the paper, ready to say the spell. Shadows creep at the edges of my vision and goose bumps rise on my arms. I stop.

"Are you okay?" Tess asks.

The shadows recede and I don't want my friends to worry, so I smile and say I'm fine. I start again and this time, I feel the warm glow that comes from magic. As I'm speaking, hand-drawn images begin to emerge on the page.

"Rhee, you were right!" Impulsively, I hug her. Just as quickly I'm not sure if I should have and I let go. "Sorry, got a little excited."

"No problem. I'm happy to be of service." She grins at me and I smile back, remembering our inside joke.

The images that we've revealed show us a very basic hand-drawn map. Two small buildings adjacent to one another sit in the middle, one smaller than the other. Wavy lines indicate the river flowing at an angle on the right side of the buildings. Only five other buildings are marked: the hardware store, the woods, the antique shop, the cemetery, and the marina.

"Five places to go with five clues." Rhia beams.

"They're all places in our town that have been here for a good long while, too," Tess says.

"And they surround these two buildings," I say, pointing at the ones in the middle.

"Not only that," Rhia says. "Look." She traces her finger from one building to the next until I recognize the shape of a star. "Those five places form a pentacle around these buildings in the middle. That's definitely some magical planning."

"Hang on!" I say, inspecting the placement of the buildings relative to the river. I touch my finger to the buildings drawn in the middle. "I'm pretty sure that's our cabin and the workshop Mom wrote about in her journal."

"Whoever did this was creating a place of power around

those buildings," Rhia says. "I've read that hiding items in the shape of a pentacle usually means that someone was performing an invocation."

My response is immediate and vehement. "No way. Mitchell magic is about balance between nature and the elements. Magic that helps and heals. My family would never engage in that sort of magic."

I knew a little of what Rhia referred to when she mentioned an invocation. Some people with innate magic can summon powers, things, the dead, even. But Mom had said it was dangerous work that ended up taking more that it gave. This was magic we were never meant to use.

Tess and Rhia look at one another.

"What?" I say.

"How do you know that for sure, E?" Tess's tone is gentle, but her point is clear.

"Who else could have done that?" Rhia says. "And why would your grandmother have needed a protection spell?"

I want to bolt, like I do whenever I'm uncomfortable. I want to run off the confusion and fear. But Tess and Rhia have shown me that I can be myself with them. And they are right. I know that they are.

"Can you think of a reason why your mom might have performed an invocation?" Tess asks.

I give a curt shake of my head. But then I think about my

mother's journal entries. How she talked about her grief over her father dying and how GG didn't speak. I whisper my answer. "Actually, yeah. Mom wanted to see her dead father again." I pause, trying to digest what's ahead. "So, if we find those five items—"

"We should be able to banish the bad magic in the cabin," Rhia says. "And that infection *should* go with it."

"Okay," I say, letting out my breath in a big exhale. "You've convinced me. Let's find some hidden items."

Chapter Nineteen
MAURA

July 7, 2003

This morning, I found Dad's lucky coin in my bag. I remembered the time that Dad took me to the racetrack with him. We stopped at the concession stand where he bought me popcorn and a Coke and himself a beer. He handed me the lucky coin and told me to blow on it three times because three times was the charm. That was funny to me. I only needed one time for a charm to work, as long as I did it correctly.

When Dad's horse came in first, he whooped and picked me up and spun me around, and when he collected his money, he told everyone how I was his lucky charm. I stored the coin in the velvet bed of my jewelry box, occasionally taking it out to rub my fingers over it.

This year, when Dad got sick, I pulled that coin from its bed of velvet and blew on it like before, then I tucked it under his pillow. But deep inside I knew that no amount of magic—not even if you performed it perfectly—could cure cancer. When he died, I retrieved the coin. Though I knew it was no more than an old coin with no luck left, I saved it, putting it in my bag before we left for the cabin.

A couple days after Fourth of July, Jamie stopped by as the sun was making her languorous journey toward the edge of the world. His T-shirt and jeans were dirty from work. His boots clomped down the steps and across the dock to me. His face was shaded by the bill of his baseball cap. He looked like someone who got things done. Someone you could depend on. I smiled at him. Smiling was getting a little bit easier each day. He gestured to the never-ending sanding that I was doing and asked if I needed a hand.

I laughed and told him that I'd probably need help with the boat until the end of time. He joked back that he only had until dark. We shared a bag of chips and he asked my favorite flavor. I told him sour cream and onion and asked his. He said barbecue unless Utz crab chips were an option. He said no one did crab chips like Utz.

I laughed and thought about how I could change these chips to be his favorite in the time it took to pass the bag from my hand to his. But I didn't. Not yet.

Jamie and I dusted our fingers on our pants and got to work. We worked on the boat until it was too dark to see clearly. Then, I pulled off my shorts for a quick dip. I still had my bathing suit on from earlier. I asked him if he was coming in as I lowered myself into the water.

He said he didn't have a suit, but I said to come in anyway, that no one would see. Jamie turned to look up at the cabin.

Butter-yellow light melted from the wide picture window that overlooked the river. I told Jamie that Mom doesn't come down here.

Jamie pulled his shirt over his head. He was built like a boy who'd already spent a life outdoors, his body honed for work. He unbuttoned and unzipped his jeans and dropped them on the deck as well. Looking up at him from in the water, seeing his barely covered body, I was seized with need. I wanted to hold him and kiss him. I wanted to be held and kissed. I couldn't remember the last time I'd felt this. It was sudden and intense. My eyes didn't leave his body as he stepped to the edge of the dock.

Jamie dropped into the water and swam to me with easy strokes. We treaded water, looking at one another. We didn't speak, but again, this wasn't my mother's silence. This silence swelled with possibility. I treaded water closer to him. He offered a small smile.

I moved closer, trying to work up my nerve to ask what I wanted to ask. The water buoyed me, and the waning light gave me a boldness that daylight never could.

I couldn't get the words out. But Jamie knew what I wanted, and I guess he wanted that too because he reached out a hand and pulled me through the water until our bodies touched. I wrapped my legs around his torso, almost sinking us both. We laughed and then my lips were pressed against his, our bodies crushed together. We maneuvered to the dock and Jamie held us up by grabbing hold of it with one hand while he held me close with his other.

I told him to be careful of barnacles and he answered by kissing me. I allowed myself to get lost in it, in the sensation of skin on skin and the water embracing us both. For the first time, I felt something besides the detonation of Dad being gone.

In the middle of a deep kiss, Jamie let go of the dock and we sunk beneath the black water. I wished I had fins and gills so that I could continue kissing him underwater. We held hands, but our bodies separated. I floated, weightless and sightless, tethered to the world by my fingers entangled in Jamie's. Our bodies rose toward the surface.

When we pulled ourselves onto the dock, slick as dolphins, I lay my towel down and pulled Jamie close.

He brushed my wet hair away from my face and touched his forehead to mine. His eyes flashed in the moonlight when he asked if this was all okay.

I wrapped my arms around his neck and pulled him against me. Jamie kissed my lips and my bare shoulder. He kissed my neck, which tickled and made me giggle.

But then he kissed my temple and said he needed to get back. I didn't want him to move away from my body. He pulled his T-shirt over his still-damp torso and wrangled into his jeans. I laid back on my elbows, watching him cover his beautiful body from my sight. I was surprised by how badly I wanted him.

After he left, my mind went back to Dad's coin and I wondered if maybe there is some luck still left inside it.

Today, I took the coin and Dad in his box into his workshop. He had everything that I needed, of course. While I worked, I felt his presence more than ever. In the worn wooden handle of his hammer. In the old welder's hat that perched on a shelf. In the vise connected to the workbench, the paint long since peeled away from the metal ball at the end of the lever that I used to tighten the clamps around the coin. When I was finished with my work, I looked at the result and I imagined that Dad would have been proud of me.

Tonight, Jamie took me back to the boathouse. After he guided me up to the loft, I handed him my gift.

He looked surprised and unwrapped the tissue paper. Holding it up by the string, he asked if it was the lucky coin that I'd told him about. My throat closed up with emotion. All I could do was nod. Jamie kissed me deeply. Then he slid the black cord over his head and touched the coin with two fingers.

We laid on the soft blanket that Jamie had brought up here for us. I settled my back against his chest. His cheek, with its hint of stubble, rested on mine. He kissed my temple.

Then he told me that he liked the photo, but I didn't know what he meant. That's when he told me that there was a photo hanging on the Wall of Fame in the hardware store of me and my father with one of the chairs that Dad had made.

I smiled, remembering the memory. I'd asked Mom to take the photo after Dad and I had finished the chairs. He'd insisted that I sit on the chair and he'd stood next to me. I frowned. I'd framed the photo and given it to Dad for Father's Day; he'd kept it on his dresser in the cabin. What was it doing at the hardware store?

I snuggled into Jamie, hoping that his arms around me could protect me from the sad thoughts, allow me to forget for a few minutes. As if he sensed what I needed, he pulled me closer to him, wrapping his arms around my midsection.

I wiggled my butt into his crotch, and I felt his body respond to me being so close. Our hands roved over one another's bodies, banishing everything beyond this boathouse. Jamie and I half-undressed beneath a blanket was my sole focus. I was trying hard not to push Jamie. He didn't seem as ready as I was. But we went further this time. He'd slid his hand down my pants and I'd slid my hand down his.

Then, he stopped. He said that I meant a lot to him, but that he'd be leaving for the Peace Corps soon and wasn't sure it made sense to get serious right now. And he wanted our time to mean something. Not just be a summer hookup.

I didn't understand the idea of applying logic to our time together. But I said okay because I'm not sure what else you can say when someone doesn't want to have sex with you. He asked if I was mad and I told him that I wasn't. *Mad* wasn't the right word. I was yearning, I think.

Chapter Twenty
EDIE

"Mom's latest journal entries definitely do *not* help us in our search," I say, when Tess and Rhia and I are once again together. What I don't tell them is that the journal entry *did* potentially fill in a huge blank in my life. Based on the timing of the entries, this Jamie guy is most likely my father. I've wondered about my father's identity for so long and now I'm seeing their relationship unfold through Mom's journal. I feel sort of guilty for finding out this way. Maybe that's why I'm not ready to tell my friends quite yet.

"Nothing about secret maps or shadow-filled cabins?" Tess asks.

"Definitely, no." I make a face when I remember Mom's entry and how I needed to go for a run to work it out of my system. I'd been hoping it would lead me to another spell, but no such luck. "The sooner we banish this thing, the sooner I can get back to normal." I rub at the lines running up toward my wrist.

"If that's what you want," Rhia says, keeping her eyes on the map. She clears her throat. "Clue number one goes with the antique shop. Should we go look for a watch there?"

"Let's do it," I say. "And clue number two, which might be keys, should be here." I tap the drawing of a cluster of trees on the map.

"The woods?" Tess says. "That sounds hopeless."

I almost agree with Tess. Then it hits me that I know exactly where in the woods my mother would have hidden something.

"It's not!" I say. "We have a place where we go."

The perpetual woods—where I'd confronted GG on the day I'd discovered the cabin—is the only place a Mitchell would hide something in the woods.

"If that one will be easy, should we do it now?" Tess asks.

"I never said easy," I say. "I said that I know where it is."

"Want to tell us what to expect?" Rhia asks.

"Well, we have to go at night."

"Okay, and why?" Tess asks.

I look at Rhia, wondering if she already knows what I'm going to say, but it seems that this bit of magic is new, even to her. "There are places that non-magic people can only see under moonlight."

"No way!" Rhia says, her face breaking into that smile that I've begun to look forward to.

"Under moonlight?" Tess squeaks. "Maybe I'll sit this one out."

"We need you," I say.

"Yeah, Tess, we're in this together now," Rhia says.

"Fiiine," Tess says. "When are we doing this moonlight walk?"

"A full moon or near-full moon would be best," I say.

"We just had a new moon a couple days ago, so the next full moon won't be for another couple weeks," Rhia says.

"So, antique shop first?" Tess says.

"Antique shop first," Rhia and I say together.

The tinkling of the bell over the door disrupts the silence of the antique shop. The space is cramped with old things. I run my fingers across the top of a smooth wooden table that holds an array of pewter and brass candelabras. A cluster of arrows mounted on the wall point toward the ceiling. Next to them is an old-fashioned rucksack. Beneath those items, a quilt stand holds a variety of handmade quilts. Each of these items had meant something to someone. Did the items still hold meaning after the people were gone? My hand goes to the acorn pendant and I think of Mom.

"Hello?" a woman's voice trills. "Hello? Hello! Hello!"

"She always does this," Tess side-whispers to me.

The woman continues to call out hello as she emerges through heavy black curtains from a back room. She is short and round. Her graying black hair is piled on her head and held there by pencils, as far as I can tell, and her bright red lipstick works with her light brown skin. She wears a multicolored loose-fitting dress. Stacks of bracelets on both wrists create a kind of music when she waves to us.

"Well, hello!" she says. "Rhia and Tess, how wonderful to see you both. And who is your friend?"

"Hi, Ms. Alvarez, this is Edie."

"Oh, you must be Geri Mitchell's granddaughter."

I'm not sure I'll ever get used to this small-town thing. I force a smile. "That's me."

"Tell her hello for me, will you, hon? And tell her that the last salve did the trick, just as she said. She'll know what I mean." She winks at me. "Now, how can I help you girls today?"

Tess speaks up. "Can you show us your men's watches?"

"Of course. Right over here." She walks us to the display case. "You take a look and if you find something, you give a little shout, okay?" She waves and then disappears back through the curtains.

"So she's always this excited?" I ask.

Rhia wiggles her eyebrows at me. "Hello, hello, yeah she is!" I can't help but snicker.

The three of us cluster around the jewelry case. Black velvet boxes divide the jewelry. There are rings, mostly set in yellow gold. Necklaces drip from little hooks. Bracelets hang from a tubular display. Watches wait beneath the bracelets on their own curved displays. My eyes scan the chunkier ones designed for men. I absently slide the acorn pendant back and forth on its chain, welcoming the warmth and comfort it brings me.

"No Timex watches," Tess says.

I'm still playing with my necklace as I lean over the counter, my heart sinking because Tess is right—when I spy a wavering area between two of the watches. I squint. I turn my head to catch it from my peripheral vision. There's something there.

I remember the spell Rhia created to reveal the images on the map. I change one word and use it here. I cross my fingers, too. That's not magic, that's just hope.

"Something erased I wish to see,

Reveal yourself anew to me."

The watch appears, filling a space that was empty a moment before. Without taking my eyes away, I point. "Look, there."

"Where?" Tess asks.

I'm staring at a men's watch. It doesn't look terribly impressive as far as watches go. It's just a Timex with a metal band.

"Do you see it?" I ask. "The Timex stopped at 9:18?"

"Yes." Rhia breathes the word.

"I see it now, too, but I swear it wasn't there before!" Tess exclaims.

A shiver of excitement runs through me.

"Tess, could you ring the bell on the counter?" I ask. "I'm

afraid it's going to disappear again if I look away."

Tess rings the bell.

"Coming!" Ms. Alvarez trills. "Coming, coming, coming!" She walks behind the counter and stops before me. "You found something?"

"May I see that men's watch, please?" I point to the watch that was invisible just a few seconds ago, but which now appears to be very solid.

"Of course!" she says. She opens the cabinet from the back and snakes her arm in to grab it. Her hand hovers over each of the two watches on either side and for a moment I'm not sure she'll see it.

"Tell her," Rhia whispers.

"It's a men's Timex with a metal band. Between those where your hand just was."

I haven't moved my eyes from the watch. I see her hand hover for a moment longer.

"Oh! I see it." Her hand lands on the watch. My relief is immediate. "I must have been looking from an odd angle," she says. "I missed it at first. Here you go." She sets the watch in its open box on the glass top of the display case.

"Do you have any way of knowing who brought this watch in originally?"

She lifts the box and looks at its underside. "Let me see if I can find some information in our files."

"Thank you."

"In the meantime, feel free to look at it more closely, if you like." She turns to head to the back room.

I lift the watch from its holder and place it on my wrist. Almost immediately, dimness clouds my eyes. When my vision clears, I don't see the antique store or Rhia or Tess. I see a girl and her father on a dock, fishing. The dock looks sturdy and freshly stained and I recognize it as the one at the cabin, before it began to submerge. This is my mother when she was a child, maybe nine years old, with her father. He's showing my mother how to hook a worm. My mom giggles and shows him her fish face. She crosses her eyes, purses her lips, and waves her arms like gills. She used to make the same fish face at me. It never failed to make me laugh. At the gong of a bell, they both look up. My grandfather consults his watch.

"Time flies when you're having fun, eh?" he says to my mother.

"Yup. Mama must have lunch ready," she says.

"Good! I'm so hungry that I almost ate this worm!" my grandfather says.

"Well, I'm so hungry that I might eat the fish who ate the worm!" Mom counters. "And the bear who ate the fish, too!"

My grandfather laughs. He ruffles her hair and they walk together toward the steps leading up to the cabin. A swell of love consumes me. I want to stay in this memory, watching my mother as a child and my grandfather, whom I never met.

"We need to get it off her," I hear a voice say.

"I can't do it."

"Let me try."

"Hurry, Ms. Alvarez will be back any minute!"

A searing white pain in my left wrist yanks me from the beautiful scene.

"Are you all right?"

I open my eyes to find Rhia and Tess peering at me. I'm on the floor of the antique shop.

"Yeah," I say. "Why did you take the watch off?" I'm missing the memory already. Wishing to be back in that place. A wave of nausea rolls over me.

Rhia and Tess look at one another. "You seemed to be in a trance or something. You went super still, but your eyes were open."

"Not gonna lie, it was pretty freaky," Rhia says.

Tess and Rhia each take one of my arms to yank me to standing. I'm overcome with a rush of vertigo.

"Are you okay?" Rhia asks. "You look really pale."

"And you're shaking," Tess says.

"I don't know. I thought I was okay. But I'm so cold."

"Oh, shit, look," Tess says. She points to my wrist where the watch had been. The fine black lines that had progressed from my palm to my wrist after the last trip to the cabin are now up to my forearm. "The watch must have made it worse."

"That's not good," Rhia says. Grasping the watch with the edge of her T-shirt, she drops it into its box and snaps it shut as if it contains an evil spirit. "What happened when you put the watch on?" she asks.

"I was looking at a moment from my mother's past. A happy memory." I smile. "It was so nice." I rub my palm and my wrist, trying to warm it up. Shadows dance at the edge of my vision, but I shut my eyes tight and when I open them, my vision is clear.

"So, that's definitely the watch we were looking for," Rhia says.

"One down, four to go," Tess says.

"But hopefully, Edie won't go into a trance every time," Rhia says.

"Ha, yeah," I say, but in truth, I can't wait to put that watch back on my wrist and see that memory again.

Chapter Twenty-One

EDIE

"Scooby Gang's all here," Tess says, when we're all gathered in front of the hardware store.

"Thanks for coming," I say.

"Anything weird after taking that watch home?" Rhia wants to know.

"Nope." I don't tell them how I spent most of the night wearing the watch, allowing the memory to play over and over. I also don't mention how I was so nauseous this morning that I couldn't eat breakfast. I'm telling myself that I must have caught a stomach bug.

"Hey, how's your wrist?" Tess asks.

I hold up my arm covered in gauze. "GG to the rescue."

GG had been perplexed when I showed her the progression. She'd muttered about how the protection spell should have halted the infection because it should have blocked any additional corrupted magic from reaching me.

"Are those black lines any better?" Rhia asks.

"I think so," I say. I'm lying because she's already worried enough and besides, we're handling this.

As if she wants to reprimand me for holding back the truth from my friends, Mom appears behind Rhia. I'm conflicted as I see her floating there. I miss the mother I knew, and I loved seeing the memory of her young with her dad. But I don't know how to integrate that with the mother who invoked the thing that inhabits our cabin. That's now infected me.

"What's the plan?" Tess asks, pulling me from my thoughts.

"Okay, so based on the map and Mom's journal, we think we're looking for a photo that should be here. There's like a Wall of Fame or something?"

"That Wall of Fame is legendary. Just saw it the other day when I was here with Jorge."

"Let's do it," Rhia says.

The guy working behind the counter barely looks up from his phone when we enter. I can't help but think that Jamie was much better at customer service. Tess leads Rhia and me to the huge display of photos in the back of the store. There are hundreds of them.

"I've got a needle in a haystack feeling," Tess says.

"Rhee, remember the Finding Something Lost spell that I wrote down?" I ask in a low voice.

"Sure, but we can't light a candle here," Rhia says.

"The note said that we didn't need the candle as long as you're specific about what you're looking for."

"But isn't it intended for like earrings or something you owned and have lost?" Tess asks. "You've never even seen this photo before."

"Well," Rhia chews her lip contemplatively, "everything I've read suggests that magic is so much about intention. The objects—like the candle or the rosemary—are often just vehicles for the intention. What did your mom's journal entry say about the photo?"

I close my eyes to remember what the journal said. "Mom is sitting in a chair that they'd built. Her dad stands nearby. They are both smiling."

"It's worth a try," Rhia says. "Tess, can you distract the guy?"

"Uh, I'm kind of seeing someone? Hello?" Tess says.

"Oh my gods, you don't need to make out with him. Just talk to him. Like a human being talks to a human being."

"Fine." Tess throws up her hands.

Rhia turns back to me. "Okay, I'll block you so no one can see."

I try to push away my overwhelming sense of self-consciousness. Magic is definitely about intention. And I already know that these spells only work well if you give them your full attention, no snark. I breathe in and breathe out. I do that two more times, centering my mind on the wall. I'm one in a long line of Mitchell women calling on their inner power, I can *do* this.

"As I hold this image in my mind, help me see what I hope to find," I intone, my eyes closed.

"As it is above, so below," Rhia whispers.

The warmth of magic glows in me, and I flutter my eyes open. As if guided by an invisible force, my hand is drawn to the top middle of the display where an image is flickers in and out of visibility. "I see it," I whisper.

"I see it, too," Rhia whispers back.

I'm dying to get that photo in my hands so I can see another memory of my mother. But even on tiptoes, I can't reach. "I need a stepladder," I say.

"No, you don't," Rhia says, excited. "I've read this one! Keep your eyes on it and ask it to come to you. Say: lost thing, come to these hands."

Feeling doubtful, I hold my hands with palms facing upward. "Lost thing, come to these hands."

"As it is above, so below," Rhia says again.

I can't bring myself to say those words that all witches say. They don't feel like my words just yet. Instead, I say, "Please."

It happens in an instant. The photo was on the display and then it is in my hand. I stare at it, faded and curled from time. My mom's child face grinning at the camera. Her father resting one hand on the back of the chair, smiling.

"Thanks, Mom," I whisper.

"You did it!" Rhia says, leaning her chin on my shoulder. I tilt my head so that it rests against hers, enjoying this rare moment of closeness. I press the photo to my chest. "I can't believe that worked."

"I had enough confidence for both of us," she whispers. Her breath tickles my ear and sends delicious shivers through my body. I could turn my face and kiss her. It would be that easy. Just as I wonder if I should, she pulls and away and calls over her shoulder, "Tess, stop flirting. We're leaving."

We leave the store giggling, a little giddy from our victory. Now that we have the second item, I only need three more. Based on our success so far, we should have all of the items before this infection even reaches my elbow, let alone my heart. I can handle the nausea and dizziness because it's all going to be over soon. As least that's what I tell myself. Though I'm finding that I'm not as focused on leaving Cedar Branch as I was when all of this began.

As we walk toward Cosmic Flow, Tess suggests we stop for iced coffee to celebrate this win.

"I can already taste that sweet, sweet iced mocha latte," Rhia says.

At the coffee shop, I order a peppermint iced tea because I'm remembering Mom's favorite summer drink. While we wait, I pull out the photo to look at it again. Everything around me fades away and a memory comes into sharp focus.

It's a sunny afternoon. My mother and my grandfather are working outside. My mother is older than the memory from the watch, maybe twelve. She and my grandfather are constructing the chairs. He's measuring wood and she seems to be sorting nails.

"Always measure twice so that you only need to cut once," he says to her.

She rolls her eyes good-naturedly. "You've told me that a hundred million times."

"Have I?" he asks, equally good-natured.

"Can we do s'mores tonight?" she asks.

"Of course! Why don't you gather up some kindling with Mama?"

"Oh, and maybe we'll collect some raspberries, too!"

I feel the summer sun and the love between my mother and her father. I want to linger, but the image strobes. I feel like I'm tumbling. I can't see and my ears are full of a loud whooshing. I land with a heavy thud and the whooshing grows louder. Rhythmic. Wings beating. Something soft and smooth falls on my face, and then another and another. At first, they tickle. Feathers. They fall one after the other until I am smothered. I can't breathe.

I hear my name from far away. I gasp for air.

"Turn her over."

I need to open my eyes. I sense a bead of warmth, but it seems so distant.

"Is she on something?"

"Is this an overdose?"

"Should we call someone?"

I fight to get to the surface. The warmth grows. I am so close. Almost there. When I come to, I'm on a couch in the coffee shop. My hand clutches the acorn charm. Nausea roils in my stomach. I feel like there's something stuck in my throat and my mouth feels dry.

"I really think we need to call someone." The manager of the coffee shop stands back, looking at me with distaste.

"Did I puke or something?" I say as I push myself to a sitting position.

"Sort of?" Tess smiles apologetically to me.

"The manager wants to call your grandmother," Rhia says.

I shake my head. "GG doesn't believe in phones. Besides, I'm fine."

I cough and pull a black feather from my mouth.

"That's what I meant by 'sort of,'" Tess says. On the floor are more tiny black feathers.

"Edie, you're not fine!" Rhia says.

Tess hands me a tall cup. "Here's your tea."

"Let's go," Rhia says, holding the door open for me.

I can't get out of that shop soon enough. I'm so embarrassed by what happened. Outside, the late afternoon heat is like a balm on my skin. I slurp at my tea gratefully. I had ordered it because Mom loved peppermint iced tea, but now I'm glad for the peppermint helping to dispel my nausea. Rhia's arms are crossed over her chest and she looks concerned.

"What?" I ask as we walk away from the shop.

We stop at a bench and sit down.

"Seriously? You ordered your tea and then dropped like a rock," Tess says.

I glance back toward the shop. "I'm mortified about that. The photo showed me the sweetest memory, though." I start to pull it out, wanting to see the memory again.

Rhia swats my hand away. "No! You can't touch that photo again."

"Right. You're totally right," I say, even as I'm yearning for that memory.

"Look at your arm," Rhia says.

The black lines which had been hidden by GG's gauze are creeping up past that point, to the midpoint of my forearm. "Oh."

Rhia shakes her head. Tess suggests that we go hang at the beech until her shift. On the way, I think about Mom building the chair with her father. I want to see the other memories, even if they make me feel sick. Seeing Mom again, even as a kid, made the missing of her just a little more bearable.

At the beech, I climb into the hammock and pull her journal from my bag. "Seems like the items used for that invocation are all mentioned in this journal. Should make it easy to figure out the rest."

Tess and Rhia talk in low voices while I begin to read the next entry.

Chapter Twenty-Two

MAURA

July 9, 2003

I was still in bed and it was already deep afternoon, maybe. It was hard to tell because of the unrelenting rain. I'd found Dad's dog tags hanging on a hook in his workshop and I'd put them around my neck. They remind me of the most vulnerable side of my strong father, at least before he got really sick. Dad never spoke of the war. But Mama and I both knew when it was on his mind. He'd go quiet while staring at the television. It wasn't simply silence; it was an absence. Like he'd left us. Other times he'd spend hours alone in his workshop.

Mama knocked on my door, pulling me from my memories. She gestured for me to get out of bed. I told her that if she wanted me to do something, then she'd need to ask me. Out loud. She looked sort of helpless after that and left.

But then Jamie was there. Jamie with his strong hands and warm eyes and I knew he could take away my pain for a little while. I told him to shut the door, but he wouldn't. Not while Mama was just outside.

Later, after he left, I thought about what had happened earlier, when I'd first woken and had planned to text Jamie and work on the boat all day. The reason that I'd hung Dad's dog tags around my neck.

After I'd gotten up, I listened to a voicemail message. It was from my new college roommate. I hadn't gotten around to forwarding our mail, so I guessed that my housing assignment letter was in whatever mountain of mail was collecting back at our house. Hearing that I had a roommate and dorm assignment made me want to talk to Dad right away. I couldn't remember which dorm he'd been in his freshman year. Why couldn't I remember? I know he told me—probably a thousand times. I held the phone in my hand, suddenly remembering that he's not back in Baltimore working. He's gone. And I couldn't remember what dorm he'd been in. I called him anyway, to hear his voice. I didn't leave a message. I never do.

Then, I called the administration offices at UPenn to tell them that I was withdrawing. I did it without talking to Mama, because what would she say? Nothing. I'd been in bed ever since and not even Jamie was willing to give me what I needed. When I leaned into the crevice between my bed and my wall for the bag where I kept Dad's things, it wasn't there. I wanted to put the dog tags in the bag. But the bag was gone.

I got up and yelled at my mom. I asked her what she'd done with my bag, what she'd done with Dad's things. Water flew from my fingertips. Mom raised her hand and I knew she was going to wrap me in vines.

I walked down to the dock and boarded the boat. Sitting on the deck, hugging my knees to my chest and letting the rain fall on me, I felt Dad with me. I was sure that he would appear to me again. If only I waited long enough. Mom had always said that it was the way of our family that our dead stay with us. It had to do with shared memories and the bond of love. So where was Dad?

Chapter Twenty-Three

EDIE

"Dog tags," I say, closing Mom's journal and tucking it next to me in the hammock. "My mom wrote about dog tags. My mother wore them to remember my grandfather, so that's got to be one of the items."

"His name, two times, hanging on a chain." Rhia looks up from drawing with a marker in the small sketchbook she carries around. "Sounds like dog tags to me."

"Yeah, for sure," Tess says. She's climbed one of the lower branches of the tree and she's perched there like an oversized, very colorful bird.

I close my eyes to take in what Mom had written. How Mom had withdrawn from UPenn before she had me. I'd always thought that I was the reason that she hadn't gone to college. But now I know it was because of her sadness and not being able to share the experience with her dad.

This is the closest I've gotten to knowing the grandfather I'd never met. It makes me wonder why GG doesn't talk about those times at all. I hear Rhia and Tess chatting, and I want to join in, but I also want to look at the photo again. I pull it from my bag and allow myself to get swept back into the memory from so many years ago.

Next thing I know, I'm being shaken. "Edie! Wake up!"

I open my eyes. Rhia's face is close to mine. I smile to see her so near. She glances at my lips, but then her eyes go to my hand where the photo is clutched there. She moves away.

"What is it? What's wrong?" I ask.

"Got to go—Tess is late for work. Lost track of time."

"Did I fall asleep?" I look around, trying to orient myself. We are at the beech. I'm in the hammock.

"I don't know." Rhia looks at the lines on my arm and bites her lip. "Come on. Tess is at the truck."

I roll out of the hammock, carefully sliding the photo into my bag. I can get back to it later.

On Wednesday morning, we're supposed to meet for our morning run, but Tess texts to say she can't make it. I'd stayed up a lot of the night, with the watch on my arm and the photo in my hand. I could almost feel like I was with them, in those memories. When I finally slept, my dreams were full of shadows.

I head out to run on my own, but I've got no gas. Unbearable nausea forces me to stop my workout early, which might be a first for me. I text Tess and Rhia, asking when we can look for the next item. I've got to stop this infection. A voice whispers that maybe I'm also eager to see the memory held by the next item.

Later, I message them again. Hours go by before I get a reply from Tess saying that she and Rhia can meet me at Cosmic Flow that afternoon. And that I should bring the watch and photo—Rhia has been reading up on dark magic and wants to take a closer look at them.

"Did you bring the things?" Tess asks as soon as I walk into the store.

I'm hesitant to pull them from my bag. I like it better when they are close to me, in my bag or in my hands, but I set the watch gently on the table and then the photograph. Nothing happens when I touch them for only a short moment. Nothing except my need to hold them longer and let the memories play.

Using a pencil, Tess slides them over to Rhia. "Be right back." Rhia scoops up the watch and photo into her gloved hands, taking them with her into the back room.

"Where is she going?" I ask. I don't like that they are going out of my sight. I rub at the black veins on my arm. I feel sick. I've barely eaten anything these last couple days.

Rhia comes back empty-handed.

"Where are they?" I feel my anxiety ratcheting up. I need that watch and the photo. I need them in my hands.

"We're keeping them locked up," Tess says.

"What do you mean, you're locking them up? Give me back my watch and photo."

"They aren't safe," Rhia says. "They're corrupted with dark magic."

A flash of irritation zips through me, followed by a tingling in my fingers. "What are you talking about? They contain beautiful memories of my mother and grandfather. That's not corrupted magic. It can't be."

"It's like you're addicted to them—that's not normal magic," Rhia says. "And we're worried."

"So this is an intervention?" The burn of betrayal ignites in me.

"We're keeping you safe," Tess says.

"Those items are not the problem!"

"You look like shit," Tess says. "And I say that with love."

"I'm stressed." I scratch my arm. "You would be too if you had a magical infection working its way to your heart." I shut down the inner voice telling me that the items are making it worse.

Rhia asks me to pull up my sleeve.

I hide my left arm behind my back. The two of them are teaming up on me and it brings me right back to when those girls yelled *freak* at me all those years ago. The tingling in my fingers grows. I clench my fists. What had Mom always said? *What can you see?* And what else? Why can't I remember now?

"Doesn't matter," Tess says. "We know the infection is getting worse."

"Those items are speeding it up, aren't they?" Rhia says.

"We just need to find the other three items. You said it yourself, Rhia. We find the items, we banish the baddie. And I'll be fine."

"And your grandmother said that if she can't stop the progression, you'll be lost to us forever." Rhia looks really upset. "We don't want to lose you, Edie."

"Please give them back. Please!" I hear the desperation in my voice. I feel pathetic, begging like this.

Tess shakes her head slowly like she feels guilty for telling me no. Rhia doesn't even look at me.

The tingling sensation spreads from my palms to my wrists and my desperation flashes into anger, hot and fast. "So you're not giving me back my property?"

"It's for your own good, Edie," Rhia says. "They're locked up where they can't hurt anyone."

I want to rip apart the store. I want to burn it down. I'm scared of these feelings. I'm scared where they could lead. "I need to leave," I say.

"Wait. Edie! Let's talk," Rhia says.

"Don't run off like you always do," Tess calls out.

"I might do something that I'll regret if I don't." I turn and leave without looking back.

When I return to our living quarters on the boat, GG looks up from a book she's reading. Temperance looks up from the window she'd been napping in.

"Do you care to talk about it?" GG asks.

My anger flares again and my hands tingle. "Would you *actually* talk to me, though? Because you've told me that I'm infected and that I could be lost forever, but you won't tell me why or how this all happened."

"I understand your frustration."

And just like that the fight goes out of me. She might as well have used Mom's element and doused me with water. GG's words have the same effect. My anger can't grow if she doesn't engage. I flop in the chair opposite GG. But I'm still craving those memories. Maybe GG can help me get back to those moments.

"Geege, Mom wrote about helping my grandfather build the chairs on the porch and making fires and having s'mores and stuff."

"Hm-mm." GG makes a noncommittal noise.

I lean forward in my chair, elbows on my knees. "What was

it like with you all back then? I feel like I never hear you tell stories."

"We had many good memories." A small smile plays at GG's lips.

I flare of hope rises in me. "Can you share some?"

A cloud passes over her features. The smile disappears. She clears her throat. "We can't dwell in the past, can we?"

Seems like an odd answer. I can't help but think about Rhia's grandmother. Does GG not share memories because she doesn't have them? Could she have dementia? GG walks over to me, leans in, and kisses me on the head.

"I love you, Edie. Never doubt that."

A rush of emotion bursts forth in me like the flowers on GG's magical hawthorn tree.

"I don't," I say. "I won't."

GG lifts her chin. "It wouldn't be a bad time to work on your element."

I curl my fingers into my palms. "I'm too agitated."

"When better to practice control? Look, I have a pail of soil here, which can put out any fire. And if all else fails, I can toss you in the river."

GG's words coax a small smile from me.

"Come." She tilts her head toward the door.

We stand on the back deck of the boat. I breathe in and

breathe out. I close my eyes. But what if the sparks catch something flammable? My eyes fly back open. "You have the dirt?"

GG nods. "I have the dirt."

"You'll put out the fire if it gets out of control?"

"I will."

"Even if it means throwing dirt in my face."

"Even then."

"What if someone sees?"

"In my experience, people don't believe what they see when it
doesn't match the way that they think the world works."

I can't think of any other excuses, so I try. I call up Mom's
guidance from three years ago. She'd said that I couldn't
be frightened—that anger and fear bring chaos to our magic.
She'd told me to slow my breathing and calm my mind. Then,
she'd said for me to hold up my palms and ask the fire to come
to me.

When my breathing is even, I take in a breath and hold my
palms up toward the sky. In my mind, I call to the fire. The tingling
returns. I open my eyes. Tiny sparks dance from my fingertips just like at the cabin that day. They are beautiful.

"Good! Now form a ball, Edie," GG coaches me.

Focusing on the sparks, I imagine them coming together to
form a ball of fire, of light. They begin to merge together. Over
each palm hovers a sparking ball about the size of a marble. The

fire tickles me but doesn't burn. The balls begin to grow larger, the tickling more intense. It's too much.

"No!" I say, dropping my hands.

"Call it back, Edie," GG commands.

But it's too late. The fire has hit the deck of the boat. GG flicks one hand and the pail full of soil smothers my flames. I curl my fingers into my palm.

"You allowed your fear to take over," GG says.

She flicks her fingers again and the soil rises and sets itself back into the pail.

"That's what happens every time," I say. "I keep hoping that the fear will go away, but it doesn't."

"It's possible that it never will," GG says. "Here." She hands me a broom and a dustpan. "For the rest," she says.

As I sweep up the remaining dirt and ash, I feel more hopeless than ever. "I'll never learn to master this element if I can't stop being scared of it. Mom said I couldn't be afraid."

"You will," GG says, taking the dustpan and broom from my hands. "It's not that you can't be afraid. You can't allow your fear to be your boss. Make friends with the fear. Tell it to step aside. And you'll master your element."

I don't know how I'm supposed to make friends with fear. My approach to uncomfortable things is either to run away or figure out a solution. Making friends with fear doesn't seem to fall into either category. And on the topic of fear and friends, I wonder how I'm going to find the last three items when I feel so betrayed by Tess and Rhia for tricking me into giving up my items. I rub at the veins webbing my skin and wonder how long I have before I'm lost and what that even means.

Chapter Twenty-Four

EDIE

On Friday before work, I pull on a long-sleeved shirt, but first examine the progression of what's happening to my arm. The lines haven't progressed any farther since Tess and Rhia took those items, but the fingers on that hand continue to feel cold. I go to GG and she covers the lines with her remedies and gives me two tablespoons of her best honey. But she shakes her head.

"It's not working, is it?" I say.

"It doesn't appear so."

"What did you mean before when you said I could be lost to you forever?"

GG sighs one of her epic sighs. "When it reaches the heart, the person becomes a shell, living in another dimension altogether."

A chill runs through me. "And you truly don't know any way to fix it?"

GG closes her eyes tight before opening them to look at me. "There is a way, but it's very dangerous and we do not have everything that we need."

* * *

My shift with Tess is stilted as each of us avoids the magical elephant in the ice cream shop. My mind is occupied with what GG meant when she said that the way is dangerous and that we don't have what we need. I'm also still angry at what Tess and Rhia pulled, double-crossing me like that. But if I'm honest, the longer I'm away from those items, the better I feel. After two days, the nausea and dizziness are pretty much gone, even though the black veins remain.

I'm not ready to admit that yet, so I'm relieved when the shift is over, and I can go back to the boat. We've just begun cleaning up for the night when her phone rings. I can hear Rhia yelling from where I stand by the sink. I turn off the water.

"What?" Tess's face shows shock. Her eyes flick over to me.

"Working. Yeah, she's here, too. What?! No! Okay. Be there as quick as I can."

"What's going on?"

Tess has trouble looking at me. "We need to leave right now. The beech is on fire."

Tess speeds down the roads and for once I don't mind. We turn off the main road and start to bump over the side road that leads us to the field where the beech stands. As we turn the corner, we both gasp. All we see are flames. The entire tree is lit and sparking. The weeping branches spill fire toward the ground and smoke billows upward to the sky.

"No!" Tess wails.

The flames are not orange, red, and yellow as they should be. The flames eating this beloved tree are a sickly green.

"Get me as close as possible," I say.

"What? No! We are calling nine-one-one," Tess says.

"Tess, get me as close as possible. Nine-one-one won't be able to help."

Tess rockets across the field toward the tree where one lone figure is on her knees. I can feel the beech dying. I don't know if I can help—I might be too late.

"Grab Rhia and get back," I say. "As far as you can. Promise me!"

"Okay, okay," Tess answers. Her face is fixed in fear.

I jump from the Jeep and sprint across the field. Rhia runs toward me. When she reaches me, she pushes me hard in the chest. I stumble backward.

"Rhia, what the fuck?"

"You did this!" she yells.

"What are you talking about?"

"You can conjure fire," she screams. "You said you'd do something you'd regret. You're getting us back for taking your things. You burned our beech!"

"Rhia, I'm trying to save it, not burn it. Go with Tess."

Rhia collapses on the ground, wailing. The air is filled with the acrid smell of burning and the popping and crackling of the fire as it roars through the tree.

"Rhee, come on," Tess yells, tugging on Rhia's arm. "It's not safe."

Rhia allows herself to be pulled up. I sprint the rest of the way to the beech where I stop and kick off my shoes. I wiggle my toes into the dirt, connecting to the earth beneath me. The tiny acorn pendant on my necklace warms. I touch my fingers to it for the comfort it always gives me.

"Help me, please," I whisper.

I raise my hands. Fire is my element, so fire should obey me. Even if it's not a natural fire. I hope I'm right. I need to be right. The green flames lick at the branches, consuming the leaves. I focus on the fire, on each molecule, and call it to leave the tree. Sparks jump and skitter toward me. I feel them hit my fingertips and enter my being. They are cold, not like my fire. It's working. I must stay focused.

My feet leave the earth, but I hardly notice. More sparks follow the first ones. The fire seems to dim, but barely. My body continues to rise. I float in the air, toward the fire and the fire flows toward me.

My arms are outstretched, doing all that I can to bring the fire to me, within me. I feel it entering my body, filling me with its cold fury. My vision grows blurry. Shadows swirl at the edges of my sight. The cold burn licks at my face and the surge of fire from the tree pushes me ever higher. My arms can't hold much longer. I try to hang on, to keep pulling fire, calling it to me, but the great tree still burns. I call with everything in me. Then I begin to fall.

"Edie."

I hear my name. The voice pounds the inside of my skull.

"Edie, Edie."

The pounding is like someone knocking on my head to be allowed in.

"Edie, wake up now!"

Someone snaps their fingers and my eyes fly open. Rhia, Tess, and GG stand over me. The stars swim behind their heads.

"Did you wake her?" Rhia asks GG.

"I did. But it won't last long." GG kneels beside me and holds my head up. "Open up, Edie." She slips a large spoonful of honey into my mouth.

"Mmm," I say. It's sweet, but also peppery. "Yummy!" Then I say to Rhia and Tess, "We've got to stop meeting like this." I giggle.

"Is she drunk?" Rhia asks.

"It's a side effect of what she's done." GG's tone is grim. "She's going to feel awful tomorrow. *If* she makes it through the night. Come on, Edie. To your feet. Let's go. That's it."

Somehow, I am upright. "Wow." I look down and wiggle my

toes. "Look! Those are my feet way down there. But where are my shoes?"

"Can you girls help me get her back to your car?" GG says.

Rhia and Tess each take one of my arms and they walk-drag me back to the Jeep. The scent of scorched wood fills my nose.

"What happened?" I ask. "Where are we? Oh, I don't feel so—" I stop, push my friends away and retch into the field.

"You've been messing with things you aren't prepared to deal with," GG says to me when I wobble my way back.

"I saved our beech!" I say. "Wait." I turn, looking for Tess. "Did I save it? The tree?"

"You tried your best. We won't know just yet."

"I didn't save it? Oh, no." I flop down on the ground, suddenly despondent. "Mom's journal was in there."

"What?" GG says.

"Mom's journal." I press the heels of my palms into my eyes.

"How long will she be like this?" Tess asks.

"Until she sleeps it off," GG says. "Then she'll need days to recover."

"Can you give her something to help?" Rhia asks.

"She'll get through it quicker if I don't."

The next thing I know, I'm in Tess's Jeep.

"If you puke in here, it will not matter that you are some magical girl with a death wish because I will kill you dead, understood?" Tess says.

I nod and everything goes double.

"Don't let her fall asleep," GG says.

"Don't you need a ride?"

"No, I'll meet you at the boat."

And then we're off.

"Bumpy, bumpy!" I say as Tess navigates through the field and back to the dirt road that leads to the highway. "Rhia?"

"Yeah?" Rhia says.

Everything dims.

"Edie!" Tess yells.

My eyes fly open. "What?"

"Don't fall asleep."

"Rhia, you're so pretty. Did anyone ever tell you how pretty you are? Because you are. So, so pretty. Man, I'd like to kiss you. I've been wanting to kiss you forever."

When I wake, I can't see. I panic before I realize that a compress lies across my eyes and forehead. I nudge it away and blink against the daylight, which feels like tiny needles stabbing into my eyes. Temperance licks a paw and looks at me as if to say it's fine if she sleeps forever, but not okay if I do. My left arm feels sort of heavy. I raise it to my eye level. It's wrapped in layers of leaves. That can only mean my veins have gotten worse. I need to use the bathroom very badly, but I can't seem to move my body.

"Geege?" I try to call loudly, but my voice is weak.

She appears at my door. "Oh, thank the gods and goddesses." She wipes her hands on a tea towel and comes into my room where she leans over to feel my forehead. Two or three ghosts float in behind her.

"Can you help me up? I can't seem to move."

"You don't need to get up."

"I do," I say. "I need to use the bathroom."

GG nods her understanding and comes to the side of my bed. She lifts my legs and turns my body so that my legs are on the floor. She guides me to sitting upright. A rush of light-headedness makes me dizzy.

"Can you stand on your own?" GG asks.

I shake my head. She helps me up and with slow steps, she guides me to our shared, tiny bathroom.

"Do you need help in there?" she asks. Her tone is so gentle.

"I'll manage."

I shut the door and fall more than sit on the toilet. When I'm done, I manage to pull myself up to standing. I peer in the mirror. The whites of my eyes have gone blood red around the hazel irises. My hair explodes around my head in a dark-brown wavy mass. When I wash my hands, I notice that my nail beds are all black. Peeling back the leaves on my left arm, I gasp. The black veins are up to my biceps now.

I emerge from the bathroom and take slow steps back to my room. It's all I can do to reach my bed.

"Why do I feel this way? Why do I look like this?"

GG tucks my covers around me. "What you did took an enormous strain on your being. After you took in that fire, it started to burn through your body." I can hear the concern in her voice as she places a new compress on my forehead. "You're lucky to be alive."

I know she's right, but the pain I'm in right now makes me wonder if death would be preferable.

"It's worse." I rest my right hand on my left arm.

GG sits at the edge of my bed. She nods.

"What's today?"

"July eighteenth."

"I've been sleeping for two days?" I try to sit up, but a wave of dizziness pushes me back onto my pillows.

"Yes," GG says. She brushes my hair from my face. "As I said, you put a great strain on your body. And Edie, we need to talk."

I fiddle with my bedspread. "You know."

"That you've been messing with things outside of your understanding? Yes. Now help me fill in the blanks. What have you and your friends been up to?"

I tell GG the whole story—how we returned to the cabin to cast the protection spell, but that we also took the paper that turned out to be a map and how we've been trying to collect the five items in an effort to banish the presence in the cabin.

"Do you think Rhia is right about all of this?" I ask when I finish talking.

"She's not wrong," GG says. "But it's a fair bit more complicated than you all realize." GG purses her lips. "Given what I saw at the beech, you must be very close. And this means that you must be careful moving forward. This sort of magic is not to be trifled with. By the way"—her eyes flick to my window—"where is your triquetra?"

I frown, trying to remember what happened to it after the last visit to the cabin. "It might be in Tess's car. I'll ask her."

"Return it to your window. Don't forget."

I nod.

She picks up my arm and examines the black veins crackling up my arm. "I'm going to prepare a fresh remedy."

Trying to take my mind off corrupted magic and infections, I think about what I know from Mom's journal. And what I suspect but have not confirmed: Jamie is my father. GG returns with a bowl. A towel is draped over her shoulder.

"Geege, did you know Mom's boyfriend from the summer that Grandfather died?"

A crease appears between GG's eyebrows. "There was a boy, yes." Her eyes cloud over. "That summer was a blur. I don't remember much from then."

I wonder, not for the first time, if GG could possibly be losing her memory. We're both quiet as GG layers the fresh salve over my arm. My thoughts take me back to Mom's notebook.

"Her journal was at the beech," I say quietly.

GG nods. "You said that on the night it happened."

I rub the fingers of my left hand, which have stayed colder than any other part of my body ever since I held that rock.

"I've lost my one way of learning from her. I was never ready when she was around, but now I am ready to learn, and she's gone."

I begin to cry.

GG sets the bowl on my bedside table and wipes her hands on her apron. She sits on the edge of my bed. "You have everything that you need. Here, here, and here." GG touches me lightly on the forehead, my heart, and Mom's necklace, resting her hand for a moment longer on the necklace.

Chapter Twenty-Five

EDIE

Another day passes before I feel well enough to get up, but I still don't leave the boat. I'm getting some strength back, thanks to GG's remedies and her honey. Even so, I spend most of my time in bed. I feel like Mom did when she wrote about staying in bed all day missing her father.

Not having the journal feels like an added physical pain. I can't believe I left it at the beech. I'd thought that the objects we'd collected were helping me deal with Mom's death by letting me be in memories. But they were also making me sick. I know GG says that I have everything in my head and my heart, but I wish I had the journal in my hands right now.

When Tess shows up the following day, I'm on the roof among GG's plants. She climbs up the ladder and stands awkwardly for a minute before she finds a place to sit. Temperance slides by her and then disappears among the plants with a flick of her tail.

"Hey!" I say, surprised.

"You said you'd never bail on me, so when you didn't show this morning, I figured you were still sick. Either that, or you're never speaking to me again."

"I've been really out of it. Sorry."

"It's okay." She shrugs. "I actually ran on my own, if you can believe that."

"That's awesome." I run my hand down the length of my ponytail. "Um, so, you two might have been right," I say. "About those items being bad for me."

Tess nods. "I know we were right. But I'm sorry we lied." She fidgets with her shoelaces for a moment. "The news trucks have been at the beech."

Grateful for the change of topic, I ask, "What're they saying?"

"That it was some sort of natural gas explosion. That's not what you think, is it?"

I shake my head. "GG figured out what we've been up to—searching for the five items. She said that the fire at the beech means that we're getting close. I wish that made me feel better, but it doesn't." I pluck a bit of rosemary from a nearby plant and break it with my fingernail, releasing the woodsy scent. "Does Rhia still believe that I did it?" It's almost painful to say the words out loud.

Tess looks down. "I'm not sure."

I flick the pieces of rosemary away and sigh.

"What do you remember from that night?" Tess asks, cocking her head.

I blink a couple times and frown. "Not much. I remember

trying to pull the fire away from the tree. And maybe I was floating or something?"

Tess nods. "Yeah, you were levitating. It was *wild*. You *did* do it, though, Edie. You were pulling the fire into your body. I've never seen anything like it."

"If the tree has died, I failed." I'm quiet for a moment.

"It was scary to see you like that," she admits.

Now I look up. "Like what?"

"Floating and having that green fire flow into you. It's like you weren't you. Like you weren't—" Tess shakes her head. "What else do you remember?"

"It's all a blur. Until I woke up in my bed two days later."

Tess bites her lip like she doesn't want to tell me something.

"What?"

"You're going to be embarrassed."

"Just tell me!"

"Well, you sort of told Rhia how pretty she was." Tess winces. "And that you wanted to kiss her."

My cheeks burn with the hot rush of embarrassment. I look down.

"I was starting to get a vibe about you two," Tess says. "I mean, I totally saw you in the boat back on Fourth of July. But since you haven't really let on what you're feeling, I thought you should know what you said."

I don't say anything. I'm not sure I *can* still feel that way after what Rhia accused me of. I rub my fingers on a lamb's ear leaf, getting small comfort from its softness. I have trouble meeting Tess's eyes.

"Talk to her," Tess says.

I chew the inside of my mouth.

Tess stands up. "I need to get ready for work."

After Tess leaves, I go back to bed. I'm pretty sure Tess was trying to say that I didn't seem human. And Rhia has accused me of using my element to destroy a tree. So there go my only friends in town. Now that I've had a taste of what it means to feel connected to people, to let them in, I feel lonelier than I've been since Mom died.

The scent of honeysuckle drifts into my room and Mom appears. I haven't seen her for a while. Looking at her floating before me like that, I wonder why she had hoped to see her Dad again. Needing my mother and not feeling her touch or being able to actually speak to her—this is so much worse than not seeing her at all.

"Go away," I say, squeezing my eyes closed. "If you can't talk to me or help me, I don't want to see you anymore."

* * *

On Wednesday, I finally get up and get dressed. I pull on the shorts I'd worn the night of the beech fire and feel something in the pocket—the map. I'd thought that I'd left it in Mom's journal so I'm relieved to have something rather than nothing. The map tells me that I need to go the cemetery and I'm sure that I'm looking for my grandfather's dog tags.

I close my eyes to bring up the spell for finding lost things, but all that appears behind my closed eyes is Rhia, looking hurt and betrayed. I hold my head in my hands.

When I come out of my room dressed, GG looks pleased. "You seem stronger."

"Yes, thanks to you."

"Going somewhere?"

"I need to take a walk."

"Remember that your body is still recovering. Don't expect more than it can give."

As soon as I walk off the boat, I soak in the July heat. Jim is spray washing the hull of a huge fishing boat. He stops the sprayer. "Edie! Good to see you up and out."

"You heard?"

"Yes, your grandmother told me. Sounds like a hell of a stomach bug."

Seriously, GG? "Yep, went right through me. Later!" I wave as Jim shakes his head and chuckles.

The cemetery sits at the top of a small hill, up and away from the river. By the time I enter through the huge wrought iron gates, I'm drenched in sweat, but I don't mind. The heat makes me feel more alive than I have in days.

I follow the winding paths aimlessly for a while until I admit to myself that there's no way that I'm going to find dog tags in a cemetery just by wandering. I'm so tired. I sit down on a stone bench planted at the foot of someone's gravestone. A cedar rises up beside the bench.

I've never spent much time in cemeteries. We don't bury the women in our family. We cremate them and on the one-year anniversary of their death, we plant a tree in their honor and sprinkle the ashes in the soil. Mom had thought it was a lovely tradition to show our connection to the earth and its elements. But when it happened to us, when Mom died, I had wished for a traditional ceremony—some songs sung, some words said—that would help me make sense of it. Mom's death anniversary is just weeks away. I can only hope that I'll be healed by then. That this will all be over.

I close my eyes to and try to hold the image of dog tags in my mind. I start to say the words of the finding spell, but they get tangled on my tongue. Mom and the lost journal fill my thoughts. Nothing is revealed to me, which isn't a surprise because I can't clear my mind long enough to focus. I stand for a moment with the sun on my face.

I miss my mother's humor. I miss her delight in life. I miss her smell. I miss her so much. I think that maybe she'll appear to me now, but she doesn't. Maybe she listened when I told her to go away. Now I regret my words.

GG climbs down from the roof of the boat when I return. "Are you okay?"

"I'm so tired. No energy."

She wipes her hands on her smock and starts the kettle. "I told you that you need to be patient with your body while it heals."

Patience is not an attribute that seems to have been passed on to me. While the water heats, she mashes something in a bowl and pulls out a fresh mug, which she pours some honey into, adding the roots and a sachet of herbs, then covers it with the now-boiling water. She brings the steaming cup to me. "Until then, rest. And this will help. Twice a day."

I peer into the mug and breathe in the vapor. There's a hint of peppermint and the sharpness of ginger and cayenne. I sip at the scalding tea, feeling the peppery burn followed by the soothing calm of honey. Thoughts of my mother in the cemetery have made her absence yawn wide. I wish for her soft touch on my hair, for the way that she'd squeeze my shoulder and kiss me good night. I miss the song that she'd sing sometimes when I was scared.

"GG, do you remember the song Mom used to sing to help me sleep?" I ask.

"Of course I do!" GG's face opens up like the sun on the river in the morning. "Darkness . . ." She purses her lips and frowns. "Maybe I don't."

I sing the song and when I'm finished, GG has tears in her eyes. She clears her throat. "Remember, I said to rest," she says, and she heads to her room.

I wish a simple song could solve my problems. I still have three items to find for this search. The girls I thought were my friends only see the worst in me now. These black veins are snaking up my arm and not even my magical grandmother seems able to cure them. One thing I am sure about—I have no time to rest.

When I get my energy back, Tess and I agree to meet for a run. I need the run to clear my head, but even more important, I don't want to lose Tess as a friend.

"How do you feel about mile repeats?" I ask.

"What doesn't kill me makes me stronger?" Tess says. "Is that the answer you were looking for?"

"That's the one!" While we warm up with an easy two-miler, Tess asks about GG.

"Is she going to help, now that she knows what's going on?"

"Seems like it. She was a little cryptic though."

We start our repeats. With each mile, I focus on running off the fear about the black veins on my arm, the betrayal of Rhia's accusation, and the sadness about the tree. When we are finished with the repeats, I slow down my pace as we return to town.

"You were on fire!" Tess says when she catches up to me.

I shoot a look at her. She holds up her hands. "Too soon?"

"A little," I say, but I give her a small smile.

We turn onto Main Street where people are starting to crowd the sidewalks, oblivious to the corrupted magic that burned the beech, that has infected me.

"Oh my gods, I've never been so happy to see the diner," Tess exclaims as we pass the coffee shop and fish market until finally we see the awning of the diner. "Because that means we are done!"

We stop in front of the plate glass window, panting to catch our breath.

"Is Jorge working?" I ask. Things so far seem pretty normal between us, which is a relief.

"He's off today. Speaking of which, you're working solo tonight. Jorge and I are going out."

"Have fun." I wiggle my eyebrows up and down.

"Oh, stop," she says, giggling. She pushes her sweaty hair from her forehead. "Have you talked to Rhia yet?"

"Nope." I adjust my cap so it sits low over my eyes.

Tess flips my cap back up so that we can make eye contact. "Talk to her."

I cross my arms over my chest. "I can't get past what she accused me of. And she hasn't reached out to me, so I guess she still thinks I'm guilty."

"Could you try? For me?"

Tess makes it sound easy. Like *trying* is no big deal. But it feels like a big deal to me. I never expected to be interested in anyone romantically. And now the one person I'd ever felt attraction for had accused me of something terrible. And yet, I can't get Rhia out of my head.

After a moment, I sigh. "For you," I say. "I'll try for you."

Before my shift at the ice cream shop, I stop by Cosmic Flow. I remind myself that I'm doing this for Tess, but if I'm honest, I want to see Rhia again.

She looks up when the door jingles. "Welcome to Cosmic—oh, it's you." She's wearing a beanie over her hair today. It's mashed low over her eyebrows. Her face gives away nothing and she looks back at whatever she was doing.

"Do you think we should talk?" I ask.

She stares at the computer screen like it's fascinating. "I'm sort of working."

"I didn't mean now. I've got to get to work, too." I hold my hands up. "But whatever. I can at least tell Tess I tried."

I start to turn to leave and then I pause. "Remember the

day that we talked under the beech, the day that I showed you how to harvest bark? Do you truly believe that I could hurt that tree, after what you know about me?" Rhia's shoulders drop, but she doesn't say anything. After a moment, I pull open the door.

Rhia calls after me. "The coffee shop."

"What?" I turn around to face her.

"We can meet at the coffee shop. What time do you get off?"

"Shop closes at nine and then I have to clean."

"I'll meet you there at nine thirty."

"Nine thirty at the coffee shop." I nod. "See you then." I'm not sure I can get all my cleaning done by then, but I'll make it work.

At the stroke of nine, I shut the windows, flip the sign to closed, and clean as fast as I can. It kills me to leave the shop in less-than-pristine condition, but no way am I going to be late to meet Rhia. I rush over to the coffee shop, but when I look through the window, Rhia isn't one of the people clustered around small tables, talking over lattes and teas. I look at my watch. 9:26. Maybe she never planned to be here at all. Maybe she was messing with me. I turn away from the door, the cold wash of rejection flowing over me.

"Edie." Her voice comes to me through the dark.

"Rhia?"

"Yeah."

Conflicting feelings rush through me. A happy quiver to be near Rhia again. Nervousness about what I said that night. And confusion about why she's being so cloak-and-dagger.

"I thought maybe you weren't going to show," I say.

She moves into the light, the lamp over the door casting half her face in shadow. "I wasn't sure I was."

"Okay." I wait for her to say more, but she doesn't. "Do you want to go in?"

"I need to tell you something." Her words fly out in a rush.

The sight of Rhia stabs me like the Ten of Swords card in her tarot deck. I wonder what she'll tell me. A couple weeks ago, I might have hoped that she would confess feelings for me. But based on the last week, I know that I shouldn't expect anything as good as that. I brace myself for whatever she's going to share.

"I'm listening," I say.

"You can't get mad."

Now I know for sure it's nothing good. "How can I promise that with all that's happened? You know what? Never mind, Rhia. You can tell Tess I'm done." I step away.

She jolts forward to stop me. "I have your mom's journal."

Whatever I thought Rhia was going to say, that was not it. I turn back. "You what?"

"I have the journal. It didn't burn in the fire."

"Were you going to keep my dead mother's journal because you thought I burned the beech?" My fingers being to tingle. I focus on my breath to try to calm myself. Rhia eyes me like I'm dangerous, which I guess I am.

She speaks fast, like she needs to let the words out. "I was so confused. At first, I thought if I had the journal, then it would somehow keep you safe. Like you would stop your search. Then, after we took the first two items and told you that we were out, you'd said that you were going to do something you'd regret. When I got to the beech and it was burning, your words kept repeating in my head." She pauses and then says, quietly, "That tree was our sanctuary, our safe place."

"I know," I say. Then I pause. "Wait, when did you take the journal?" I'm trying to put together a timeline in my mind and it doesn't add up.

Rhia presses her lips together. "I grabbed it when we were leaving that afternoon that we got the photo. Remember? We went to the beech. You fell asleep in the hammock. We left in a hurry because Tess was late for work. I grabbed it from the hammock when I realized you'd left it behind."

"Why didn't you give it to me then?"

"I wanted—" She puts her hands to her face. "This is so hard and sort of embarrassing."

I look around to make sure no one is in earshot before I speak.

"Rhia, you've accused me of using my power to do a terrible thing. And now you're talking about something embarrassing? I'm lost," I say. But I'm also frustrated.

"Okay, fine." She drops her hands from her face. "I knew the journal had spells in it."

The pieces slide together. "And you wanted to try them. Did you?"

She nods and manages to look miserable. She pushes her beanie up high to her hairline.

Something is different and it takes me a moment to realize what's missing. "What happened to your eyebrows?"

"I tried a spell?"

Despite myself, I start laughing.

"It's not funny!"

"It sort of is."

Rhia breaks into a smile. Then we are both cackling and we can't stop. When we finally catch our breath, I step toward her.

"Do you still believe that I could have burned the beech?"

Rhia shakes her head. "I know you didn't. When I saw you practically sacrifice yourself to try to save it, I knew it hadn't been you."

"It hurt that you thought that, even for a minute."

"I get that. But Edie, you were so angry when we took those items. We don't know each other that well, you know?"

"I guess." I've gotten so close with Rhia and Tess over these last weeks that I feel like I've known them forever. But I've really only known them for the summer. For all Rhia knew, I'd gone over the edge.

"And that night—it had been really hard with my grandma. Something called sundowning. My mom said she couldn't handle it. We were all crying and now my parents want to put her in a nursing home. I went to the tree to get away. When I saw it burning, I wanted to blame someone. Anyone. I'm sorry."

I'm caught short by her honesty and embarrassed that I haven't been sensitive to what's going on in Rhia's life.

"Shit, I have been *so* self-centered," I say. "I'm sorry about everything going on with your grandmother. That sounds really hard. And anyway, you were right about those items messing with me." I sigh. "I shouldn't have tried to involve you and Tess in the first place—it's my problem and I'll deal with it."

"No way," Rhia says vehemently.

"No way what?" I'm so confused.

"The fire at the beech is connected to the search we're doing. I will not give up until we get rid of this messed-up magic motherfucker."

"Are you sure?" I ask.

"Absolutely. Are you?" she asks.

"I don't have a choice."

Rhia steps closer. "So you want to kiss me, huh?"

I start to stammer out something in my massively awkward way.

"How do you know I don't want that, too?"

She holds the journal out to me. I grab it and then her hands are in mine and we both go still. Rhia's looking into my eyes and I'm looking into hers. She licks her lips, drawing my eyes to them. My breath quickens. She takes a small step closer to me so that I feel the toe of her flip-flop against my sneaker. If I stepped any closer, our thighs would touch. I lean toward her. She parts her lips. But instead of the kiss I'm anticipating, she speaks.

"But I sort of need something from you."

"Okay." I breathe the word out.

Just then, the door to the coffee shop opens, letting an air-conditioned breeze out into the humid night. Two ladies emerge from the shop. Rhia steps away from me and mashes the beanie low on her head.

"Rhia," a lady says. "Hello, hello, hello! How are you?"

"Hi, Ms. Alvarez. Good, thanks."

"Edie, I didn't realize that was you. Tell your grandmother hello for me, will you?"

"Sure," I say. I'm glad that Ms. Alvarez can't tell how fast my heart is beating from being so close to kissing Rhia. Once she's made sure they've walked off, Rhia turns back to me.

"So, could you help a girl out?" Rhia says.

I look at her blankly until she points to the place on her head where the hat hides her absent eyebrows. And I almost howl with laughter. "I'll try."

"Good enough for me. I tried the reversal spell we made up, but it's not working."

On the walk home, I clutch the journal to my chest, relieved to have it back. I try to make sense of my roller-coaster feelings about Rhia, feeling betrayed one minute and wanting to kiss her the next. I wish again that I had Mom with me to talk through my first crush.

Chapter Twenty-Six

MAURA

July 12, 2003

I've moved onto the boat, which is one part freeing, two parts lonely. Dad's ashes are gone. I know Mama took them, but of course she wouldn't admit it because she's not talking. That was it. If Mama won't speak and won't give me back Dad's items, I won't live with her.

I walked by the cabin on my way into town. I tried not to look in the windows to catch a glimpse of her, but I couldn't help it. She wasn't there, though. Then, when I walked by Dad's workshop, I heard a peculiar noise. I peered through the window and saw her leaning over the boxes of items she'd placed there when we'd first arrived. I hadn't seen her set foot near Dad's workshop since then, just as she hadn't set foot on the dock. I stepped away before she could see me.

I found Jamie at the hardware store. He was shy at first, asking what I needed. I told him that I didn't need any supplies. I wanted to apologize for how I'd acted before. I told him about how I have bad days and unfortunately, he'd stopped by on a bad day. He nodded his understanding. I told him that I'd love to see him, but that I understood if he wasn't up for it. Looking at him there, all I wanted was to be wrapped in his arms and feel his lips on my skin.

Jamie looked so serious when he said that he wanted me to talk to him, to tell him what's going on. We took a walk and I shared with him how sad I feel about my Dad and how Mom's silence makes it even worse. But being held feels good. He told me how he'd never felt for anyone the way that he feels about me. But he's so conflicted because he's leaving soon for the Peace Corps and we're getting serious so fast.

I told him that spending time with him was the best thing for me—however we spent it. When we finally returned to the hardware store, I felt so much better. He hugged me tight and told me he'd be over later.

Early in the evening when I pulled myself from the water after my afternoon swim, he was on the dock. My heart started beating a little faster. Still dripping with river water, I led him into the interior of the boat, locking the latch behind me. He followed me to the narrow bed where I'd been sleeping. I tugged his T-shirt off. He untied my bathing suit top and let it drop. I unzipped his jeans. He hooked his thumbs into my bathing suit bottoms and slowly pulled them over my hips and down my legs until I stepped out of them. We kissed and stumbled and sort of fell on my bed. We both started laughing. I asked if Jamie was sure and he said he was, and he asked me, and I said I was.

We were gentle with each other, but so awkward. It wasn't

my first time, but I wouldn't call myself experienced. Jamie was so worried that he wasn't doing it right, but I told him it was perfect. And after, we stayed tangled together in that narrow bed all night long. After Jamie left this morning, I lay in bed a while longer, feeling so happy. Jamie had shown me that I could talk to him. I've decided to tell him about the magic. We love each other and I can't hide this part of me from someone so important.

Later, when I knew Mama had gone to the perpetual woods and would be gone for a while, I went to the cabin and opened her recipe box. I closed my eyes and willed the recipe I needed to present itself. The cards flipped themselves forward and back but did not settle. I tried two more times and when still no solution presented itself, I resorted to my own knowledge. I grabbed yarrow, peppermint, and ginger, and I set about creating something that I hoped would work.

Chapter Twenty-Seven

EDIE

It's Saturday night, and to celebrate the successful return of Rhia's eyebrows, she, Tess, and I are inhaling a pizza, chicken wings, and hush puppies in the back room of Cosmic Flow. I'm happy for the distraction. After reading the most recent entry in Mom's journal, any possible doubts have been removed. Jamie *must* be my father. It seems that it's taken losing my mother to finally learn about my father. At the same time, I still do not know his full identity. This is all too big; I'm still not ready to talk about it. Instead, I'm focusing on repairing my friendship with Tess and Rhia. I eat a drumstick, and sneeze.

"God bless you," Tess says.

"Goddess blessings upon you," Rhia says. "I've never met anyone who sneezes when they eat chicken wings."

"It makes me special and unique. And—okay, maybe a little weird."

"Lucky for you, we are all about weird." Rhia's smile causes a flutter inside me. We had that almost moment in front of the coffee shop. But at the same time, I know I'm holding part of me back. I don't feel the same ease between all of us as I did before the beech burned, before they lied to me to get those objects. Maybe we all need to work on some trust. I bite into a slice of pizza.

Tess holds a hush puppy in one hand and a chicken wing in the other. She dips the hush puppy in the sauce first. "Yum." Then she dips the wing in the hot sauce and eats that. "Mmm. Sweet and spicy heaven."

Although fixing Rhia's eyebrows and sharing all this junk food is helping to bond us again, I can't help but consider what Rhia said about us not knowing one another that well. I wipe my hands clean. "Listen, I've been thinking," I say.

"Sounds serious. What's up?" Rhia asks as she grabs a hush puppy.

"So, I've told you each that I get why you took those items from me. That you were right about how they were affecting me. But"—I take in a breath and let it out—"it hurt that you made me think you were helping me just to take them."

Rhia and Tess stop eating. They look at one another and have one of those unspoken conversations. Rhia speaks.

"We *were* helping you. We were worried," she says. "What would you have done in our place?"

"I don't know. Maybe tell the person that they are in danger, that the items were having a bad effect on them?"

"Do you think you would have listened though?" Tess asks. "You were basically obsessed with that watch and picture." She sets down her chicken wing.

They aren't wrong. I smush my mouth to the side. "Yeah, I'm not sure I would've listened."

Rhia speaks up. "Besides, we didn't know what to expect. We weren't sure how much those things were affecting you—what they may have caused you to do."

I wipe my mouth with a napkin. "Well, because of that— maybe you both should have some sort of protection. I don't want either of you to ever feel afraid of me." I look from one to the other.

"We don't—" Tess starts to protest, but I level a look at her.

"You were. You basically told me you were," I say.

"What do you have in mind?" Rhia asks, licking hush puppy sauce from her fingers.

"I found this." I pull out a protection spell I'd jotted down and hand it over. "What do you think?"

Rhia reads it carefully. "With these ingredients and the right words, this spell should protect against possession, related mind control attempts, and unwanted magical influence in general. I'm willing to try it. Tess?" Rhia asks.

"I am definitely down with locking out any mind control attempts," Tess says, as she starts to gather up the trash from our meal. "But is it necessary?"

"If you two are serious about continuing this search with me, let's be as prepared as possible," I say. I pile up our paper plates and toss them in the trash.

"Speaking of being prepared, this might help you, too, Edie," Rhia says, as she rereads the spell.

"Really? How?"

"I'm not totally sure, but it sounds like it could protect you from the corrupted magic in those items. So you're safe to find the rest of them."

"Let's do it," I say.

"Mind if I take the lead?" Rhia asks.

"Lead away," I say.

"Magical protection bags coming up!" Rhia says.

"*After* we get the rest of this mess cleaned up," Tess adds.

"Sure thing, Mom," Rhia says. Tess throws a balled-up napkin at her. I down the rest of my root beer and let out a big burp.

"Nice one!" Rhia says.

"Root beer burps are the most impressive of all burps," I say.

"Cheers to that." Rhia tips her bottle to me, drinks it, and lets out her own big burp. We both start giggling.

"You're both gross," Tess says.

After we clean everything up, Rhia gets started on the protection bags. "First, I need three hairs from a witch. Edie, would you do the honors?"

I tilt my head toward Rhia so that she can pull out three

hairs. I feel her hands in my hair and I wish that it was for a different reason.

"Got it," Rhia says.

"Ow!" I say, rubbing my head. "That was more than three!"

"I needed three for each bag. And stop complaining. You've got plenty more."

Rhia separates the hair and adds some to each bag. Tess has donned a paper flower crown from one of the baskets in the shop and she's admiring the look in a mirror. "Tess, can you grab three pieces of obsidian?"

"What can I do?" I ask.

"The hawk feathers are near the checkout counter. I need three of those as well."

Tess brings the obsidian and I hand over the feathers.

"What's next?" Tess says.

"Are there any robin's eggs? Maybe on top of the tincture display?"

"They're blue, right?" Tess calls from across the store.

"Pale blue, yeah," Rhia answers.

"You have one here."

"That'll be enough."

I drift around tables and wander by bookshelves and wall hangings. I see this store and everything in it so differently than the first time I stepped foot inside, wearing the armor of a skeptic. Rhia, it seems, has disarmed me in more ways than one. I look at her. Her head is bent in concentration, her beautiful curls a cloud, just like the first time I saw her. I think of the close moments we've had. Could there be more between us? I'm scared to hope.

"Okay," she says, looking up. Her eyes catch mine. "What?" she says, smiling. "Do I have something on my face?"

I shake my head, embarrassed to have been caught looking.

"I need nail clippings from each person," Rhia announces.

"Ew, really?" I ask.

Rhia shrugs. "Unless you'd rather contribute a tooth or some bone."

"I second Edie's ew. How did I end up with you two weirdos?" Tess says.

"Well, you were my first friend when I moved here when I was eight, so I'd say it was Fate," Rhia says.

"And I found you on the bike trail. Again, Fate," I say to Tess.

She holds out her hand to allow Rhia to clip her nails. "I need to talk to this Fate person."

Rhia catches the nail clippings and places them in each bag. She then ties the bags three times with a white silk string and then does the same thing again with a black silk string.

"For increased protection," she says. "It's perfect that the moon is basically still full tonight because this will be stronger."

"It's a full moon?" I had lost track of the lunar cycle.

"Technically, it was full last night. Hey, didn't you say that getting to the magical place in the woods is best on a full moon?" Rhia asks.

"I can *only* take people with me on a full moon."

"Oh, well, too bad it was technically full *last* night," Tess says.

Rhia narrows her eyes at Tess. "That didn't sound sincere. What's up?"

"The party at the barn!" Tess says. "Plus, I thought you wanted to get the dog tags next."

"Let's wait on the dog tags. GG said not to be in the cemetery at night right now."

"Also because of the full moon?"

"Yeah." I frown. "Who knew that magic is so connected to the moon cycle?"

Rhia stops what she's doing to give me a look. "Um, only everyone everywhere."

Tess starts laughing. "Yeah, E, even I know that the moon is like *the* feminine power center."

"Does that make it a witch thing though?" I ask. "Seems like just a female thing."

"Witches are like next-level humans, so yeah," Rhia says.

For so long I'd resisted what I am. After what had happened with fire back in middle school, I decided it would be best if I were like everyone else. But the thing is, I'm starting to see there is no *everyone else*. Every person is an individual with some attributes that they like about themselves and others that they struggle with. Maybe my attributes and struggles are pretty different from other people's, but that didn't mean that I need to be alone with them.

Rhia hands the spell bags to me. I look at her blankly.

"Say something," Rhia says.

I stare at the bags in my hands like they are going to sprout teeth and bite me. To be honest, I'm not sure that they won't. "Like what?"

"Words for protection." Rhia pushes a stray curl away from her face.

"Seriously? Just make up a spell?"

Tess slides into the chair next me and starts shuffling a deck of tarot cards that sits nearby.

"Why not?" Rhia says.

"I don't know, I thought that maybe there's some Supreme Court of Witches who makes them up or approves them or something."

"Remember about intention?" Rhia lights a stick of incense, blows out the flame, and waves the smoke toward her face. "Breathe in. Center yourself. Hold your intention in your mind and let the spell come out."

Rhia's supportive guidance brings to mind Mom's calming technique. Despite that, I'm not feeling encouraged. "But I haven't been able to do any real magic at all since the tree."

"What about these?" Rhia points to her eyebrows.

"That was basic magic."

"Says the witch who couldn't perform any spells only a few weeks ago."

"Fair," I say.

I hold the bags in one hand for a moment. I center my mind and consider my intention and then find the words that match it best. When I'm ready, I place my other hand over the bags. "May these bags extend protection to me, Rhia, and Tess, so that we may be immune from unwanted magical duress."

The bags glow with golden light.

"There," Rhia says. "You did it."

"I did it?"

She takes two of the bags from my hands, but I'm still stunned. "Didn't you see the glow?" she asks.

"Yeah, but I didn't believe that I could."

"I never doubted," Rhia says. "Duress, though?"

"Yeah," I say. "Making someone do something against their will."

"I know what duress means. Way to work an SAT word into a spell." She rolls her eyes.

I stick my tongue out and she laughs.

She hands one bag to Tess. "Make sure to keep this on you at all times."

"Even when I'm with Jorge?" Tess cocks her head and stares at the bag, no doubt trying to figure out how to keep it on her when she has nothing else on her.

"No, not when you're with Jorge, I guess." Rhia sighs out her exasperation. "Let's go."

"Where are we going?" I ask.

"Oh my gods, seriously? We are going to your magical woods to find the key. Keep up!" Rhia says.

"I should have been more specific. The full moon needs to be in the sky. It needs to be dark," I say.

"Guess I can't convince you to go to the barn instead?" Tess asks. "Jorge says the party is already bumping."

"Bumping, really?" Rhia says.

"Guess that's a no, then," Tess says.

While we wait for the moon to rise, Rhia reads our tarot with a simple three-card spread. After reading Tess's, Rhia shuffles and reads mine. "This first card, the Eight of Swords, suggests that you've been standing in your own way."

I wobble my head back and forth. "Probably."

She points to the card in the center position. "The Moon is about anxiety or wariness. Like you know something bad is coming and you can't do much about it."

All I can do is laugh nervously.

When she gets to the final card, she laughs. I smile in response. "What is it?"

"Well, the Three of Wands is sort of like a group project card. Like you've got a plan and then you need to pull in some people to help."

"Tarot for the win!" Tess says.

The discomfort I had from hearing about the first two cards dissolves. Maybe I *was* stubborn in the past, getting in my own way. But *now*, no matter what's coming my way, I've got people. That simple truth glows in me like the spell I just performed.

"There was something I wanted to ask about your mom's journal," Rhia says to me as she's putting her deck away.

"What's that?"

"It was about the titles of the charms. Do you have the journal with you?"

"Always." I pull it from my bag.

Rhia flips through the pages until she reached the first spell. "See this?" She points to the title of the spell. The first letter is bigger than the others and it's in green ink, not like the rest of the purple ink in the book. "And then look here and here." Rhia shows me the next two spells. "Did it seem strange to you that the titles didn't follow a pattern?"

"Didn't give it a thought. Figured Mom made up the titles as she went along."

"It's awkward, though, right? Like the first one says 'A Charm for Stubborn Locks' but the next one says 'Charm to Keep Dry.' Then the third one is 'Old Bind-Breaking Ritual' but the fourth one says 'Retrieval Charms' and then 'No Unwanted Marks Charm.'"

Tess leans over to look as Rhia flips from one to the next to the next.

"That last one did stop me," I admit. "Like why didn't she just call it Erasure Charm or something else more straightforward?"

"Acorn!" Tess says.

"What?" Rhia and I both turn to look at Tess like she's on another planet altogether.

Tess points to the first letter of each spell. "When you put them all together, the first letters spell acorn. Does that mean anything to you?"

A shiver runs through me. "You, Tess Sullivan, are a genius," I say.

"Ooooh, no one's ever called me that before!"

I pull the necklace from beneath my shirt. "My mother made this for me. It came with a note that said 'For when you need me with you.' She could infuse jewelry with emotion. And I swear that sometimes when I'm feeling most alone, this acorn gives me comfort."

"No way!" Tess says, her eyes growing big.

Rhia raises an eyebrow. "Maybe your mom infused this one with something stronger than just emotion."

I pull the necklace from over my head so that we can look at it more closely.

"Hang on a minute," I say, getting an idea. I take the acorn in my hand and give a little twist to the cap. It comes off like a lid.

"What's in there?" Tess asks, leaning in.

Using my fingernails, I tug out a tiny vial sealed with a rubber stopper. I hold it up to the light.

"I'm not one hundred percent sure, but this might be my mother's—"

"Blood," Rhia finishes.

Chapter Twenty-Eight

EDIE

"I'm missing a great party for this," Tess says as Rhia locks up the shop.

"First—we're all missing the party," Rhia says. "Second, I doubt it'll be better than visiting magical woods. And third, there's always another party."

"But Jorge is leaving for boot camp soon, and I want to spend every possible minute with him."

"If you all don't want to come, I can find the key alone," I say, though I'm not 100 percent sure that's true. Tess and Rhia helped me find the first two items—plus the map. I haven't done any of this on my own. And if the key is corrupted like the photo and the watch, I hate to admit it, but I'll probably need backup.

"She can be with Jorge anytime," Rhia says. "It's a nearly full moon tonight. And besides, don't fall for it. This isn't about Jorge. It's about fear."

"Fine," Tess says, as she unlocks the Jeep. "It's about fear. *Healthy* fear."

"Speaking of which, do you two have your protection bags?" Rhia asks.

"Right here," I say, patting my backpack.

"Yup," Tess says, patting her front pocket.

"Let's go."

We pile into Tess's Jeep and head for the entrance to the woods. From there, I lead the way, and it feels even more natural than it did last time, like we're living that Three of Wands card, in this together as it should be.

"This is the spot," I say when we reach the old hawthorn tree.

"This is the magical woods?" Rhia looks around. I can tell that she's disappointed, though she's not saying so.

"No, this is the magical spot where we need to be to enter the magical woods."

"Like a portal?" Tess asks.

"Yes, like a portal. We need to hold hands and close our eyes."

Rhia, Tess, and I join hands. I chant the words that I remember from the night of solstice, when I confronted GG. "With secrets deep, woods wise and tall, keep our garden hidden from all. Know me as a Daughter in this place; reveal to me now our sacred space."

I feel the rippling sensation and the brightness on the other side of my closed eyelids. I squeeze the girls' hands and we open our eyes.

"Whoa," Tess says.

"It's beautiful." Rhia breathes out the words as she turns in a big circle.

Seeing it through their eyes, as though for the first time, I'm reminded of the beauty of magic and the power of this place. The cherry blossoms fall like blessings while the hawthorn shows off her magical perpetual cycling through seasons.

"All we need to do is find a single key hidden somewhere here," I say. "How hard could that be?"

"Yeah, piece of cake," Rhia adds.

"I mean, what could go wrong?" Tess asks.

We all laugh at our own string of clichés, but I hear the nervousness in my own laugh. Last time I touched an item, I passed out in a public place.

"Seriously, though, how could you leave all this behind?" Rhia says. "I mean, I get what happened and everything. I do. But still."

"Haven't you ever wanted to be normal?" I ask Rhia.

"God, no. Normal is boring."

"Liar," Tess says with a smile. "In sixth grade, you tried to tell everyone that your real name was Emily."

"Oh, man, I totally forgot that. My name was so different. No one could spell it. Teachers never knew how to say it. There were already like three Emilys in the class, so it seemed like a good bet. Now, though, I love my name and I'm glad it's different."

I think of similar times I tried to blend in. Truth is, I'm

relieved not to be pretending anymore, not to be hiding who and what I am. Blending in means erasing what's special about each of us. I walk to the middle of the clearing and kneel. I dig in my bag for the candle and rosemary, and something else tumbles out. I pat the ground, but I can't find what fell. It seems like I still have all the ingredients I need, though, so I don't worry about it. I'm focused on this moment of seeking the key. I set the candle on the ground, lighting it with a match because I'm still hesitant about making fire, especially after the beech. I crumble rosemary into the flame and when I smell its fragrance, I repeat the incantation for finding a lost item:

"As I hold this image in my mind,

Help me see what I hope to find."

Behind me, I hear Rhia say, "As it is above, so below."

The illumination that comes from magic is followed by an image appearing in my mind: a long skinny skeleton key tied to a tree branch with a red satin ribbon. "The key must be attached to the hawthorn, on one of the branches."

"Wow, your mom was not messing around when she hid stuff, was she?" Tess mumbles.

"Guess not," I say, still uncomfortable with what my mother had done.

"She couldn't risk someone finding all of the five items and dismantling what she'd created," Rhia said.

"At least the hawthorn isn't a tall tree," I say. "But it has thorns, so be careful." I tuck my long ponytail under a baseball cap.

"Good thing I brought these!" Tess holds up three pairs of work gloves. "I really brought them so that none of us has to touch the key, but they'll help with thorns, too."

"Always thinking, Tess," Rhia says.

The bright moon is our light as we peer up through the branches seeking the key.

"Ow," Rhia exclaims. "Damn branch caught on my hair."

"Let me help," I say, moving to where Rhia stands. I work to disentangle her hair from the thorny branch. Standing so close to Rhia here in the dark awakens every part of me. I wonder how long I can drag this out because I don't want to step away from her. But a moment later, she's free. "All set."

"Thanks," Rhia says, turning to face me while rubbing the spot at the back of her head. "Maybe the tree was getting me back for taking your hair earlier."

I laugh. "I'm not sure this tree is that protective of me, but who knows?"

"How's it going, Tess?" Rhia calls.

"I think I found the key!"

We gather around her and she guides my hand. There it

is, the skeleton key protruding from the branch. It had been here so long that the wood had begun to consume it. I tug gently and the tree releases the key to me. I pull off one glove to touch my palm against the trunk in thanks.

"See, no need to be afraid of witchy clearings in moonlight," Rhia says to Tess. "And we will get back in time for you to jump Jorge, if you're so desperate."

Tess punches Rhia playfully in the shoulder. "Jealous! You wish you were getting some."

"Not some of that," Rhia counters.

I blow out the candle and place it and the matches in my backpack along with the key. As I zip up the bag, I wonder once more what fell out earlier. I'm pretty certain I have everything I came here with, so I don't dwell on it. I take a last look around and my thoughts naturally turn to Mom and how much she loved this place.

"Okay, to get back to the ordinary woods, we need to do the same thing in reverse." I shrug the bag onto my shoulder. Then I grab Tess's hand and Rhia's in each of my own. I say the reverse chant. Nothing happens.

"Let me try again."

I repeat the chant and suddenly there's a rushing sensation that has nothing to do with this place or our ritual. There's a roaring in my ears and bone-rattling cold envelopes me. Before I know it, I feel as though I'm falling. And I'm bringing Rhia and Tess with me.

When I open my eyes, Rhia is lying on her back and Tess is slumped on her side. The cold clutches me and I begin to shake. Tendrils of dark swirl toward us from all sides. I crawl toward Rhia. Her eyes are closed. I manage to pull Rhia close enough that I have her on one side of me and Tess on the other. Maybe my hands on their skin will keep them safe or at least limit any damage.

I place my left palm on Rhia's bare shoulder and my right palm on Tess's bare forearm. The susurration of a thousand feathers fills my ears. I continue to press my hands to the girls' skin and close my eyes tight, hoping to concentrate on a magic that can help us.

"Deliver us from this place," I yell. "Please hear me!"

"Don't worry."

I flicker my eyes open. Rhia stands before me.

I look down where my hand had gripped her shoulder. Rhia's body is not there.

"Come here," she says.

I stand. "We need to leave. It's not safe here," I say. Tess remains slumped and unconscious on the ground. She's beginning to sink, the ground turning viscous like tar.

"You don't need to leave," Rhia says. "Come here."

This doesn't make sense, does it? And yet, I step closer.

"Haven't you dreamed of this?" Rhia says. She reaches out to touch my face. She runs her finger down my arm. I recoil.

But I like Rhia. I like her a lot. Don't I?

"Haven't you been waiting for my touch?" she asks.

"Yes," I whisper.

"Come closer."

I am hesitant, but I step forward.

She leans in like she wants to kiss me. She's right. I've been dreaming of Rhia wanting me, and I can't resist her. I incline my head toward hers. My mind wonders why this is happening now. But my body wants what it wants. I part my lips.

She whispers, "Yes, that's it. Take what you deserve."

My head snaps back. Rhia would never speak like that. And Rhia isn't something to take. My eyes fly open to look at her. But it's not Rhia. The eyes of the thing looking back at me are black all the way through. And its smile twists into an awful grimace. I stumble backward. Falling, I land on something soft. I turn. It's Rhia. Still unconscious where I'd left her and now, she's sinking, too.

"No!" I lean over Rhia. "Wake up, Rhee."

"I was so very close." The not-Rhia thing's voice has changed into a thousand, thousand voices. Its shape swirls into something undefinable, not a coherent form so much as a loose manifestation of all things shadowy, unknowable. There is a hint of wings and deadly claws. "You're more intuitive than I had guessed."

"What are you?" I ask.

"I am ancient, child. As old as death yet called by the living. Your grief." The thing sighs in pleasure and my skin breaks out in goose bumps. "Your grief sustains me."

This thing is feeding off my grief—I need to block it somehow, to stop it. I remember Mom's song. I open my mouth and I begin to sing.

> "Darkness, darkness, not welcome here,
> Return from where you came.
> Sunlight, starlight, please be near,
> I call you in my name."

I finish singing, but nothing happens. There is no burst of bright light and no shrinking of these shadows from us.

"That little spell won't work here, child. This *is* where I came from."

Tess's legs are fully submerged. Rhia's left arm and leg are sinking fast. If I don't do something soon, they'll be gone.

I grip the acorn pendant in my hand. *Think, Edie, think.* The first time I went to the cabin, I did something that made the shadows back off. What was it? The blackened handprints on the floor rise up in my mind. GG has told me that I need to master my element. She said to make friends with fear and I've never been more afraid that I am right now. I hold my palms up.

"What do you think you're doing, girl?" the thousand, thousand voices ask.

I don't answer. I calm my mind. And I call the fire.

"Magic is about intention." Repeating Rhia's words gives me confidence. "And I intend to get us out of here!" Power surges through me. I hope that I don't hurt my friends with this magic. But right now, I'm more worried about them dying down here. I clap my hands together and a burst of sparks fly out.

"Send us home," I yell. "Now!"

The world spins around me. The ground disappears beneath my feet. Rhia is tugged in one direction and Tess in the other. There is a rushing in my ears. My stomach is pushed to my throat.

"She's back!" I hear Rhia's voice, but I won't be tricked a second time. "Hey, hey." Her voice is closer to my ear now.

I am screaming.

"Edie!" That's Tess's voice.

Suddenly, there is the bright sting of a smack on my cheek. My eyes fly open and I jump to my feet. My surroundings come into focus. There is no tar-like ground. No enveloping blackness.

No shadowy being floating near me, mocking my desires. We're in the forest, beside the hawthorn tree that marks the entrance to the perpetual woods. My eyes skip from Tess to Rhia.

"How do I know you are you?" I ask.

Rhia frowns at me, not understanding. "What happened to you?"

Shame burns my face at the memory of almost kissing that thing. "How do I know?"

Rhia holds out her hands. "Um, you always sneeze after you eat chicken wings."

I sigh out my fear. That doesn't seem like something that the shadow being would say. A wave of dizziness—from adrenaline or magic leaving my system, I don't know—forces me to grab onto the closest tree.

"Are you two okay?" I ask.

"Are *you*?" Rhia asks me. "Looks like your shirt is singed. Did you call your fire?"

"I didn't know what else to do. We were trapped in that nightmarish place and you two were sinking. And there was this—thing—trying to keep me there. Do either of you remember anything?" I ask.

Tess and Rhia look at one another.

"What?" I say.

"We weren't with you," Tess says.

"I'm sorry, what?"

Tess shakes her head. Rhia says, "It was a bumpy ride—the transition from the magical woods to here. Nothing like when we entered. But we were here, and you weren't. For a long time. We weren't sure what to do. I was getting ready to go get Miss Geraldine. Then there was a *bang* and you appeared."

"I thought you both were trapped. I thought you were going to die." My breath hitches when I say the words out loud. I was so scared, but Rhia and Tess being in danger had been an illusion.

"What was the thing? Have you ever seen it before?" Rhia asks.

I shudder to remember it. "Definitely not. It looked human at first"—I don't say that it took Rhia's shape—"but then it was sort of a collection of shadows. It said"—I frown as I try to remember—"that it's as old as death yet called by the living. And then it seemed like it was feeding on my emotions, my feeling of missing Mom." I shudder at the memory.

Rhia purses her lips. "I'll have to do some research."

"Edie, look." Tess gestures to my arm. "The black veins have reached your shoulder. I *knew* I was right to be scared."

"How long was I gone?"

"Over an hour," Tess says.

"It felt like a few minutes," I whisper, shocked. Then I shake my head to clear it. I can't dwell on what could happen to me if I get stuck in that place, if the veins reach my heart. I've got to focus on the finish line. "At least we've got one more item," I say, trying to convey the positive outlook that I need if I'm going to get through this.

"There is maybe one more tiny silver lining," Tess says.

"What's that?" Rhia asks.

Tess holds up her protection bag. "Seemed like these worked."

I cock my head in thought and then poke through the items in my pack. No protection bag. "I must have lost mine."

"Where?"

"How?"

"Maybe back in the perpetual woods. I heard something fall from my bag, but I couldn't see it in the dark."

"Should we go back?" Rhia asks.

I run my hand over my mouth. "I can't magic us back there right now."

I am so weak when Rhia and Tess drop me off at the marina that I can barely get myself to my room. I could use some of GG's curative tea, but I don't want to wake her and I'm not up for making it for myself. The nausea and dizziness are way more intense than when I'd held the watch or the photograph. But the bone-chilling cold is truly awful. I wonder if I'll ever feel normal again.

As I burrow under my covers, I file away a new piece of information. The song Mom used to sing to me, which I thought was a lullaby, turns out to be a spell. And that creature—whatever it is—knew that it was a spell. I curl up with Mom's journal. I haven't read it since Rhia gave it back and I wonder what light she might shed on what I'm going through.

Chapter Twenty-Nine

MAURA

July 19, 2003

Jamie and I are together every chance we get. Now that we finally had sex, we can't keep our hands off each other. He comes to the boat most nights. Mama never comes down, so we have all the privacy that we need. Nothing allays my pain like Jamie's touch. The world with its chasms of loss washes away when we shed our clothes and find solace in skin against skin. And at that moment when I shudder with the force of the storm that rolls through me, I forget myself completely.

But . . . almost as soon as we're done, even before he leaves, the razor-edge of reality carves into me once more.

I'm starting to crave being with Jamie as soon as I wake up. I'll need more yarrow, though!

We're going to move the boat to the marina soon. Jamie is going to have it pulled out of the water so that we can work on the hull. I'm sure that the shade of purple I picked is perfect. Of course, I could always change it if I don't like it.

I'm getting close to telling him. I almost told him last night. But he started talking about the Peace Corps and I wanted to listen.

I don't know what Mama is doing. The few times I've gone up to the cabin, she's not around. I guess she's out gathering herbs or something.

July 24

Jamie has a team of guys working on sanding and painting the hull of the boat. It's going to be finished before he leaves.

We do it almost every night now. I'm actually a little sore down there. But when we skip a day, the emptiness yawns its jaws wide and threatens to consume me. My father dead, his ghost not appearing, and my mother barely here as well. She is gone more and more. I want to know where she's going and how she's filling her time. But she's still not speaking. The other night I thought I saw flickering lights—like candles—in Dad's workshop. I meant to check it out, but then Jamie showed up.

I'm going to tell Jamie about my magic soon. I can feel it. I can't wait to see his face when he knows what I can do. Last night, after we finished, I joked that the only thing he was wearing was the coin necklace I'd given him. He lifted it up and asked me to kiss it so that he could always have my kiss near his heart. I cried a little when I kissed the coin, out of joy. Then we fell asleep together.

Chapter Thirty

EDIE

The morning after our trip to the perpetual woods, I'm very weak. GG helps me to a chair and starts a pot of tea. I tell her about the shadow world and the spirit, or whatever it was, holding me there.

I force out the question that's been on my mind since my ordeal. "Is that where I'll be stuck if we don't stop the infection?"

GG shuts her eyes tight and gives one curt nod. Then I tell her how I called fire and got out. She lights up a little when she hears that.

She places her warm hand on mine. "That's good, Edie! Exactly what you need to do."

But I sense the fear she's trying to hold back.

"Do you know what it is?" I ask, as I sip the green tea she gives me. "That shadow thing?"

GG seems lost in the stirring of her tea for a moment. Finally she speaks. "Luctus spirit." GG practically spits the words out, like they burn her lips just to say them. "Awful thing."

"And that is what we are going to banish?" Candles flicker, casting dancing shadows on our walls and catching on the witch balls hanging in front of our now-dark windows.

"We will try." She lets out a long exhale. "We will try."

GG's age is showing tonight in her stooped shoulders and down-turned mouth. Her natural vigorous nature seems tapped out. At this moment, I can relate.

"Oh, I almost forgot!" I take off my necklace and I show GG the tiny vial of Mom's blood hidden in the acorn. GG's eyes widen.

"Oh, Maura, you clever, clever witch!" she says.

"What?" I ask.

"*This* is what we need," she says, holding up the tiny vial. "Keep this safe and I'll get to work on the final step." She hands me the vial. Then she cups my face with her palm, her energetic nature returning. "*Now* we can dare to hope, Edie. Now we dare to hope."

On Wednesday, I go to Cosmic Flow in response to a text from Rhia that she needs help with a project. Tess has a family thing, so she's out. I'm sort of nervous and excited to be alone with Rhia. I find her outside the back entrance up to her elbows in a huge tub of dirt. "Ready to help?" she asks.

"Sure, what is it today? Witchy bridal shower? Wiccan naming ceremony? Earth goddess spell bottles?"

"Not spell bottles," she says. "Flower bombs. And you look better."

"Thanks." Days after my forced trip into the shadow world, I'm starting to feel like myself again. As much of myself as possible while a magical infection works its way into my body. For just a moment, I'd like not to think about it. So I focus on Rhia. "What exactly are flower bombs?"

She motions with a dirt-covered hand for me to come join her. "Did the journal reveal anything?"

"Way too much," I say. "Remind me to never write down my sexcapades. I do not want any future children of mine reading about my hookups."

Rhia laughs. I shoot a look at her.

"Sorry!" she says. "But it is sort of funny that you're reading about your mom's teenage sex life."

It feels somehow bold to talk about this with Rhia, who I've wanted to kiss more than once. Who I wouldn't mind kissing now as I watch her blow a curl away from her face. Nothing has happened since our close moment in front of the coffee shop.

"Let me help," I say. "My hands are clean."

She tilts her face toward me, and I brush the curl back, letting my fingers linger on her warm skin. Her eyes catch mine and my body responds with a roller-coaster swoop somewhere deep and low inside me.

"Thanks," she whispers. Her hands have stilled their work. My eyes go to her lips. Her eyes go to my arm where those awful lines snake their way up to my shoulder. I drop my hand and step back. No wonder nothing has happened—why would she want to kiss someone who is infected with corrupted magic?

"I meant to tell you a while back," I say, to change the subject. "I think I know what my mother used for the invocation spell. She talks about pulling together yarrow, peppermint, and ginger."

Rhia shakes her head a little bit. "Doesn't make sense," Rhia says. "Yarrow reduces swelling and can also bring on a late menstrual cycle. Peppermint and ginger are good for calming nausea and cramps. I don't see how those three things would be used to call a spirit."

I frown, digesting this new information. So Mom *had* tried birth control. A natural remedy that failed. But if that yarrow concoction was used for birth control, then when and how did she perform the invocation that called the spirit?

"You know what? Enough about my family and my problems. What's going on with your grandmother?"

Rhia bites her lip and exhales through her nose. "My parents are looking at places tomorrow."

I see how hard this is for her. I wish I could help.

"Do you think it would make you feel better to go with them? So you can check them out, too? Maybe they won't be awful."

Rhia presses her lips together and gives me a brief nod. "Maybe. I'll think about it. Thanks for asking. Means a lot." Then she clears her throat. "Let me tell you about these flower bombs," she says, and it's clear that I'm not the only one who wants to change the subject.

"I was visiting the beech to see how it's doing," she says. "There's actually new growth where the tree had burned. Did I tell you?"

"No! Really?"

"Yeah! I'm sure it's because of Miss Geraldine's brew. Anyway, being there, seeing the burned-out area looking so dead got me thinking about how to make areas beautiful again. People can throw these flower bombs out their car windows or toss them into fields when they're hiking. They will beautify areas that have been neglected. Wherever people drop them, flowers will come up next year."

"Like magic," I say.

"Ordinary magic."

"Still magic."

Rhia smiles and that feels like magic, too. Nothing ordinary about it. She shows me what she's doing. "I've got dirt and seeds and stuff all mixed up in here. I'm molding it into these balls and then I'm setting them on those cookie sheets. Got it?"

I plunge my hands in and after a while I'm surprised by how calming it is to immerse my hands in dirt. Maybe, when all this is over, I'll ask GG to teach me about gardening. I cling to the hope that we'll conquer this magic and I'll be okay.

"Another thing did come up from the journal," I say as I'm molding a ball.

Rhia glances at me. "What's that?"

"Jamie asked my mom to kiss the coin that she'd made into a necklace for him. Could that be the 'love, worn in a never-ending circle'? It's round. And she loved him."

"Maybe," Rhia says. "Where is that one supposed to be hidden?"

"According to the map, it should be somewhere on the marina."

I mold more balls, my mind stuck on the hamster wheel of wondering if we can collect the last two items and banish the spirit before these veins reach my heart. Knowing that I was in that shadow world for over an hour when it felt like minutes scares me more than I've been letting on. My hand meets Rhia's beneath the dirt. I want to grab her fingers in mine, but I think about how she eyed my arm. She's probably repulsed. I move my hand away and start forming a new ball.

"How do you think we can find that coin?" I ask.

"What did you say his name was?"

"Jamie."

"Last name?"

I shrug. "She never mentioned it."

"But he worked at the hardware store?"

"Yeah, and the marina, I think."

My hands stop molding flower bombs. Rhia stands up straighter. We both speak at once.

"That coin is in the marina office!"

"I think Jamie is Jim!"

"Wait. What?" I'm not sure I heard Rhia right.

"Jim. His dad used to own the hardware store ages ago. I heard Jim had gone overseas for years. He came back—when was it?" Rhia looks up at the ceiling. "Last year some time? He rolled back into town and everyone was so surprised that he'd returned."

"Jamie is Jim?" I can't even imagine Jim as a teenage boy, let alone one that my mom had fallen in love with. And if Jamie *is* Jim, then Jim is my father. I don't say this part out loud just yet, though.

"That definitely tracks," I say, "because I'm sure that I saw a coin like the one my mom mentions when I went into Jim's office the other day. I didn't think anything of it at the time."

"Do you want to go ask him about it?" Rhia asks.

"Guess we should."

"Don't be nervous," Rhia says, mistaking the source of my feelings.

I don't correct her. I need to digest this huge new truth before I share it. For so long I've wondered about the identity of my father and now I find out that he's been right beneath my nose for as long as I've been on GG's houseboat.

We finish molding flower bombs and leave them out to harden in the July sun. After we wash up, we walk over to the marina.

My stomach is rolling over itself as we get close. I shake out my hands to try to get rid of my nervous energy. We find Jim in a rare moment of stillness. He's sitting on a chair in front of his office wearing his old O's hat and his marina T-shirt. I see him differently now. That's probably the same hat he wore when he knew my mother. The same hair that curls around his ears.

"Edie! Rhia! How I can I help you both today?"

I can't speak. I'm just staring at Jim and inside my head all I hear is: That's *your father, that's your* father, *that's* your *father!*

"Edie needs a life jacket," Rhia blurts. "We're going out on a boat tonight and we're short one jacket. Could you spare one?"

Jim—my father, I'm still processing—offers a slightly confused smile. "Well, sure. That's no problem. Give me a minute."

He gets up and heads toward the back area where he stores the life jackets, paddles, and floats.

"Why are you asking about a life jacket?" I whisper.

"Because you weren't talking," she whispers back. "Go get the coin."

"What?"

"Go," Rhia whispers. "Grab the coin from his office."

"I can't do that!"

"You have about twenty-seven seconds. Go!"

Rhia pushes me toward the office. I slip in. The room is dim after leaving the bright sun of the dock, but even so, right away I make out the coin still hanging from the frame where I'd first noticed it. I slip it off the frame and into my pocket. I manage to make it out just as Jim is coming back with a life jacket in one hand. "Did you need something else?" he asks, looking from me to the office.

"Nope, only the life jacket."

He hands it to me.

"Thanks, Jim," I say.

"Sure."

"No, I mean I really appreciate it."

Jim chuckles. "It's only a life jacket, Edie. Bring it back when you're finished."

"I will." We turn to leave.

"Edie!"

I freeze. Did he realize I'd taken the coin so quickly? Did

he know I might be his daughter? I turn toward him. "Yes?"

"Have fun!"

All my breath leaves me. "We will."

Rhia and I start giggling to the point of hyperventilation when we're out of Jim's earshot. Rhia doesn't know that some of this nervous energy is from talking to the man who I now know is my father. I refuse to pull the coin from my pocket until we get back to Cosmic Flow.

"I can't believe you talked me into doing that!" I whisper as we round the corner, out of sight of the marina.

"What were you going to do?" Rhia asks.

I shrug. "I don't know! Tell him the truth?"

We pass by the diner, busy with the lunch rush. I don't see Jorge working and I wonder if he's with Tess at her family thing.

"What truth, though? Were you going to tell him that you've spent your summer here trying to dismantle some freaky magic?" Rhia lets her hand drift over the flowers overflowing the window boxes at the coffee shop.

"'Course not! I would've said that I've been learning about my mom."

Rhia stops in front of Cosmic Flow. "And what? That you know your mom and him knocked boots when they were your age? Awkward!" She unlocks the door and, once we're inside, flips on the lights of the darkened shop.

"Yeah, you're right. I feel terrible, though."

"But not terrible enough not to take it." Rhia bumps her shoulder against mine. "You can give it back when all this is over."

When all this is over. That cannot come soon enough.

"Are you ready to take this away if something happens to me?"

"I'm your girl." Rhia gives me a reassuring smile.

I hold the coin in my hand, rubbing the face with my thumb. Mom touched this. She blew on it for her father. Probably the first piece of jewelry she'd created—a necklace for Jamie. And she kissed it. My mother's gift—being able to infuse jewelry with emotion—is present in this coin. I feel joy and love and anticipation. I'm holding the coin in my hand for a while before something hits me.

"This isn't the right item," I say. "Nothing's happened. Every other item I've touched has shown me a memory or sent me to that shadowed place. I'm holding this one, and nothing."

"Okay, true." Rhia puts her hands on her hips. "What could it be then?"

I lean against the table. "I have no idea. What else could be at the marina that fits that description?"

"Back to the journal?" Rhia says.

"Back to the journal."

Chapter Thirty-One

MAURA

August 5, 2003

Telling Jamie didn't go well. It didn't go well at all.

I was so excited to let him into this part of my life, to know the full me. After we were together last night, while we were still wrapped in one another's arms, I started to tell him how I was different from other people. He chuckled and kissed me and said that he knew that already. I asked what he knew, and he talked about how I was rehabbing a boat by myself and I was basically dealing with my dad's death on my own and how strong he thought that I was. I told him that I meant I was different in another way. He asked what I meant, and I said I would show him. I figured that I'd start small. I said a few words and changed the lights in the room to different colors. He laughed and asked how I did that. I told him that I could do things. Magical things. He laughed again and said that there is no such thing as magic.

I tried to talk to him, tried to show him more things that I could do. But then he got up, dressed himself, and said he didn't know what was going on, but he needed to go home. He said that it was all too strange. That *I* was too strange.

I went up to the cabin to find Mama, but she wasn't there. I cried myself to sleep.

It's raining again.

August 15

I said goodbye to Jamie today. It was awful. I was crying and clinging to him and he would barely touch me. I've tried to talk to him, but he kept making excuses. He didn't even bring the boat back. He had it parked at the marina and sent some guy to tell me. I gave him an herb bundle for safe travel and watched him hand it to his mom like it was something he didn't want to touch.

Loving Jamie so soon after Daddy died and then being rejected like this feels like being buried under the rubble of loss.

I tried talking to Dad, like I had that one time. But he didn't appear again. Not even the pale, flickering version. I need to figure out why he's not showing himself to us. I need to find a way to make him appear.

August 25

Felt sick again this morning. But in the afternoon, I biked up to the post office to check our box. Now that the rain has let up, people filled the sidewalks, holding ice cream cones or wandering past the shops. The beachy areas were packed, and the river roared with motorboats. All these people enjoying their lives while mine felt ripped apart.

I'd finally forwarded our mail and the post office box was packed. Neither Mama nor I had checked it in a while. I rifled through, tossing the junk. Amid the flyers and bills, and a couple letters from UPenn, was a postcard featuring the Horn of Africa from a satellite. My heartbeat sped up.

Dear Maura,

I've landed. I spent the entire flight thinking about you. About us. You meant so much to me. I'd never felt about anyone the way that I felt about you. What we had was real. I don't know what happened, why you started talking about magic. Maybe it was your dad dying and your mom not speaking. Maybe I was not enough for you. But Maura, magic is make-believe. A game that children play. It's not real. I'm sorry that things ended the way that they did, but I didn't know how to handle the change in you. I hope that you find the help that you need to get through this difficult time.

—Jamie

I threw the postcard in the trash and biked home. I should never have shared my magic. It only led to hurt.

Chapter Thirty-Two

MAURA

August 27, 2003

I'm pregnant.

After I realized the date and that I hadn't had my period in a while, I took a pregnancy test. Then I went to the Planned Parenthood clinic. A nurse in blue scrubs came out with a clipboard and called my name. She ushered me into a bland exam room where I told her about my pregnancy test. I heard myself saying the words, but it was as though I was up above watching this happen to someone else. The nurse nodded and made a note on my file.

"The doctor will be right in," the nurse said.

I wished I had something to distract me. I wished that I wasn't alone.

When the doctor finally came in, a tall thin woman with a hawkish nose and a kind smile, she looked over my file and then told me that she was going to do an exam. A nurse stood by while she told me to put my feet in the stirrups and performed the exam. She asked if I'd used protection and I knew she meant condoms, not yarrow tea, so I said no.

"You're early on," the doctor said when she was finished. "You have options."

The doctor told me about those options while she pulled plastic gloves off one at a time and dropped them efficiently in a nearby trashcan. I lay on the exam table in a paper gown, my knees pressed together. The nurse asked if I wanted to call the father.

The father.

Of my baby.

Jamie.

Jamie who was in South Africa. Who had sent me a postcard on the day that he landed basically telling me that our relationship was over. I shook my head no.

The doctor told me they would give me some time to think over what I wanted to do and then she and the nurse left, shutting the door behind them.

The obvious choice was to terminate the pregnancy. If you'd asked me three months ago what I'd do if this happened, I may have laughed. It wouldn't have seemed possible to me then.

But a lot can change in three months.

Three months ago, I assumed that my father would be around for a very long time. I assumed that I would go to UPenn, as he'd hoped. But he's gone.

And in a way, his death led me to Jamie.

I rest my hand on my abdomen.

And here we are.

I slid off the exam table and removed my paper gown, using it to wipe away the goo from my privates. I pulled my clothes back on.

"I'm going home," I said to the woman at the front desk.

"Are you sure?" she asked.

"I'm sure."

When I got back to the cabin, I wrote a letter to Jamie. He deserves to know, I guess. I wrote the letter and told him that I'm having the baby and I don't need or want his support. I wrote it. I sealed it. And I mailed it before I could change my mind. When I returned, I looked for Mama.

Chapter Thirty-Three

EDIE

I shut the journal and sit for a moment, allowing this new truth to settle. I'd realized that Jamie must be my father. But now Jamie was no longer a dim figure from Mom's past. He was someone who broke my mother's heart. Someone I knew, who I'd seen every day of my time in Cedar Branch.

"What is it?" Rhia looks up from doing inventory. "Did you figure it out? Was something revealed?"

This new bit of information makes me want to share what I've realized. "Rhee," I say. "Jim is . . . my father."

"What?" Rhia breathes out the word. "What are you saying right now?"

"Jamie, my mom's big summer love, is Jim. And Jamie is my father. Which means *Jim* is my father."

"Holy shit," Rhia says, lowering her clipboard. "You never knew?"

"I mean, I was starting to put things together. I figured Jamie to be my father. But I didn't know until today that Jamie was Jim. Maybe I should have, but I wasn't ready to face it full-on, you know?"

"You never knew your dad at all?"

I shake my head again. "My mom used to tell me this fairy tale about how there once was a girl-woman who was so sad and who wished for a girl-baby and then the girl-baby arrived. And that was supposed to be where I came from. When I got old enough, we fought about it. I told her that I wanted to know who my father was. Not some magical story. But she never told me."

"I wonder why?" Rhia says thoughtfully. "I mean, Jim seems like a good guy."

"I think I know why," I say, tapping the cover of the journal with my finger. "Mom had told him about her magic. He didn't believe her. Told her that she needed help."

"No, he did not!" Rhia slams her pen on her clipboard.

I toss Mom's journal on the table. "Yeah, he sure did."

"That's bananas!" Rhia says. "Are you okay? This is a lot."

"It *is* a lot, isn't it?" My breathing hitches slightly.

"Yeah, it is." She reaches out and squeezes my hand. "Are you going to talk to him?"

"I have to."

"Back so soon?" Jim asks when I show up at the marina again.

My stomach jumps with nerves. I rub my hands together and remind myself that I've spoken to this man almost every day since

I moved here in June. "I have something to talk to you about."

His nod suggests that maybe he knows.

I hand him the life jacket. "I didn't actually need this."

"Okay." Jim accepts the life jacket and walks into the back area with all of the rental gear. I follow him in.

"And I took this." I hold up the necklace.

Jim's eyebrows go up. "I see."

I shift on my feet. "You used to be called Jamie?"

"Yes." He whispers the word out. He clears his throat. "Yes, a long time ago."

"My mother"—my voice cracks—"got pregnant with a boy named Jamie. Here in Cedar Branch." I feel tears filling my eyes. "Pregnant with me."

We stand face-to-face and it's like we're actually seeing one another for the first time.

Jim places his hand against his mouth. "You're my daughter. You're really my daughter." His voice is clouded with emotion.

"You didn't know, either?" I ask.

"That I might be your father?" Jim takes his cap off, rubs his hand across his hair, and mashes his cap back on. This is a habit I know and recognize. Now I see it in a new way. It's not just Jim's habit, this is my father's habit. He shakes his head. "Not for sure. You've got my hazel eyes." His eyes crinkle when he says it. "And I hoped. I mean, you're an amazing kid. But I didn't know for sure."

"What happened?"

Jim squints at the shining river, but I imagine that he's picturing the past. "That summer, she'd just lost her dad." Jim looks at me. "Your grandfather. She and I were like magnets. Couldn't stay apart. But I had already signed up for the Peace Corps and I had to leave. Then she told me something about herself that I couldn't accept."

"She told you that she could do magic."

Jim nods. "I didn't believe her. Didn't believe in magic."

"Her journal says that she wrote a letter to you telling you about me."

His brow wrinkles. "I never received it. But I'm not surprised. There was barely phone service and the mail was not reliable."

"And you'd ended it anyway."

"Yeah, I guess I had ended it."

"Have you been married?" I ask. "Have kids? Other kids, I mean." Maybe it's rude to ask this, but I feel that I have a right to know.

Jim shakes his head. "No, I guess I was married to work and travel." He smiles then, a sad smile. "But I never forgot Maura. From time to time, I'd try to look her up."

"Mom didn't have an online presence."

Jim's eyes sparkle when he smiles for real. "No, she sure did not."

"Are you still skeptical of what she told you?"

He holds my gaze for a moment before he breaks it. "No, no I'm not. During all the travel I did, engaging in so many different cultures and belief systems, I came to realize that there is more to this world than what meets the eye. I only wish I'd realized it much sooner."

"I asked Mom from time to time who my father was, but she never told me. She also said I should never mix magic with relationships, which sort of makes sense now."

Jim looks at me and his eyes are full of shame. "Edie, I'm so sorry."

Something flashes in my mind, a connection. "She wrote that you didn't bring the boat back to the dock after the work was done. You parked it here at the marina?"

Jim stares at his feet. "There's nothing that I can say. I was young and stupid."

"No, that's not what I'm saying." If the houseboat has been at the marina all this time, then maybe the last item is on the boat. I clarify. "Has our houseboat been docked here ever since then?"

Jim's brow furrows as he thinks. "I was gone for years, but I'm pretty sure it's stayed here all that time. Why?"

I grin. "You may have helped me figure something out. I've got to go." I turn to leave.

"I'll see you again, right?" Jim calls after me.

I turn back. "I live on the purple boat parked at your marina, so yeah."

"I mean, will you speak to me? You have every right to turn your back on me like I did your mother."

I pause. "I'm young, but not stupid."

He smiles to hear his words turned around. "At least I didn't pass on my stupidity to you."

At the idea of DNA being passed on, something occurs to me. I walk slowly back to Jim. "Do I have grandparents?"

His eyes fill with tears then and he's laughing at the same time. My heart opens up. "Yup." He nods. "You've got a cranky but loveable grandfather. And an aunt who likes to boss me around—even though she's younger than me—and a couple annoying and adorable cousins, too."

I realize I'm smiling. "I'd like to meet them sometime."

"And they will love meeting you."

Chapter Thirty-Four

EDIE

It's Friday and we've all gathered at Cosmic Flow. Tess has brought chips, I've brought Gummis, and Rhia has brought root beer.

"How was your grandfather's birthday party?" I ask Tess.

She takes a handful of chips. "Well, you probably shouldn't do a surprise party for an eighty-year-old man. I thought he was going to have a heart attack. Other than that, it was really nice. Except for my little brother smashing cake in my hair. But, oh my gods, enough of that, Edie—I can't believe that Jim's your dad!"

"I know, right? I went to the perpetual woods yesterday just to be alone with my thoughts," I say. "Oh, and I found this there, too!" I pull the protection bag from my pocket to show Rhia and Tess.

"Nice," Rhia says.

"Are you feeling okay about Jim?" Tess asks.

"I don't hate the idea. Turns out I even have some relatives. But I can't even think about all of that until I know that we've dealt with all of this." I gesture to the protection bag and my arm. "But something Jim said made me pretty certain that the final item, the 'love, worn in a never-ending circle,' could be on the boat."

"I've been thinking—it might be a ring," Tess says, touching a ring on her hand. "That's like a never-ending circle, isn't it?"

"Wait, yes, it totally is," I say, watching Tess spin the ring around on her finger.

"I didn't say anything before because you and Rhee know so much more than I do."

"We don't, though," I say to Tess. "You don't give yourself enough credit."

"I've also been researching the lore," Rhia says, popping a red Gummi in her mouth. "And I found references to the Luctus spirit your grandmother mentioned. It's attracted to grief and it feeds on memories."

"That's awful!" Tess says.

"Yeah," Rhia goes on. "And it can only manifest in liminal spaces."

"What does that mean?" Tess asks.

"In-between places," I say. "Thresholds, places of crossing over."

"That's why it could get to you when we were leaving the perpetual woods," Rhia says to me. "And when you'd hold those items, because you were between the present and the past."

"But how did it attack the beech?" Tess asks.

"Maybe because it's a *weeping* beech. It has the space underneath that's sort of between places," I say. "GG was really excited when I showed her the vial of blood. She said she's working on the final step. Whatever that means."

"A few accounts of dealing with this spirit say that you need a holy relic to banish it. Others say you need three witches from the same bloodline. And they all say that ashes of the dead are required."

"Like any dead person?" Tess asks.

We look at her. "What? Not like I have any ashes on hand. Just trying to understand what we need."

"Ashes of the person who caused the grief that called the Luctus spirit," Rhia clarifies.

Not that the clarification matters because none of those solutions seem possible for us. There are only two witches alive in my family, we definitely do not have access to any relics, and I have no idea where the ashes of my grandfather are.

"Let's gather the last two items," I say. "If GG feels like we have a shot, we need to trust her. She's my grandmother. She only wants me to be safe."

As we walk into the cemetery, Tess asks if we are going to the war memorial. When Rhia and I both give her blank stares, she rolls her eyes and says that it's a statue for fallen soldiers.

"Maybe your grandfather's dog tags are somewhere around there."

Rhia points to a sign for the office. "Let's ask about it."

It hadn't occurred to me that the cemetery would have an office with a living person in it. Rhia's idea is a good one. We go in and ask the woman working at the desk.

"Oh, yes. The war memorial was created after the First World War. People started leaving dog tags on there and now it's pretty much covered in them."

We all look at one another with eyes wide. The woman gives us a map with the spot marked. Following a winding path through the cemetery, we find it.

The war memorial is nothing like I expect. It's a granite statue of an angel at least fifteen feet tall with her arms outstretched and face inclined downward, beneath a huge old ash tree. As the office lady told us, from her arms hang hundreds of sets of dog tags. It's an amazing sight.

"I guess we need to start looking," I say. "This could take a while."

"Edie, Edie, Edie, when will you ever learn?" Rhia asks.

"Learn what?"

"What you are. What you can do. Tell the dog tags to present themselves to you."

"Like with the photograph at the hardware store?"

"Exactly."

I take a deep breath, close my eyes and hold out my hand.

"Wait!" Tess says.

My eyes fly open. "What?"

"Here." She hands me a pair of oven mitts.

I close my eyes again.

"Wait!"

I open my eyes.

"Do you have your protection bag?" Rhia asks.

I pat my pocket.

Rhia and Tess both nod at me.

I close my eyes to envision the dog tags and I open my eyes again. "What if I end up in the Luctus spirit realm again?"

"Call your fire, like you did before," Rhia reassures me.

Finally, I close my eyes, picture the dog tags, and chant the words, "Lost thing, come to these hands."

I open my eyes. The dog tags sit in the oven mitt and I have not gone to the shadowed place.

"I think we've finally got the hang of this!" Tess says.

I'm so relieved that I don't even speak. I just give Tess and Rhia a nervous smile and we walk back to Main Street. I hand Rhia the dog tags in the safety of the oven mitt and she takes them to wherever she's keeping the rest of the items locked up.

One more keepsake and we'll be that much closer. I rub the arm that's always cold now and I'm reminded that we're far from finished.

I wake to the rude call of crows. The sun is beginning its confident march across a cloudless sky. The river rocks our boat gently. I lock my door and light a candle and crumble some lavender in it. This morning I want the calm of lavender over the sharpness of the rosemary that I usually use.

I sit cross-legged on my bed and close my eyes to bring up the image of a ring. I open them. I can't remember the last time I saw Mom. She used to appear to me every day and I couldn't take it, but now I need her. I think back. It was after the beech. She'd appeared and I told her to go away.

My hand goes to the acorn charm. I force myself to let it go. It's Mom's fault that I'm in this mess. If she'd never invoked the Luctus spirit, I wouldn't be infected, and I'd probably be home by now.

I close my eyes to push away the thought of my mother with her big smile and floating hair. I'm determined to focus on the finding charm again. Behind my closed eyes, I imagine a ring. I whisper the finding spell.

All that comes to me is shades of blue and purple. I try again with the same result. The third time I try, I can't focus because the rocking of the boat, usually barely noticeable, is increasing to the point that items on my dresser are actually sliding. I peer through my small window. Thick clouds, heavy with rain, race toward us. I climb up to the roof of the boat.

"What's going on?" I ask GG. "It was a clear sky like five minutes ago."

A gust of sudden wind whips my hair around my face. The clouds grow bigger and closer by the second. The river, reacting to the wind, turns black and angry. The boat rocks on its moorings. I can feel the tug as the river tries to pull the boat out into her flow. I squint at the sky.

"We should go below," she says.

The plants are swaying, threatening to topple in their planters. Lightning cracks the sky, followed quickly by a boom of thunder so loud and so close that I feel it in my chest.

GG frowns. "Go below, Edie." Her voice is stern.

I turn to the ladder. My hair flies around my face, defying gravity, like Mom's hair whenever she appears. As I start to climb down, I feel light, like I'm not attached to the boat. I look down and realize that I'm not. I'm floating away from the ladder.

"GG, help!" The wind consumes my words.

The water roils itself into whitecaps. I hang in midair for a fraction of a second. Then I'm falling fast. The words of the

Charm to Keep Dry come to me. I shout them before I plunge into the water.

I bounce back up as though I'm in a plastic bubble. That spell came to me quicker than any other spell. All of these weeks and the magic is beginning to come naturally. I think about Mom embedding those spells in the journal for me to find. Despite my earlier anger, I'm seized with a missing of her so deep, that I feel as though I'm sinking. Suddenly, the bubble disappears and the black river swallows me whole.

Underwater there is no sense of the sudden storm raging above. I'm not a great swimmer to begin with and now I'm weak from this infection, bone-tired from seeking hidden items and dealing with magic above my pay grade. Shadows flow toward me, ribboning around my body.

My limbs feel too heavy to move. The shadows tighten around my midsection. Bubbles of oxygen leave my nose and rise to the surface as I sink. My acorn necklace floats upward as well, and I remember the note that came with it: *For when you need me with you.*

But she's not with me. I'm on my own. I give an angry kick. My body begins to rise. I kick again and pull water with my hands. My right hand breaks through the surface of the water. My face is free. I gulp air. Up here on the surface, the river is wild. The flow, usually barely noticeable, pushes me away from our boat.

Jim runs down the dock, tearing off his shirt. He leaps onto the stern of our boat. GG seems to study the water for a moment before she climbs to the roof. Jim kicks off his shoes and dives into the river.

A swell slams into me and I'm plunged beneath the water. I kick and swim, ignited by my anger. I reach the surface. The boat is farther away. Jim swims toward me. I catch glimpses of him over the swells. GG stands on the roof of the boat. Her long braid has come undone and her gray hair blows all around her. She holds her hand over the water, a branch sitting on her open palm.

Jim is closer. The water tosses me. My lungs are hungry for oxygen. Jim reaches for me. My body is lifted with another swell. I take in water and I'm under again. My lungs feel tight. I kick again, but weakly. When I break the surface this time, Jim is there. He grabs me in a lifeguard hold and begins to swim back to the boat. GG drops the branch into the water and raises her arms in great sweeping movements. Her lips move, casting some spell. I kick to help Jim along. The swells seem to be calming a bit. There are no longer whitecaps. My lungs still burn. But the squall is moving out. Jim and I make it to the boat.

By the time we reach the ladder at the back, GG is there. Jim climbs up first and then reaches down to pull me up. He holds me and I collapse against him.

"Are you okay?" His eyes, full of concern, inspect me.

"Think so."

Jim releases me and I go down on my hands and knees on the deck of the boat coughing and spitting river water. The wind has completely stopped, leaving the air oddly still. The river, too, is calm now, its surface a mirror.

I roll over so that I'm staring at the sky. My chest heaves. "GG, what just happened?"

"Nothing good." GG squints at the horizon, at the clouds rushing away as fast as they rode in.

Jim kneels beside me. "Are you sure you're okay?"

"I'm shaken up, but I don't think I'm hurt."

"It's best to leave us now," GG says.

He shakes his head, like he doesn't understand what just happened. "This is my daughter. I'm not going to leave until I know she's okay."

GG looks from Jim to me and back again. I nod.

"Well, that's a question answered. Thank you, Jim," GG says. "I'll take it from here."

"Edie, if you need anything, you give me a shout."

I nod. "I will."

When he's out of earshot, I ask, "What just happened?"

"You're very close and the spirit is fighting back."

I push myself to standing. "What do I do?"

"You keep going."

"I almost died."

"But you didn't. And you won't, now that I know we've got some of your mother's blood. Find the last of the items, Edie. This is very nearly over."

I shiver standing before my grandmother despite the late July heat.

"You can't say anything more than that? How will we banish the Luctus spirit? What should I expect? I don't even know where to find the last item."

GG wraps me in a towel. "I find that in times like these, a good peppermint tea with fortifying honey does wonders. Why don't you go make yourself some now?"

My eyebrows fly up. "Seriously?"

GG nods at me. "Quite seriously."

After I've dried off and put on fresh clothes, I set the kettle to boil and lean my elbows on the counter. I feel chilled to the bone and sick, like I do every time the Luctus spirit tries to reach me. GG says we are close, but at this moment, I've never felt further from the goal.

I reach for the tea tin, and the twirling of the handblown witch ball catches my eye as it casts shades of purple and blue whenever the light hits it. Purple and blue were the colors that came to me when I tried to cast the spell. Something glints inside the ball. I stand up. Holding the fishing line from which it hangs, I lift the ball from its hook. Peering through the colored glass, I see a simple gold band sitting inside the ball.

Chapter Thirty-Five

EDIE

We all get out of the car. I carry the five items. Rhia has her bag of supplies. Tess wears a necklace of garlic along with the spell bag that Rhia made. Rhia and I had tried to tell Tess that there aren't any vampires involved, but she wouldn't be moved.

We've spent the last week preparing for our next step. I was excited to find the ring, but after my near-drowning, I was weak—as I am after every interaction with the shadow world. Then, when I told GG that we'd found the fifth item, her eyes lit up. But just as quickly, they clouded over. She frowned then and said that she couldn't remember what she needed to do next. Couldn't remember an important thing. Knowing what Rhia's been through with her grandmother, I knew that I should be patient with GG. It wasn't her fault that she couldn't remember. I tried to show her patience and compassion.

But inside, I was the opposite of patient. I was in turmoil. I'd been frozen, nearly burned, nearly drowned, and temporarily paralyzed. I have black veins working their way toward my heart. Patient is definitely not what I was.

Rhia hit the books, looking to fill in GG's missing memories. I paced, wondering if the key was something that GG had shared with me in the past. Tess mostly fretted. We all agreed that we needed to return to the cabin with the five items and perform a powerful ritual spell. We knew that we needed to break the bind of the Luctus spirit to the cabin, to the Mitchell bloodline. So we collected what we needed and here we are on a Saturday morning staring at the overgrown cabin.

"I guess this is the end of the road," I say.

"Let's hope for the best," Rhia adds.

"It's always darkest before the dawn," Tess says.

Rhia and I stare are her. "What?" she says, "I couldn't think of a good cliché that matched."

That gets a smile out of me. A small one at least. Remembering what happened last time Rhia tried to enter the cabin, we go in with me holding Rhia's hand on one side and Tess's on the other. It takes some awkward shuffling, but then we're in.

Rhia creates a circle of salt and we all sit. She pulls a bowl and the rest of the ingredients from her bag. Wearing Tess's oven mitts, I take each item out one by one. The watch that my grandfather wore every day. The photo of him and my mom finishing a big project. The key to the place where he did all of his work. The dog tags that showed Mom and GG the most vulnerable side of him. And the gold wedding band that represented the love between him and GG.

Into the bowl I place soil from the perpetual woods along with some hawthorn bark that I harvested. Rhia adds a piece of black amber. Tess contributes the feather of a red hawk. I add three strands of my hair as well as GG's, for good measure. I add a drop of Mom's blood from the vial in the acorn charm. Rhia drips oil over all of it.

I look at my hands and take in a deep breath to calm my mind. I envision a tiny flame, nothing big. Nothing dangerous. Tiny sparks dance from my fingers. A spasm of fear zips through me. I greet it as an old, annoying friend. Then, I send my sparks into the concoction. The blaze is quick and hot. Our faces are illuminated in the flames.

"You did it," Rhia says.

I nod. "Me and fear, besties now."

All those weeks ago enclosed in the weeping arms of the beech tree, Rhia encouraged me to conjure fire. I had been so afraid. This time I was afraid again, but I didn't give fear my power. I held on.

We chant the spell that we'd written based around one found in Mom's journal:

"With these items we have found,

Through their power you've been bound.

With my words I set you free.

Depart from here; leave us be.

Dirt of earth and feather of sky,

With bark and crystal here do lie.

Hairs of witches in my line,

Hear my words and break this bind."

We look at each other across the circle. Nothing has happened. No banging doors, no creeping vines, no shadows. We try
two more times. Still nothing.

"Did we do something wrong?" Tess asks.

I drop my head. All of the danger I faced since June was for
this moment. I believed that we would dispel the dark magic
connected to the Luctus spirit when we completed this ritual.
I'd been willing to place myself in harm's way knowing that I
would be able to restore order and balance. That I would cure
myself of this infection. I hadn't allowed myself to dwell on any
other outcome.

We wait a few moments longer, hoping. But the veins that had
worked their way across my collarbone after the near-drowning
have not receded at all. I say nothing as Rhia gathers her things
and holds them awkwardly under one arm while grasping my
hand with the other. Tess grabs my other hand and we make it
to the door. We all step outside. Rhia drops her bowl and all its
contents.

"Whoa," Tess says.

"That's unexpected," I say. "Do you think our spell actually worked?"

Inside the cabin, there had been no clue that the ritual made any difference. No shadows. No fire. No unexpected squall. No flickering of my vision. But behind the cabin, where there had been nothing, now stood a large workshop.

"*Something* obviously worked," Rhia says.

"We did it!" Tess jumps up and down. Then she looks at me. "Why aren't you excited?"

"I don't know what I expected, but it wasn't for a workshop to magically appear. And I don't know what's in there, but I'm pretty sure it's not unicorns and rainbows." I steady my breath and walk toward the building. Rhia and Tess follow close behind. I turn to them.

"I think I should go in alone," I say. "You two have done so much already. I don't want to put you at more risk. But if something goes wrong, will you get my grandmother?"

Rhia nods. Tess squeezes my hand. "Just don't die, okay?"

"I'll do my best."

The workshop is unlocked. No need to lock it when it's a hidden building. I push open the door and step into the dimness.

There's a simple altar on a wooden stand and candles in various stages of use, a few photographs, and some other items I can't yet make out. I walk closer. The photographs are of my grandfather. One of him alone, smiling from the deck down by the water. One of him and GG. He smiles at the camera while she kisses him on the cheek. The third photo is of him and my mom when she was a little kid. She digs in the sand while he sits nearby, smiling at her.

In front of the photos and interspersed with candles are various items. I reach out to pick up a pocketknife and it cuts me. A drop of my blood lands on the cloth of the altar.

The candles flicker to life one by one. The entire cloth is riddled with spots of blood. I step back.

I bump into something. I turn to see what I've run into. And I scream.

An older man looks at me with confusion. A glow emanates from him and ripples out, altering the environment in its path. What had been a dark, dusty space with a few grimy windows morphs into the living room of the Baltimore house. Not as it is now, but maybe as it was before I was born.

"Who might you be?" the man asks.

I don't need to ask who he is. I've seen him in photos and memories. I've seen him floating around GG on our houseboat. He's my dead grandfather, not aged a day since the photos were taken. And he appears real. He's talking to me.

"I'm—I'm Edie," I stutter. "Your . . . granddaughter."

He frowns, inspecting me. "But that's impossible. My daughter is graduating from high school today. I have a gift for her. See?" He dips his hand into his jacket pocket. "Where is it? I just had it."

My breath chokes in my chest. "Do you know where you are?" I ask.

His laugh is big and confident. "Why would you ask such a question?"

"Where are you?"

"I'm—" He looks around. "I'm in our house. In Baltimore." He looks at me then, confusion clouding his eyes. "Aren't I?" He looks around some more. "But it doesn't, something isn't quite . . ." He clears his throat and offers a polite smile. "Forgive me. Are you a friend of Maura's? Going to graduation with us?" He frowns, then the polite smile is once again pasted onto his face.

"I'm so sorry to be rude, but I must be going. We're in a hurry. To get to the graduation." Then to himself. "That's where we're going, right? To Maura's graduation?" He shakes his head. "I can't seem to . . ."

He begins to fade away and the scene fades with him. Then he appears again. This time he believes that he's on his way to build furniture. Once again, he gets confused and disappears. He appears three more times. Each manifestation seems to be a different memory. I'm overwhelmed with seeing him relive old memories that I've heard about or read about in Mom's journal. My heart aches as he becomes confused at the end of each moment.

I begin to whisper the words that we said in the cabin. My grandfather looks baffled as I begin to speak.

"With these items we have found."

His image flickers like Mom spoke about in her journal entry that day that she spoke to her father's ashes with her whole heart.

"Through their power you've been bound."

The words lodge themselves in my throat. Here is the grandfather I've only known as a ghost. How is he also here? I focus so that I can continue.

"With my words I set you free."

His image strobes through all of the memories that have held him captive.

"Depart from here; leave us be. I release you, Grandfather Edward," I say through tears. "I release you to go where you belong."

His figure ripples and brightens before bursting into a thousand tiny balls of light. A whisper of wind caresses my cheek and the lights fly out into the afternoon sky.

I'm once again staring at the altar in a workshop that had been hidden for years. The candles have gone out and the space is dim with afternoon light trying to break through the dirt on the window. Deep in the corner of the workshop, I make out the shape of something dark and hulking. I hear a scratch and a rasp. I don't wait to find out what it is, I race out as fast as I can.

"I saw my grandfather," I say. "Not like the ghosts I usually see. He had a physical presence." I try to catch my breath. "He talked to me. He was solid. But he was so confused. Like he was reliving moments from the past. I think I released him from whatever was holding him here."

"That sounds like what we hoped we were doing," Rhia says. "But I have some bad news."

"I do too," I say. "You first."

"We're not finished." Rhia points. "Do you see those stones? One at the corner there and then another over this way?"

"I never noticed them before," I say. "Are those crystals?"

Rhia nods. "There are three buried around the property as I'd expect for a containment spell, halfway out and halfway in," she says. "But this one"—she toes the area—"seems like it's been messed with."

My stomach drops. "Oh my gods, Tess."

"What?"

"Remember the first day we came here? That morning on our run?"

"Yeah!" Her face goes white and her hands fly to her mouth. "That stone. I said it was pretty."

I nod. "I found it right here." I look at Rhia. "I had no idea what it was. I barely knew anything about how magic worked then."

"So you removed a crystal from here?" Rhia asks, pointing at the spot.

I nod. "But it had bad energy. I knew that much at least. And I came back and buried it again. That must be how everything started. And all this time, I thought it was because I'd taken a photo of my mom from the cabin."

"Maybe it doesn't matter," Tess says. "You said you released your grandfather's spirit. Maybe we're done!"

"We're not done," I say, looking at the cabin. "My grandfather disappeared, but something else was in there. Something I didn't wait to see."

Chapter Thirty-Six

EDIE

"GG, Mom magically hid Grandfather's workshop," I blurt out to GG when I return to the boat just before noon. "And she trapped Grandfather's spirit there."

"Nonsense," GG says from behind the book she's reading. "Your mother couldn't have done that sort of magic. Besides, Edward's spirit is here."

GG drops the book into her lap, as if she's realized what she's said and what it means. I feel as though the floor has been pulled out from under me. All this summer as I've read about Mom's grief and her memories associated with her father's belongings, I assumed it was she who had invoked the Luctus spirit so that she could see her father again. And when GG said that she was limited in how she could help or that she couldn't remember, I thought it was because it was Mom who had created this terrible situation.

I never guessed that it could have been my grandmother.

"It was you?" I ask. "You hid those items and invoked the Luctus spirit?"

GG looks down at her hands.

"I did, yes. A very long time ago and I've been paying for it ever since."

"*You've* been paying for it? Look at this!" I say, I say, yanking the collar of my T-shirt over to reveal the black veins. "How exactly have *you* been paying? I'm the one in danger. And you allowed me to think that my mother—my dead mother—was to blame."

"Edie, don't—"

"No! You withheld the truth. You don't get to tell me what to do now."

I walk over to GG's workspace and I pick up her recipe box. I start to look through all of the recipes, reading them and tossing them to the floor as I dismiss them. "Calming Nerves, Quieting Nausea, Ceasing Cough. None of these actually help, GG. These are *useless*. Just like you! You're the witch who created this; *you* need to end it."

"Edie!"

I run out of the boat and up the dock. I don't stop when Jim calls after me. It's the middle of the day and he's surrounded by people eager to rent equipment. I clutch my sparking fingers into fists. I pump my legs and they burn with effort as I continue to run.

Before I know it, I'm at the entrance to the perpetual woods, the magical clearing. I whisper the words. Nothing happens. I sigh and collapse on soft pine needles carpeting the forest floor at the base of the hawthorn. I press the back of my head against the old tree and clutch the acorn charm.

"Please help me," I say. "I know I told you to go away. But I thought this was all your fault. I was wrong. I need you."

The charm warms in my fingers and at the same time, I sense a rippling all around me, like a soft breeze. A warm glow caresses me. The magical clearing has opened up. The flowering trees continue to flower and the bees are busy at their work. The hawthorn moves through her seasons one after the next.

How could it have been my grandmother who had invoked such awful magic? My mother had been young. She'd been missing her father and then she'd been heartbroken by Jim. I could almost forgive her. But my grandmother was a grown woman, a mother, skilled in magic, and she knew exactly what she was doing.

Anger spikes followed by the tingling. My fingers spark again and once more I close my hands into fists and hold them against my chest. GG had let me believe that it had been Mom to blame. And she'd had me working to right this terrible wrong on my own. Me. Not even a legal adult and most definitely not skilled in magic.

I unfold my hands again and look at my fingers. I focus on control and allow sparks to jump from my fingertips. My stomach clenches.

"Hello, Fear," I whisper. I focus, like I did when we

performed the ritual, but this time, I don't stop when the sparks dance. I imagine the sparks merging. A crackling ball of fire appears over each hand. Just like when GG was coaching me that day on the back of the boat. Not much larger than a grape. I blink rapidly, surprised. I give the ball in my left hand a slight bump with my palm, and it leaps to the other hand, joining that one. I let out a quavering breath.

Now I have a ball of fire the size of an orange floating above my cupped palms. I hold it there, hanging in the air. I override the instinct to clench my hands closed. Instead, I remain still, sensing the power that flows out of me and into this fire. I spread my arms out and the ball grows wider. I huff out a nervous breath. I press my hands toward one another, and the ball becomes elongated.

When the urge to stop becomes a dim hum in the background, I look around for a safe place to send my fire. My eyes land on the large slab of stone that GG uses to cut herbs. I stand, guiding the orb of fire toward the stone. When I'm near enough, I slam the fire ball into it.

The ball explodes, dissolving into tiny sparks once again. They migrate to my fingers like magnetic filings. I breathe deeply in and out. When I look at my hands, they're no longer sparking. I touch my fingers to the acorn charm.

My grandmother has betrayed me, but I still need her.

Whatever we did, it didn't work. The lines on my arm are just as bad as they had been. I have to go back, and I have to ask for her help. At least now I understand why she never shared memories of the past. The spirit had stolen them from her. I turn slowly in this space, taking in all the plants and trees and their meanings. I've come so far from the person I was when I arrived in Cedar Branch. And I've learned so much. Maybe even enough to help my grandmother.

I walk GG's maze and harvest some herbs and leaves from nearby trees. I bundle them together with a thin green branch. I hold up my hands, sense the familiar nervousness alongside the power flowing in me, and then I light the bundle on fire. After I blow out the flames, I breathe in the smoke, feeling the curative properties of GG's plants work in my system, giving me the energy that I need to face this next step.

When I return to the marina, it's early evening and all the day rentals have returned. I find GG sitting in her chair in the living quarters. I walk over to the Brigid candle and light it with a touch of my fingers.

"All those weeks ago, you told me to learn the magic and then we'd talk about me going home. Did you know then that I'd be in danger trying to fix this terrible magic that you'd allowed into our lives?" I pause. "Did you ever have any intention of allowing me to go home?"

"My intention—now and always—has been to keep you safe," GG says.

"Well, you've been pretty shit at it."

"I can't argue with you."

"I'm really angry with you, but I still need your help. And I have an idea."

Sitting before GG, I place into a bowl herbs I harvested as well as soil from the perpetual woods. I select two crystals from GG's collection. I hold my palms up.

"Place your hands in mine and call your element," I say to my grandmother. She quirks an eyebrow but doesn't object. Resting her palms on mine, she closes her eyes and the soil swirls upward like smoke from an extinguished candle. She opens her eyes to watch me. I call my fire and the two dance together, flames twining around the spinning soil. Then I speak the spell I created:

> "For memories stolen by means impure,
>
> May our Mitchell magic be the cure.
>
> With power of fire and strength of earth,
>
> We call the memories, we know their worth."

As the words flow out of me, a glow emanates from us. GG's eyes widen. Her mouth trembles. My fire extinguishes and her soil drops back into the bowl. GG clutches me to her. "I remember," she whispers into my hair. "I remember everything now." She pulls back from me. "And I know where they are!"

Before I can ask what she's talking about, the wind chimes on our deck start to send off a cacophony of sound. GG looks in the direction of the sound with a worried expression. Something dark and fluid dances at the edge of my vision. GG and I both turn toward my bedroom door to look at the same time. There's nothing there.

"Did you see—?" I start to ask.

"The iron talisman. The triquetra. Did you put it back over your window?" GG asks, standing so suddenly that her chair topples backward.

My eyes go wide. I'd forgotten. I shake my head. GG and I rush toward my room. Tendrils of shadow curl from beneath my door. I step back.

"Can you tell me now?" I ask. "What magic still needs to be undone?"

GG pauses and turns toward me. "Still?"

"We performed a bind-breaking ritual. From Mom's journal. Because you said you couldn't help."

"You released the bind?" GG looks very pale all of a sudden.

My bedroom door flies open. The room is black with shadows. They rush toward us. I stumble backward.

"Yes, I freed Grandfather and I revealed the workshop."

GG raises her arms and vines start to grow across my door. The shadows seep through the barrier she's creating.

"The bind you broke, what you've freed—that was not your grandfather!" GG continues building vines. "You need to get out of here."

"I want to help you!"

"Go! You'll be helping me by keeping yourself safe. And Edie—here!"

She throws something to me, and I catch it. It's small silver sphere like a tea ball.

"What do I do with this?" I call back to GG.

"Keep that safe. Only the power of three will work! I'll be there. I promise!" GG can barely get the words out. Feathers protrude from her mouth. The shadows twist around her legs. She goes down on one knee. Inky feathers swirl around the room like a cyclone. GG is barely visible now. She's raising her hands to fight back. The shadows begin to slink toward me.

I pocket the silver ball and fling open the door leading out of our living quarters, bracing myself for shadows. But there is nothing. Even the wind chimes have stopped their noise. I look over my shoulder to see how GG is managing to fight the shadows.

But my grandmother is gone.

Chapter Thirty-Seven

EDIE

Sprinting at full speed, I'm well away from the marina before I realize that I don't have my phone or my bag. I left with nothing except the clothes on my body, the protection bag, and GG's silver ball. I almost stop at Jim's, but I can't imagine that he could help. I should have stayed to help GG. I know how to make fire now—I could have saved her. But now she's gone. I run to Tess's house where I pound on the door.

"Hi. Mrs. Sullivan." I pant between each word. "Is. Tess. Here?" I continue to pant.

"Hi, Edie. Come on in. Tess wasn't kidding when she said you love to run. Even at dinnertime, huh?" She laughs like running is a silly idea. "Tess?" she calls. "Edie is here."

I hear Tess yell that she's coming.

"She'll be right here, hon." Tess's mom smiles and disappears into the house. A second later, Tess opens the door and steps onto the porch. I already feel a tiny bit better, seeing my friend.

"You look like shit. What's going on?" Tess asks.

I stand up and wince. I have a stitch in my side. "GG disappeared. I think the Luctus spirit took her."

"What!? Should I text Rhia?"

I nod. "Forgot my phone."

Tess's thumbs fly across the face of her phone. "Meet at Cosmic Flow?"

I clutch my head in my hands. "I guess?"

"Where else?"

"Cabin?"

"Cosmic Flow first."

Tess sticks her head back in the house to tell her mom that we are going out. Then I'm in her Jeep. Everything blurs by me.

Rhia is already at the shop when we arrive. I tell both of them what happened on the boat and that my grandmother is to blame. It was never my mother. Then I tell them what GG said before she disappeared.

"She said she remembered everything, that she knew where *they* were, whatever that means. And we need the power of three."

"Miss Geraldine—cryptic to the end," Rhia muses. "What could she mean? What are we supposed to do?"

"We know that the acorn has Edie's mom's blood in it," Tess says. "And Edie's element is fire."

"And we've spent the summer learning spells from her mother's journal," Rhia says.

"So Mom's blood plus my fire plus some unidentified spell and what? We either fix this or burn down the world?"

"We need to figure out which spell," Tess says.

"And what did Miss Geraldine mean when she said the power of three? Does she mean us three?"

I walk in circles, tugging my hair back from my face. "I don't know, and we don't have time to figure it out." I stop my pacing when I remember what GG tossed at me on my way out. "Wait, she also gave me this." I pull the silver ball from my pocket.

Rhia almost smiles. "Oh! I read about these."

"What is it?" I ask.

"A spell ball." Rhia clicks the clasp and opens the ball, showing us the contents. "This must be what we need." She pulls something from the ball and holds it up.

"Ew!" Tess says, stepping back.

"That's GG's hair!" I say.

"Perfect. Let's find out where she is," Rhia says.

We use a strand of hair from the spell ball, crystals from the shop, and the chain from my acorn necklace to cast the finding spell from Mom's journal.

All those weeks ago, I saw this spell as the only useful one in the book. I hadn't realized then that most of Mom's spells had bigger uses. I hadn't imagined that a silly acne hiding spell could end up revealing a hidden map. I hadn't expected the keep dry charm to give me protection from drowning. And I definitely hadn't expected to use this one to find my grandmother who has been taken by shadows. My hands shake as I hold the chain above the map. My voice shakes, too. I can't say the words.

"Will you all say it with me?" I ask.

They both nod and we begin, our three voices joining together for this one purpose. "With this crystal and the items I bind, reveal to me the one I wish to find."

The crystal swings for a moment before it stops dead and pulls itself down to a spot on the map.

We're quiet as we drive. No music, no chatter. Apparently, my grandmother is at the beech, but I don't know why or what I'm supposed to do when we arrive. Tess makes the bone-jarring drive across the field as the sun crashes into the horizon, leaving a blaze of color in its wake.

"There she is!"

GG is bent over at the base of the burn-scarred tree. I jump out of the Jeep and run to her. She's holding her athame above the dirt where a large root forks into two.

"What are you doing?"

"Seeking."

"Seeking what, GG?" I kneel beside her. "What are you looking for?"

"The ashes. I buried them here."

"What ashes?"

GG turns a determined face to me. "My dead husband's ashes."

The same green fire that took the beech tree sparks then, along the exposed roots just next to my grandmother. She doesn't even jump. "I must be very close." She drops the athame and holds her palms out to direct the earth. The flames grow bigger, their crackling loud.

"What can I do?" I call to her.

"Keep it at bay," she yells back.

The fire spikes waist-high flames, fed by our own power and this liminal space. Last time, I tried to pull it from the beech and I nearly died. This time I know better. I'll fight fire with fire. I flick my hands and the sparks answer immediately. I imagine flames and they come. Holding my palms outward, I press my fire against the green flames. My arms ache from the effort. GG moves her hands as though weaving. The earth obeys, rising from the hole and landing in a pile. Tess has brought a shovel from her Jeep but tosses it aside when she sees GG in action.

I continue to press back the cold, green flame of the Luctus spirit. I lean into the fire as if I'm pushing against a heavy wind. The fires crackle and spit at one another, sparks flying. The green fire continues to rage, but my fire banks it, preventing it from reaching my grandmother.

"I've got them!" GG shouts.

"What do I do now?"

GG hands the dirt-covered box to Rhia. "On my count, step away."

I nod my understanding.

"One," GG yells as she sweeps her arms up. The earth follows her movements, rising from the ground. "Two." She swirls her arms and the dirt sweeps itself into a wall. "Three!"

I leap away and GG throws her arms forward. The wall of earth smothers the green flames as well as my orange ones.

My chest heaves with effort. GG braces her hands on her knees, breathing heavy. "I'm getting too old for this," she says. But then she stands up, brushes herself off, and then says to all three of us, as though we're planning a simple outing to the store. "Ready, girls?"

As we bump our way across the field and then up to Shaw Road, GG explains that when we performed the bind-breaking ritual in the cabin, we released the final bind on the Luctus spirit. When I did my spell, it brought GG's memories back. But it also called the spirit to our boat. She shares all that rushed back to her. The ashes were the final element needed. Along with Mom's blood and hair from me and GG, we could call on the power of our line and finally dispel this spirit.

The old oak tree comes into sight. Tess stops the Jeep at the rock cairn. The evening sky darkens with an oncoming storm; the trees sway as a fierce wind picks up. GG and I get out of the Jeep.

"I'll go ahead to give you time to perform the ritual to forge the acorn into a vessel for our magic. Remember that you will need your mother's blood, your fire, and my husband's ashes," GG says. "Where are they?"

"Rhia has them." I raise my voice to be heard over the unnatural wind rushing around us. My grandmother's hair ripples around her head. She looks every inch the witch that she is.

"After the ritual, when you come into the workshop, create a circle of protection right away." She gestures around herself to show me what she means.

"With salt?" I ask. "Like Rhia does?"

"With fire. Like only *you* can do."

"I've never done that before."

GG steps closer to me. "You just held back a magical blaze with your fire and you'd never done that before, right?" I nod. "Good. Now, whatever you do, keep the acorn close. If the Luctus spirit gets ahold of the acorn, the spirit will have a way into our ancestral line. Do you understand?"

"I understand." My stomach is in knots imagining what the spirit could do with access to the Mitchell line, what sort of havoc and misery it could create. And I'm supposed to be the witch to stop it.

"When you've completed your circle of fire, start the incantation."

I nod, but GG must see how terrified I am. She grabs me in a tight hug. "You can do this! You're a Mitchell." She lets me go. "And you will not be alone. Not for long anyway."

GG whispers a few words, flicks her hand and the chain across the drive falls to the ground. She disappears down the driveway. I poke my head back into the Jeep.

"I love you guys," Tess says, practically in tears.

"We love you, too!" Rhia says. "It'll be okay."

"You're just saying that," Tess says. "But I like it. Could you keep saying it?"

"It'll be okay," Rhia repeats calmly.

I speak up. "Look, I couldn't have done any of this without both of you. I just need to—"

"Nope." Tess holds up her hand. "No dramatic monologues in case we all die. Listen to Rhia. It's going to be fine. You and I will be slinging ice cream cones in three days tops. And Rhia will be back to selling candles to wannabe witches. You'll go back to Baltimore and Rhia and I will come visit you."

"Talk about dramatic monologues," I say. "All I wanted to say is that I need to harvest some bark from the oak tree. But— you'll visit me?"

"Yes, dork!" She wiggles her hands at me. "Go harvest bark."

Rhia gets out and joins me. "Are you sure about this?" she asks.

"Yeah, we need this bark."

Rhia crosses her hands over her chest. "You know that's not what I mean."

I kneel at the base of the tree. "Will you do this with me?" I ask, to avoid her bigger question.

Rhia kneels next to me. Spontaneously, I catch hold of her hand in mine. The feel of her fingers entwined in mine, her palm against mine, grounds me the same way as Mom's words: *What can you see? What can you hear? What can you smell? What can you touch?* We each place our free hand on the bark of the tree. Together we say the words of request and gratitude. The words carry a heavy weight this time—beyond this simple action. This time after I take the bark, I don't have one of GG's salves to place on the wound I've created. So, I simply whisper my thanks and we both get up. The wind whips leaves from trees and sends small branches flying.

"We're doing this, then," Rhia says.

I face her, hair blowing across my face. "I don't have a choice. You know that."

"Sorry. I guess reality is setting in. It's just—" Rhia shakes her head.

"What are you trying to say?" I ask, stepping closer.

"You've said all along that when we finish this"—Rhia gestures down the drive—"that life could go back to how it was." Rhia looks away and then back again. "What if I don't want to go back to how I was, sitting behind a counter?" She clears her throat. "Not seeing you every day."

I feel a warm glow extend from my chest outward. It's not magic. It's hope. The headlights of Tess's Jeep give off a feeble light illuminating one side of Rhia as she stands before me. When this summer started, I saw my life and the people in it in simple, one-sided terms. But I've learned that we can have many sides. We can be more than one thing. I step closer. I place my palms on Rhia's cheeks and look into her eyes.

"Everything has changed. *I* have changed. I don't want to be how I was before either—fearful of my magic, hiding the real me." I drop my hands to her shoulders. "But we can talk about what comes next after we kick this spirit's ass."

"*If* we make it out," Rhia says, sighing.

I give her shoulders a squeeze. "We will. You told Tess it will be okay. It will be."

She reaches up and catches my hand in hers. She squeezes and nods at me.

"Ready?" I say.

"Ready," Rhia says.

At that moment a crack of lightning spears down, hitting

the massive oak. The noise is like nothing I've heard before. The great tree screams as it splits and falls, only barely missing us, and landing across the entrance to the driveway.

"Not an omen. Not an omen. Not an omen," Tess says as we pull all of our supplies from the Jeep and start to walk down the drive.

The growth that had nearly obscured this path weeks ago now hangs brown and dead. When we make it to the property, the vines covering the cabin have blackened. The mushrooms that had bloomed on the front steps are rotting and oozing. The moss on the roof has also shrunk and shriveled.

We turn our attention to the workshop, which has become a monstrous thing. Whatever we unbound has fully taken over the space. Blackened exterior walls pulse and ooze rhythmically. The windows rattle like sick lungs. The door creaks open and a gust of dank air spews out.

"Let's get started," I say.

Rhia creates a circle of salt on the ground. Using supplies that we grabbed from Cosmic Flow, I pour GG's ingredients into the bowl. There is angelica root and rose oil and a bit of quartz. The soil that GG provided, as well as several strands of her hair. I add the oak bark and some of my own hair. We light incense and smudge it around us and over the bowl.

I open the box and sprinkle some of my grandfather's ashes

in. I take off my necklace, unscrew the cap of the acorn, and drip the last of my mother's blood over the items. Then, with care, I lay the silver acorn on top of everything else.

Elements of me, my mother, my grandmother, and my grandfather rest together in this bowl. I'm overcome with the enormity of the moment.

Pulling in a steadying breath, I remind myself that I can do this because I did it already. But at the beech I didn't need to be precise like I do here. "Here goes nothing." I give Tess and Rhia a wobbly smile and they nod at me to go ahead. At the flick my fingers, sparks appear. I breathe in. And out. I focus the sparks into a small ball of light and heat and send it into the bowl. The contents ignite in a bright and sudden blast of fire.

We grab hands and begin to chant. "With the power of three, we beseech thee."

The words feel stilted in my mouth, like I'm repeating someone else's lines. When we finish, nothing happens. The trees bend and sway at alarming angles. I'm not convinced that this circle of protection will helps us if one of them falls like the oak just did. We try again.

"With the power of three, we beseech thee."

And again. "With the power of three, we beseech thee."

I drop the girls' hands and hiss out my frustration. If I'm going to embrace who I am, what I am, I should do it on my terms. I can't pretend that I'm a typical human because I'm not. And I can't pretend to be like GG or Rhia either. I need to be me, wholly and completely me. And in this moment, that means not saying some old-fashioned words that don't feel right. I grab my friends' hands again. Rhia and Tess continue the chant while I speak from the heart.

"Mom, things are pretty bad over here. I really need you right now. And bring everyone with you. Bring all the witches that have come before us and have mastered their arts. The witches who were celebrated and revered. The witches who were judged and scorned. The witches who hid among typical people and the witches who let their freak flags fly. Bring them all, Mom. We need to end this."

The fire leaps high before it suddenly extinguishes, leaving behind only the acorn, burnished and shining with a white gold light.

"It worked!" I say to Rhia and Tess.

I pick up the acorn and spoon the ashes from the ritual into the cavity, sealing it. I hold it reverently in my cupped palms.

"Sisters, mothers, and daughters—I know who I am now. I am a Mitchell woman. I am one of you." The golden light brightens. "I call on you now in our time of need."

The light shoots out from the spaces between my fingers, sending rays all around us. I am infused with love. I can't help the smile that comes to my face. Tess and Rhia smile, too. I pull the necklace over my head and feel the blazing heat of the acorn against my chest, touching it with my fingertips.

"As it is above, so below," I whisper.

Then I turn to face the workshop and whatever waits for me inside.

Chapter Thirty-Eight

EDIE

"I'm coming in," I say.

The workshop is silent, as though it's waiting. The wheezing and pulsing have quieted. Dark clouds squat overhead. I walk a few steps and stop to turn my ear toward the woods, which are also silent. The trees have stopped their frightening dance. The absence of the incessant buzz of the summer insects is chilling.

I force myself to step closer.

"You've held my family hostage long enough. You're no longer welcome here."

The building remains silent.

"Don't say you weren't warned."

The doorknob turns and I push my way in. The altar to my grandfather pulses like a heartbeat. The items that had been placed on it are slowly being consumed. Part of the pocketknife protrudes from a side of the table. Photos are curled and peeling. An oily substance, thick and black, slowly drips down the sides of the altar. Something that looks like human hair grows from one end. Something like an eye is lodged deep in the middle of the thing. One bit of bright white that might be bone protrudes from the bottom.

I hope that's not GG. I swallow back bile.

I stand in the center of the room. "This is ending now," I say. I flick my fingers to create a circle of protection made of my fire.

The pulsing quickens and a rancid smell fills the room.

The acorn glows.

The pulsing becomes more rapid like a heartbeat inside my head.

I am a quarter way around the circle and the acorn glows more brightly.

Blackness lurches toward me from the altar. Shadows coalesce, forming a misshapen figure.

I am halfway around the circle. I close my eyes. I don't know if I'm more terrified to see or not to see.

I feel a cold, wet grip on my ankle. I begin to shake, fear taking root in my body.

I place one hand around the acorn, keeping it safe. With the other, I try to finish my circle.

Another wet grip on my wrist. The cold invisible fingers invite fear to grow. I try to push through the fear, believing in my family line, believing in myself, but I'm already panting with the effort.

Something presses on my back, pushing me down. I tighten

my grip on the acorn and curve my body into a ball. I try again. I'm nearly finished. A quarter of a circle to go.

I feel hands on either side of my face. I start to weep.

Fingers reach around my neck. Long fingers with sharp nails. I shake my head, trying to get rid of the thing. I know I can't let go of the acorn. The fingers travel over my ears, my eyes. They cover my nose.

"Please, please, please," I whimper. "Mom, please."

I keep the acorn tight in one palm. It's not working. I don't have protection. The spirit has me. Clawed hands cover my mouth. I can't breathe. I feel as though I've been plunged beneath black water. I'm thrashing my legs and whipping my body, just trying to get oxygen to my lungs. I don't let go of the acorn. I keep thrashing.

How could I believe that a tiny silver piece of jewelry was the answer to all of this? How could I believe that *I* could be the answer?

A cold explosion of white, green, and blue light blinds me.

My body is thrown up, up, up. I gasp for air. I flick my free hand to call up the fire and I shout words. I'm not sure it rhymes, but I shout the words in desperation. And suddenly, there is an answering blast of yellows, oranges, and reds. Then everything goes dark.

* * *

The world is burning. The acrid smell of smoke pulls me to consciousness. Hungry flames consume everything around me. The workshop is engulfed in a green inferno. I am in the center of it, not burning, encircled in my yellow flames. The words worked. I can breathe again.

Flames lick up the walls of the workshop, catching on the shelves, melting plastic containers of screws and nails. Popping glass jars of nuts and bolts. The windows ripple in the heat for a moment before they explode outward in a storm of flying glass. I raise my arm to shield my eyes and turn toward the door, but it is a wall of flame as well.

Bits of the altar crackle and crunch, bitten by flames. The blackness melts, pouring down the sides and pooling on the floor. The altar cracks down the middle and crashes to the ground. A great rustling reaches my ears through the sparking and hissing of the fire.

A concentrated mass of oily feathers swirls before me. They whip like a tornado, rising up from the dripping liquid until a loose shape of an enormous raven begins to emerge. Taller than I am, it's covered in feathers the deep shade of the night sky. Its great wings give way to long, sharp claws. Black eyes peer at me. The menacing beak yawns open and screeches. I want to press my hands over my ears, but I still hold the acorn protected in one hand. I'm supposed to start the incantation, but the words have left my mind.

I curl into a ball, making myself as small as possible and squish my eyes shut. I don't know what else to do. The piercing screech stops, prompting me to open my eyes. There before me stands my mother. She smiles at me. I frown in confusion.

"Come," she says. "We don't have much time."

I peer at her from my crouched position. "It's not you. I fell for this before. With Rhia."

Shame drips over me when I recall nearly falling for the Luctus spirit's play on my desires that night in the woods.

"I heard your call," my mother says. "You need to come with me."

I have seen my mother every day since the first time her ghost appeared almost a year ago—until she stopped showing up after the beech—but the last time I heard her voice was the day that she left for her bike ride. Hearing her now carves a new mark in my heart.

She holds her hand out.

"I've missed you," I say, and the words are choked in tears. "Mom, I've missed you so much." My sense of loss is a storm obliterating everything in its path. I forget about the incantation. I've missed teas and talks. I've missed kisses on my forehead and her palm on my cheek. I've missed adventures. I have missed everything. I want my mother. My hand drops from protecting the acorn. I reach out my hand.

"Let's get you out of here."

I push myself to standing.

Her eyes plead me to come. She sounds like my mother and looks like her. Could this be the answer to my call?

I step forward, holding my hand out.

The acorn burns against my chest. I stop. I snatch my hand back.

"Come! We are running out of time."

I look down at the circle of golden fire surrounding me.

"If you are my mother, come into the circle. We're protected here."

"I'm not coming into that circle." She sounds angry. "We need to leave!"

I turn my palms to face her. "I miss my mother, but *you* are not *her*!" I press both palms forward as though I'm pushing this thing out the window.

> "Truth hidden I wish to see,
> Reveal yourself now to me."

My not-mother flickers and seizes until it dissolves into a thousand feathers that once again swirl themselves into the raven thing.

"You've been learning." The flames die down and the room grows as cold as an underground cavern.

"Yes, I have."

"And yet, you're no matter to me."

"Underestimate me," I say. "That'll be fun."

"I see only one young witch before me. One is not enough. Two witches of your line isn't even enough." The ancient voice scrapes at the inside of my mind, taunting.

"But my mother left something of herself behind." I hold up the necklace. The acorn hangs from its chain, not looking very exceptional at all. And yet.

The voice screeches and the thing that was never my mother lurches toward me as though to snatch the acorn, but she stops short of the circle. The thing is so close that I can smell its putrid breath.

Everything in my body wants to run, but I stay in the circle.

"Give me back my grandmother. Give us back our life."

"Or what, child? You are nothing. Your family is nothing. I have seen your kind come and go for thousands of years. I remain. I was here when man fought one another on battlefields and when people like you were burned. I'll be here when you and yours are dead and buried. You are a few weak humans who play at magic. Nothing more."

"We. Don't. Play." I yank the acorn from its chain and squeeze it in my palm, encouraging it to do what an acorn is meant to do.

"Sisters, mothers, daughters, in the name of Mitchell magic, I call on you now."

Golden light shines forth through my clenched hand.

"Sisters, mothers, daughters, in the name of Mitchell magic, I call on you now."

The acorn cracks open. Roots slide down between my fingers and branches sprout upward. I feel a warm hand on my shoulder. I turn to look.

"Mom!" I say. "Is it really you?"

"It's me, Edie." Her smile glows like the magic I've been working on all summer.

More of our line extends outward from Mom. The roots from the acorn reach down through the burned floor seeking the soil beneath. The branches soar into the sky, decimating the roof in its path. My ancestors with hands upon shoulders ripple out before me until a circle is formed. Leaves bud and unfurl in dizzying speed until an oak tree stands in the middle of this burned-out workshop. The Luctus spirit shrinks back, squealing.

"It worked!" I call to Mom's ghost, who nods knowingly to me.

A low hum starts somewhere in the circle and I take it up. All the while the tree continues to grow.

In a rustle of feathers, the raven thing flies toward the edge of the circle only to be repelled back to the center. It shrieks, leaning away from the tree and finding itself trapped once more. It rushes to another part seeking its way out. The body of the spirit ripples and bulges. It tears open, the thousands of feathers scattering to reveal GG on the ground.

"GG?" I call to her. I can't tell if she's alive. *Oh gods, please.*

One of her hands moves.

"GG!"

Slowly she opens her eyes. Finally, she pushes up to her hands and knees. The spirit whirls around her until she's down again.

"Mom, we need to help her." I start to step forward.

"You must stay in the circle, Edie. You're the one making this possible." Mom gestures to the oak and light and the ancestors. "It's your power that gives your grandmother a chance."

"And your acorn."

"Each of us was needed. Three generations. Three phases of magic. Now your grandmother needs to fight this part of the battle herself."

I do as my mother says. I hold on, the acorn still clutched in my hand and still spilling its glorious light across our circle. GG is upright now. She moves toward the tree as though she's pushing against a gale force wind. The spirit is now half woman, half raven. It stands on human legs, but its arms extend into vast wings. Midnight feathers flow over its human head and down its back. Below yellow eyes, its nose extends in a sharp beak.

"You've stolen so much from me," GG says to the Luctus spirit. "And now it's time that you go."

"I was called by your mourning," it says. "I stayed because you invited me."

"You lied to me."

"I gave you what I told you I would give you," the spirit says. "You wanted to see your husband again and I granted you that."

"All you granted me was pain and regret. You used me so that you could corrupt my magic and steal my memories." GG's body vibrates with anger.

"And you trapped me in this awful place."

"I was willing to use my magic to keep you contained. Until you harmed my granddaughter. That is a line that you should not have crossed." GG presses her palms against the tree. "Sisters, mothers, daughters, help me banish the dark."

GG begins to speak the lullaby spell and we all join in.

"Darkness, darkness, not welcome here,

Return from whsplease be near,

Sunlight, starlight, please be near,

I call you in my name."

The ancestors repeat the words over and over.

GG yells, "Let this oak, full of strength, envelop this spirit."

The ancestors cry out in approval.

The Luctus spirit's keening is so sharp and loud that it could split my eardrums. But the ancestors' circle-chanting neutralizes the unnatural sound.

"That which has been called in mourning must now depart in the face of hope and love," GG calls out.

The spirit's image flickers, moving through all the masks she's worn. My grandfather, my mother, my friends, people I don't recognize. Wind whips through the room. Feathers fly around us. Items that hadn't gone up in flame are tossed around. I duck away from a flying hammer. A broken chair and some planters rip through my ghostly ancestors who continue to chant. The feathers fly in a faster, more furious circle until they're swept into the tree's trunk like a swarm of bees into a hive. GG closes the hole with quick movements of her hands along with murmured chants.

For a moment, the spirit's visage appears in the trunk of the tree, frozen in anguish. Then that too melts into the bark.

The flames have flickered out. The altar is ash. The black viscous liquid is gone. Only the mess remains.

"Edie, are you okay?" GG asks. Her long hair is a matted mess. Her coat is ripped in the shoulder and she has a gash on her forehead. But she still inspects me, squeezing my arms and touching my face as if to make sure that all of my parts are where they're supposed to be.

I nod. "What about you?"

"This?" She gestures to herself. "Nothing a good salve can't fix."

GG turns and cups my mother's cheeks in her palms. "I'm so sorry, my daughter. This is *not* the magic I taught you."

"I know, Mama," my mother says. "And I'm sorry that I didn't tell you that I knew or about the acorn and the magic I'd infused in it and in the journal. There was no time."

"It pains me to know that you didn't feel that you could trust me. But I understand why. I couldn't banish it on my own." GG turns to me. "But your smart daughter figured it out."

They both smile at me.

"Not by myself," I say.

GG nods. "We need people. When Edie said she knew the acorn was instrumental, I had an inkling of what you'd done, and I knew I needed to contribute as well."

I hesitate before I speak again. "Mom, it turns out that sharing our magic with the people we love doesn't need to end in pain."

"I'm so happy your experience has been different than my own." Mom's eyes are full of love.

There is one question related to all of this that I haven't been able to figure out. "When did you make the map?" I ask Mom. "I found it in your bedroom in the cabin. But you haven't been back here for years, right?"

GG speaks up. "I made the map when I realized that the spirit had tricked me and was stealing my memories. I'd already forgotten where I'd buried Ed's ashes by that point."

"I found the paper when we were cleaning up to leave the cabin and move onto the boat for good," Mom says. "I sensed powerful magic attached to it and I hid it in my room."

"How did you know I'd find it?" I ask.

My mother shakes her head and shrugs. "I didn't."

I'm struck by how much of this whole experience hinged

on chance. If I hadn't moved the rock on the first day, I would not have disrupted the protections and gotten infected by the magic. But I also would not have been motivated to learn our family's craft. I wouldn't have gotten close to Rhia and Tess by searching for hidden items and I wouldn't have helped my grandmother free all of us from the curse of the Luctus spirit.

GG pats my shoulder. "Fire trucks are sure to be here soon, Edie."

I look around at what the workshop has become. "How do we explain this tree that just grew in the middle of a workshop that was on fire?"

"We don't. People will create a story that makes sense to them," GG says. "I'll give you a moment." She leaves through the burned-out doorway and I can't help but notice a limp.

I turn to face my mother. "I need Tea and a Talk."

There is so much to say, so much to tell her about what has happened in the year since she died suddenly. But we don't have time to cover all those moments, the emptiness and the confusion and the wishing that she was still alive.

"It would be wonderful if we could do that, wouldn't it?"

I nod, trying to keep the tears from flowing.

"I'm sorry that I never told you who your father was," she says.

"I wish you had, but I sort of understand now that I read your journal. And Mom, I'm sorry, too."

"For what?"

"That I couldn't accept who I am."

"I know, sweetie."

"I thought I wanted to be normal, but it was actually fear."

Mom wraps her arms around me. "Don't be sorry. Just embrace who you are now." For one moment, I am enveloped in my mother's hug, feeling her body against mine. Her curls tickle my face and her smell is just as I remembered. Her real smell—fresh lemons and mint from the garden—not the honeysuckle that reminds me of her death. She lets go and steps back to look at me.

"I'm sorry that I can't be here to walk your path with you. But you're doing well on your own. I'm so proud." She kisses my forehead and I begin to weep.

"I wish you could stay," I say.

I'm only now learning to accept who and what I am, and Mom could teach me so much more. But I'd seen what happened when GG tried to change the natural order of things. Our magic is about balance and order, about using nature in ways that help and heal. Upsetting that balance is not what I'm meant to do. That sort of magic takes much more than it gives.

"But I know you can't. Not in this form."

I open my palm and the ancestors begin to disappear one by one. My mother is last. She stays, moving from solid to transparent, a moment longer than the rest.

"I will always love you," I say to her.

"And I you," she says.

She smiles her big smile. Then she flickers out and she's gone. When I look at my palm, there is only ash. This tiny acorn did its monumental job. It held Mom's blood until we needed it and it served as a vessel to call our ancestors and to trap the Luctus spirit. But I'm sad not to have the silver acorn resting against my collarbone anymore, giving me comfort in my time of need. At the same time, I know my mother is with me. I close my palm around the ashes and leave this burned-out workshop.

Chapter Thirty-Nine

EDIE

I blink against the morning light. Were we in there all night? It felt like minutes. Tess and Rhia rush toward me. I freeze, the events of the night washing over me as adrenaline leaves my system. I tell myself that I am in the real world, but my brain is not so certain. Tess and Rhia fold me into a hug, squishing me and talking over one another. Rhia's hair tickles my face and I breathe in deeply hers and Tess's human girl smells.

"We're so relieved!"

"Was it awful?"

"Are you hungry?"

"Do you need to pee?"

This last one makes me laugh out loud. If I hadn't been certain that I was in the real world, I am now. "Just shaken up. I need to be with GG right now. Can I call you both later?"

"Of course."

They each give me one more squeeze and let go.

GG sits on the steps of the cabin. The fungi beside her are returning to life and new vines curl around the handrail. She looks small, but still mighty, and I curl myself up beside her.

"Let me see your arm," GG says.

I hold out my left arm and pull the collar of my shirt back for her inspection. I tilt my head at an awkward angle to try to see as well. The black web of veins that had been steadily creeping up my arm for these last weeks, that had spread across my collarbone just days ago, is receding. Even as we look, the lines have disappeared down to my biceps. She nods and makes a grunt of approval. Then she squeezes me tight to her body.

"You've done it, Edie. You're going to be okay."

I sink into the comfort of my grandmother's body, the softness and the angles. I can't quite believe that our ordeal is over. It'll probably take a while before I'm certain that the infection is gone, that I won't be pulled into a shadow world. My stomach growls, bringing me back to the simple needs of my human body.

"I'm starving," I say. "Want to go home?"

GG leans away to gives me an odd look.

"What?" I ask.

"That is the first time that you've referred to the boat as home."

I offer my hand to my grandmother. "Let's go home, GG."

After we've showered and eaten and GG has made a pot of her most refreshing tea, we both agree it's time for a real talk. We sit at the small dinette.

"I'm still upset that you let me think that it was Mom who

invoked that spirit for all this time," I say as I stir honey into my tea.

GG sips from her cup. "I understand. It may take time for you to fully build your trust in me again."

"Why did you do it, though?" I set my spoon on the table. "Invoke that spirit."

GG lets out a puff of air. "After my husband died, I was so angry."

"Angry?" This takes me by surprise.

"Yes!" She sets her teacup down. "We were supposed to grow old together. He was the love of my life and then he was stolen from me. I was so angry. I know that sounds illogical, but grief is not logical." Her fists are balled on the table.

"I get that." I add a drop of milk and watch it swirl through my cup like smoke.

"I couldn't speak. Nothing but feathers and ash came from my mouth."

"I know," I say. "From Mom's journal." I reach out to place my hand on hers.

"Maura thought it was a choice. Me not speaking after Ed died. But it wasn't. I knew your mother needed me. She'd lost her father. But my grief had a stranglehold on me. I did that spell out of desperation. I thought that living in the memories would allow me to speak again, to say Ed's name without the bitter taste of death in my mouth. But you can't invoke dark magic without paying a price. I'm relieved that it's over now. I'd been working in service to that dark magic for long enough. And it never did what was promised in the first place, not really."

"What do you mean?" I look up at my grandmother.

"I thought that I could use magic as a way around the pain of my grief and then Ed's ghost would appear like all our ghosts have always appeared. But when I spent time with those memories, it only made me more bitter over what I'd lost. Until you."

"I don't understand."

"It was a hot August day when Maura came to me. I remember that it was the first day in a long while that the sun had come out. Maura needed to tell me something important, but she was having trouble getting the words out. I was no comfort because I couldn't speak."

GG looks out over the water, no doubt remembering a moment from years ago.

"Then Maura said that she was pregnant and that she wanted to have the baby. My immediate response was joy, an emotion I hadn't felt since before my husband had become so ill. Realization dawned on me. Grief is a red silk ribbon tied to love. The pain seemed insurmountable, but I would not have experienced grief if I hadn't loved your grandfather so deeply. And that love led to your mother and to you.

"That happy news from your mother showed me that eventually love would overcome grief. For the first time since my husband had died, I spoke. I hugged her and I told her how thrilled I was and that I just knew that her father, my beloved Edward, would have been overjoyed, too. It was no accident that at that very moment your grandfather appeared. He's been with us ever since. You see? *You* were the miracle that kept our Edward close."

I frown. "But Mom didn't want a baby. She never planned on me."

"Not wanting and not planning are different things. Your mother may not have planned on having you when she did, but she surely wanted you."

I put my head in my hands. "Her dad had died, and the father of her baby had rejected her. I was a reminder of the worst time in her life."

"No, Edie. You weren't. You were a reminder to *live* life. To your mother and to me."

Chapter Forty

EDIE

"You're sure." Rhia says this as a fact, not a question because she's already asked me like twenty-seven times. I'm sitting on the bench seat of the breakfast nook on the boat. Rhia has set her bag on the table and is waiting for my go-ahead.

"Why do you doubt that I'm sure?" I ask.

"Because you're so straight-edge. And tattoos are permanent."

"Permanent is exactly what I need," I say. "And I'm a witch. How straight-edge can I be?"

"You're the most straight-edge witch I've ever met."

"Yeah, out of two. Not exactly a large sample size."

"And I would not describe your gran as straight-edge. Didn't you say she danced naked under the moonlight?"

"No, I said I *wondered* if she did." I laugh. "But I'm ready and I'm certain about this tattoo. I want to own the part of my body that the spirit infected. And I want something that will be with me always."

I leave it at that. She was there; she knows what I mean.

"Okay," Rhia says. "Are you comfortable? Because we are going to be here awhile."

I wiggle my butt in the seat and set my arm on the table, supported by a cushion. "Yup. I'm good. We have peppermint iced tea and a bag of Gummis, what else could we need?"

Rhia smiles. "We'll get started then."

"And you don't mind using my ink?" I ask.

I look at Rhia beside me, her neck bent in concentration as she sets out her supplies. We've come so far from the first night we met when I ran out of the barn. It hasn't even been two full months and we've been through more than some people go through in years. Rhia had caught my eye on that first night because she seemed so carefree, so fully herself, and I wanted to be near that. And I still do, but there's so much more to Rhia, too.

Rhia shrugs. "It's a little unusual, but if that's what you want, that's what I'll do."

I pull the ink from my bag and set it on the table next to Rhia's supplies. She probably wouldn't think twice about the protective charms that GG and I wove into the ink, but I wasn't sure how she'd react to knowing that the ink was also infused with the ashes of our dead relatives.

"Is she here?" Rhia asks as she sets out her tools.

I know who she means. "She is." Mom hovers nearby, smiling at me. I smile back. I'll never be able to touch her or talk to her again like I was able to two nights ago when we banished the Luctus spirit. But seeing her is enough now.

Rhia takes my arm with a gentle touch. She turns it so that the pale, vulnerable part of my inner forearm faces. The black veins receded after the spirit was trapped, but the arm is still a little cold sometimes. GG says that it'll be back to normal eventually, but I wonder.

Rhia soaks a cotton ball in alcohol and rubs the area in circular motions. I watch as she sterilizes the needle and wraps it in thread. She dips the needle into my ink.

"Ready?" Rhia asks.

"I'm ready," I say. "And Rhee?"

She looks up, needle poised, brown eyes catching mine.

"Thank you," I say.

She shakes her head, her curls shaking with her. "No, thank *you*."

"For what?"

"For trusting me."

"I do."

"I won't hurt you, Edie. At least I'll try my best not to."

"I'll try not to hurt you, either."

We hold one another's gaze, both of us recognizing that we aren't talking about the tattoo, but something much bigger.

Rhia makes the first poke and I relax into my chair. There's nothing that Rhia can do to me with a needle that's worse than what I've been through already. We sit like that for a long time, while the boat gently rocks and the sun moves through the prisms, glancing through all the witch balls draped in the windows. The sun is starting to angle through the opposite windows by the time Rhia stands up.

"It's complete."

I look at the image of an acorn on my inner forearm, a reminder of my own power and courage. A reminder of my mother.

"Oh my gods, Rhia, it's beautiful," I say. "You're the best."

Rhia smiles as she collects her supplies. "Really? You're happy with it?"

"I can't stop looking at it! You are so talented."

"You'll need to stop looking at it for a couple hours at least," Rhia says as she spreads antibacterial ointment on it and then covers it with a bandage. Her hands are gentle.

Rhia strips the gloves from her hands and arches her back in a stretch. My eyes follow the long line of her neck to the deep vee of her T-shirt and the curves hidden beneath. She catches me staring and I don't bother to hide it the way that I would have a few weeks ago. Life is too short. I stand and realize that I'm stiff, too.

"Let's go for a walk," I say.

I help Rhia finish gathering her tools and we clean the area before we leave. As we walk off the boat, Rhia catches my hand in hers. She squeezes and I squeeze back.

"Is this okay?" she asks.

"More than okay."

We head to the bike trail. The hot August sun slants through the trees and wood chips soften our footsteps. When we reach the footbridge, Rhia turns to me, pushing a stray strand of hair from my face. The afternoon sun is warm on my shoulders. My arm stings from the work Rhia did over the past few hours, but I don't regret a moment of it. Rhia's fingers are gentle on my cheek. I can't wait any longer.

"Would it be okay if I kissed you?" I ask.

"I was going to ask you the same thing." Rhia's smile is soft. "Is she here?" Rhia says, looking around, as if she'd be able to see Mom. "I'd feel weird if she saw us kissing."

"She's not here right now," I say. "But . . ."

"But what?" Rhia asks, the question wrinkling her brow.

I look down, embarrassed. "I've never kissed anyone before."

Her laugh is full and warm, not at all judgmental, and I can feel my fear melt away. "Let's fix that," Rhia says. She leans in without any hesitation and presses her lips to mine. Her lips are so soft, then her tongue coaxes my lips open and I can't believe I've been missing out on this for so long. Rhia wraps her arms around my waist, pulling me to her so that her full breasts press against mine. I run my hands up her back. We bump noses and giggle and we continue kissing. I slide my thigh between her legs. I am tingling all over and I know it has nothing to do with my magic and everything to do with my skin against Rhia's, my lips on hers, our arms wrapped around one another as if there were no one else in the world.

But the sounds around us intrude, reminding me that we are entangled in a way that maybe isn't entirely suitable for a public park. We pull apart.

My eyes drink her in. "Man, that Wheel of Fortune card wasn't wrong."

"What do you mean?" She twines her hand in mine as we begin to walk again.

"When we first met, you gave me that card."

"I remember."

"You said it suggested that there were forces coming at me out of my control and they could be good or bad." I stop and turn toward her. "You were the *good* forces out of my control."

Rhia's grin is a little bit wicked. "Maybe not *all* good." She leans over to kiss my neck and the sensations that run through my body make me wish that we were somewhere very private.

Both of our phones ping at the same time and we start to laugh.

"Leave it to Tess to kill the moment," Rhia says.

Over what's become a weekly tradition of chicken wings, pizza, and hush puppies, we update one another.

"How are you doing?" I ask Tess.

She makes an exaggerated sad face. "I went with Jorge to see him off for boot camp. We're going to try to stay together, but I don't know. Long distance seems hard."

"Have another hush puppy," Rhia says. "You need it."

"Thanks to running with Edie all summer, my metabolism could burn up *all* these hush puppies." She pops one in her mouth.

"You could join us, Rhee," I say, picking up a chicken wing. "Tomorrow, eight sharp. Speed workout."

I bite the chicken wing and promptly sneeze.

"Goddess blessings upon you," Rhia says. "But eight *in the morning?* Not a chance. You are the most early-bird witch I know."

"I'm the only—you know what? Scratch that. After all this, you two are definitely witches."

"Yeah, we are!" Rhia says, beaming.

"Oh, that reminds me," Tess says. "Rhee and I got you something."

"What? I got something for each of you, too!"

"You first!" Tess hands me a paper gift bag.

I shake my head. "You two did so much for me this whole

time and you barely knew me at all. Now I can't imagine not having you both in my life."

I hand them each a small bag.

Rhia peers into hers and then gives me a big smile. She pulls out the hollow silver sphere GG had given me just for Rhia. "My own spell ball?"

I nod.

She clutches it to her chest. "Thank you."

"Me next!" Tess tosses aside tissue paper to pull out the little gift. "Ah! I love it!" She places the hot pink headband on her head. Across her forehead in gold script it says WILL RUN FOR ICE CREAM.

"Now you. Open it! Open it! Open it!" Tess squeals, jumping up and down.

Inside the bag is something black. I pull it out to find a tank top with the words 100% THAT WITCH on the front in white hand-lettered writing. I start laughing and then all three of us are cackling, and maybe I am the only one here with actual witch DNA, but this summer has shown me that we're *all* magical, each in our own way.

Chapter Forty-One

EDIE

"I thought you might want this." I pull a velvet pouch from my pocket and place it in GG's hand. Her fingers curl around it and her eyes light up. It's twilight and GG sits on her rocking chair on the back deck of our boat. I sit on the bench nearby.

GG tips the velvet pouch into her hand and the simple gold ring spills onto her palm.

"My wedding ring?" she asks.

"Yes, I cleansed it."

She holds it up between two fingers so that she can peer through the circle. She closes her fingers around it and closes her eyes as well. She presses it to her lips. "Well done. It is cleansed indeed."

The ring slips easily onto the ring finger of GG's left hand.

"I'm so sorry for your losses," I say to my grandmother.

GG nods. "You and I have both born more loss than many others. But I have you." She reaches out and cups my cheek in her palm.

"And I have you." I smile at my grandmother.

"By the way, how did you figure this one out?" GG asks, tapping the ring.

"Love, worn in a never-ending circle?" I smile. "Tess figured out that it must be a ring and then I think maybe Mom gave me the final hint."

GG sits back in her chair. "What does your future hold, now that you and your friends have mastered all of the magic?" She smiles at me again.

"Well, I'm not going to go get pregnant and live off the grid, if that's what you're thinking."

GG chuckles. "That doesn't seem especially likely. What *would* you like to do?"

I pause before saying the words. I'm not sure what GG will say. "I want to go back to Baltimore."

"I see."

"For school. But I want to come live here with you on weekends. And holidays and summers, if that's okay."

"It is." She smiles at me. "Of course, it is. We will need to figure out your living arrangements."

"I've thought about that." I take a moment before I share my idea. "I could board at school," I say. "If we sell the house, we could afford it."

GG inspects me with her sharp eyes. "You're ready to sell the house?"

I nod because the rush of emotion clogs my throat. "I know

Mom isn't in that house and I know that the life I lived with her is over. I can't live in the past. I need to look ahead."

GG grabs my hand and squeezes it. "You can't live in the past, but the past lives in you."

"I know." I'm smiling through tears now. "How could I forget?" I gesture to the ghosts that have been keeping their distance but are now drifting closer. "All of these ancestors here with us. Your parents and cousins. Mildred and Grandfather. And Mom."

GG looks around us at all of the ghosts and smiles.

"About Mom, her anniversary is in a few days."

GG nods and knots her hands in her lap. "Yes, this Sunday."

"Have you decided what type of tree to plant?" I ask.

"I thought I'd leave that to you."

"What do you think of an ash tree? Near the weeping beech?"

The beech was showing signs of life, but GG had explained that it would take years to revive and, in the meantime, the soil would be very fertile for new growth.

"The tree of life. That sounds perfect."

GG, Rhia, Tess, and I are in the kitchen of the houseboat along with many, many ancestors, though, of course, Rhia and Tess can't see the ghosts. GG is showing Rhia how to prepare a particularly tricky spell to help preserve some of Rhia's grandmother's memories before they are all gone. Tess is trying to put a flower crown on Temperance. It is August fifteenth, the one-year anniversary of my mother's death, and I am putting the finishing touches on a ten-layer cake.

"What do you think, Mom?" I say to the ghost floating beside me. I know that she will not answer, but I've learned that it's comforting to talk to her. "It's for you, you know. Well, in honor of you, I guess, since you can't eat."

"Mildred, stop being a busybody!" GG says behind me.

"Mildred?" Rhia asks.

"My sister," GG answers.

Rhia looks around, pulling her elbows in. "Let me know if I'm stepping on her or anything weird."

"They get out of our way," GG says. "Don't worry."

"You'd be a total queen with the crown on!" Tess says, following Temperance down the hallway.

"I think that's it, then," GG says, giving their pot one last stir.

"Thanks for the lesson," Rhia says. "Edie's inspired me to use all of the knowledge that I have. Not just keep it behind the counter."

"Really?" I say. "I thought I was the most scared witch you knew."

"Exactly. Feel the fear but do it anyway." Rhia leans over my shoulder and pecks me on the cheek. I dot her nose with icing.

She slides a hand around to my belly sending delicious goose bumps everywhere.

"Later," I whisper. Rhia giggles and steps away from me.

"Are you all ready?" GG asks as she removes her smock.

"Almost," I say. I spread the last of the icing across the top of the cake.

Tess drops the kitty crown on the table. "No luck with Tempy."

"Definitely not if you're calling her that," I say.

Tess swipes at some icing dripping from the cake and licks her finger.

"Hey!" I swat at her.

"Yum," she says. She closes her eyes. "So much more than yum, actually."

"Yeah, the Ice Cream Alchemist has found her talent," Rhia says.

"Because I can bake a good cake?"

After Tess had mentioned how happy my ice cream customers always seemed to be, Rhia got it in her head that infusing emotions into food was my special talent.

"Only a witch could bake a deathday cake that tastes like memories."

I stand back to examine the whole effect, now that the chocolate icing is finished. It's a little lopsided, but I don't care. I'm not so sure I agree with Rhia that I can infuse food with emotion, but she's not wrong about the memories. As I pulled together all of the ingredients, measured and stirred and baked this cake, I was filled with good memories of Mom. Each layer is a different color, a nod to the quirkiness Mom brought to so many of our shared experiences.

"It's ready," I say to GG.

"Wonderful," she says. "Shall we?"

When we arrive at the site of the burned beech tree, GG says, "Are we all here?"

I look around at the large group gathered together. Rhia holds my hand. Tess is on her other side. Jim stands nearby, holding up a sapling. I recognize Ms. Alvarez from the antique store and the woman from the cemetery. Tess's mom and uncle, who owns this land, are here. Rhia's mom and grandma are even here. There are other people who I haven't met yet, but I'm certain that I will.

"I don't think there's anyone else left in town," Tess says.

"Let's begin, then," GG says.

GG digs the shovel into the ground and tosses a pile of dirt to the side. She could, of course, just move all the dirt with a flick of her hand. But this is supposed to be a shared experience, and besides, not everyone gathered here knows *all* about us. GG hands me the shovel and I do the same. The shovel makes its way around the whole circle until we have a hole large enough to plant the sapling. Into the hole, GG pours some water mixed with her own concoction that will soon be for sale at Cosmic Flow. She nods to Jim.

He lifts the sapling and maneuvers the root ball into the hole. Then we all do the reverse, each tossing one shovelful of dirt back into the hole until the roots are covered. GG and I get on our hands and knees to pat the dirt down, with everyone else joining in.

"Not too hard," GG orders us. "Gentle pats. We do not want to suffocate the roots."

GG and I sprinkle Mom's ashes at the base of the new tree. Tess waters it. We stand and grab hands in a circle. When I arrived in Cedar Branch, I was certain that the magical life was not for me. I wanted to be back in the house I'd shared with Mom, running with my cross-country team and trying to score higher on the ACT. I didn't realize then that my craving for these things was an escape from missing Mom. I couldn't face the fact that I'd taken Mom's presence for granted. I'd always thought that she'd be there when I was finally ready to learn the magic. I thought she'd be around forever. And then she wasn't. And I was stuck in an in-between place, wishing for the past and unable to move forward.

Now I understand that memories can transcend death. They are their own sort of magic. And I can still learn even without my mother by my side. The absence remains. It won't ever go away. But as GG had said: grief is a red silk ribbon tied to love. The pain of grief is hard to bear, but it's also proof that I had a mother who loved me and who I loved. That will always be true.

"From the earth we come and to the earth we shall return," GG says. "But in between, may we grow roots to know our past and branches to seek our path forward. May this ash tree honor the memory of Maura Mitchell: daughter, mother, friend. Though her life was cut short, we hold her in our hearts, and we will remember her always as we watch this strong sapling grow into a great tree."

GG looks at me and I hold her gaze. "As it is above, so below," we say together. Rhia hands out flower bombs. Our ancestors surround us. Those I know and many I don't hover nearby, a reminder of what I am connected to, what lives on through me.

"For you, Mom," I whisper. I throw my flower bomb as far as I can and watch where it lands. I can't wait to come back next year and see wildflowers covering the burned-out patches of grass. We all gather around the makeshift table and I carve up slices of cake for each person.

As I stick my fork into the last piece of rainbow cake, the scent of lemons and mint fills the air and Mom shimmers next to me, with her perfect smile and her wild blowing hair. Always with me. Always within me.

ACKNOWLEDGMENTS

Edie's story has changed dramatically from the first draft that suggested only a hint of magic. The version you hold in your hand is what I needed to write during a time of lockdown and uncertainty. I hope it's what you've needed to read. Books, alas, are not conjured from thin air, they are made real through the work of many people.

Thanks first to my mother, Kathy Yeager. The initial spark of this book and the first version I wrote were inspired years ago by wondering what it was like for my mother to lose her father when she was just nineteen years old. Only the whisper of that original story is present in this current version. What remained is my interest in exploring how people navigate grief in unexpected ways.

But my mother inspired more than just the grief narrative. She inspired Maura's closeness to Edie. She also inspired GG's magical way with plants. My mother can grow anything. She even seems to bring dead plants back to life. My grandmother, her mother, had the same talent. And this always seemed like a bit of ordinary magic to me.

And to my uncle, John Harlan. The setting—the Western Shore of the Chesapeake Bay region of Maryland—came directly from my own childhood. When I was young, we camped on a piece of property on the Magothy River, a tributary to the Chesapeake. I have wonderful memories of those days, and in them my beloved Uncle John looms large. He taught me how to paddle a canoe and sail a sunfish; we crabbed and fished. I learned to swim there. My uncle built Adirondack chairs, an outhouse, and eventually even a gazebo! He inspired the sense of place in this novel and specifically the way that Edie's grandfather could build anything.

Deep gratitude to the sensitivity readers who helped me with the sexuality and racial aspects of the book. Linda Washington identified for me ways that I could improve Rhia's character and Edie's relationship to Rhia. Dr. Jeanne Stanley provided feedback related to Edie's emerging sense of being queer and her budding relationship with Rhia. Rosie Asmar helped me with a later version of the story, highlighting areas related to Rhia, as well as Edie's relationship to her. Any errors are mine alone. Also, thank you to Cordelia Jensen for always talking through my stories with me and for reading when I needed new eyes on the manuscript. And thank you to Laurie Morrison for cheering me through deadlines.

Thanks also to Margaret Ennis, who shared the experience of losing her husband when their daughter was a teen. She inspired a tender moment between Maura and her mother. And to Rosella Hughes, whose gift of a hand-blown glass ball inspired the witch ball in the story.

One September day toward the end of the drafting process, my mother and I drove down to the Magothy River so that I could revive my sense of the place. While exploring a local marina, we met Sheryl and Dave Parks, who invited us for a boat ride. Afterward, I mentioned how amazing it was that they would take us—strangers—onto their boat. Dave replied that there are no strangers on the water. Their easy friendliness inspired the sense that there are no strangers in Cedar Branch.

Sincere appreciation to my editor, Maggie Rosenthal, for editorial wizardry. Even when I was unsure that I could achieve what I'd hoped, your belief in me never wavered. Thanks especially for the note suggesting that I lean into the magical underpinnings of the story. What fun we've had! The ten-layer rainbow cake is for you.

The interior and exterior of the book are completely enchanting, thanks to the work of many magical people. Jessica Jenkins's cover design and Lisa Sterle's artwork perfectly capture the sense of witchy mystery that I wanted for this book. Opal Roengchai created an equally enchanting title page and brought a gentle sense of whimsy throughout the interior.

I marvel at the coven of copy editors who improved my prose: Maddie Newquist, Abigail Powers, Michelle Millet, and Marinda Valenti. Also, thanks to managing editor Mia Alberro, whose sorcery somehow keeps track of us all and keeps us all on track. Thanks also to my favorite book shouter, Tessa Meischeid. I'm so lucky to have you on the team again.

Deep appreciation to my very witchy agent, Brianne Johnson, for cackling with me when I needed a laugh and for listening when things were challenging.

Thanks as well to Rosemary Gladstar for her book *Medicinal Herbs: A Beginner's Guide*, which shaped the ways that GG uses plants and herbs for healing. And to Coven's Cottage in Salem, Massachusetts. The witchy interior of that shop inspired the inside of GG's houseboat.

And of course to my husband, Tom, and my two grown children—for always supporting my writing and for ordering lots of take-out when I was on deadline. A special thanks to Zach for answering my running-related questions.

And finally, you, the reader. This book is for you. Thank you for picking it up and for joining Edie on her journey. I hope you've found your own magic along the way.